The Hengest and Horsa Trilogy
A Brother's Oath
A Warlord's Bargain
A King's Legacy

The Arthur of the Cymry Trilogy
Sign of the White Foal
Banner of the Red Dragon
Field of the Black Raven
Drustan and Esyllt: Wolves of the Sea (novella)

The Rebel and the Runaway
Lords of the Greenwood

https://christhorndycroft.wordpress.com/

As P. J. Thorndyke

The Lazarus Longman Chronicles
Through Mines of Deception (novella)
On Rails of Gold (novella)
Golden Heart
Silver Tomb
Onyx City

Celluloid Terrors
Curse of the Blood Fiends

https://pjthorndyke.wordpress.com/

Sign of the White Foal

CHRIS THORNDYCROFT

Sign of the White Foal
By Chris Thorndycroft

For Maia for her constant encouragement and my parents for their unwavering support.

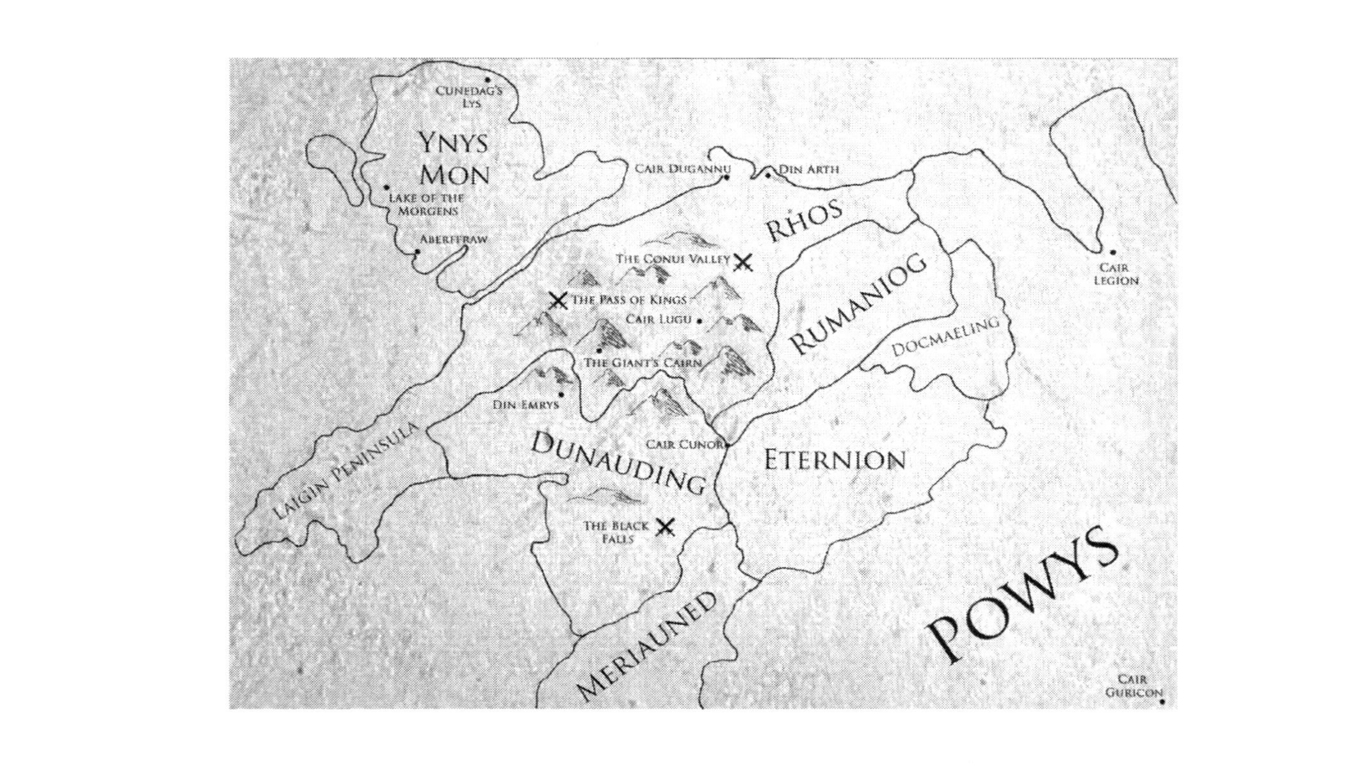
Cunedag's Lys
Ynys Mon
Lake of the Morgens
Aberffraw
Cair Dugannu
Din Arth
Rhos
The Conui Valley
The Pass of Kings
Cair Lugu
The Giant's Cairn
Din Emrys
Rumaniog
Docmaeling
Cair Legion
Laigin Peninsula
Cair Cunor
Dunauding
Eternion
The Black Falls
Meriauned
Powys
Cair Guricon

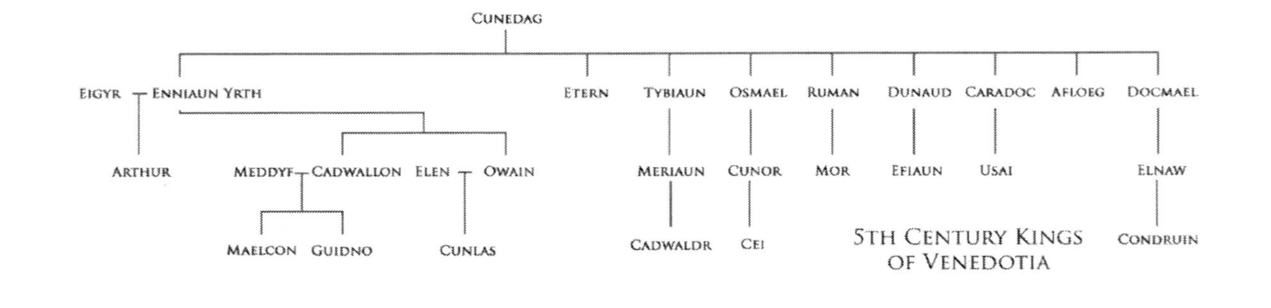

5th Century Kings of Venedotia

GLOSSARY

Albion – The island of Britain
Teulu – Warband
Penteulu – Commander of a king's teulu
Saeson – Saxons (singular – Sais)
Saesneg – The Saxon language (Old English)
Commote – A division of land within a kingdom.
Cair – Fortress
Din – Fort
Afon – River
Lin- Lake
Coed – Forest

"Then Arthur along with the kings of Britain fought against them in those days, but Arthur himself was the leader of battles."- The History of the Britons

PART I

"My poetry,
from the cauldron
it was uttered.
From the breath of nine maidens
it was kindled."
- The Spoils of Annwn, The Book of Taliesin (trans. Sarah Higley, 2007)

Venedotia (Gwynedd), 480 A.D.

Cadwallon

Night cloaked the coast, turning sand to silver and the hills to slumbering shadows. The moon was shrouded by shifting clouds and beyond the lapping waves the sea was an impenetrable, black void. Cadwallon mab Enniaun sniffed the air. The tide was going out; there was no mistaking that stink. But there was something else there too. Perhaps it was his imagination but there was something on the wind that was not *right.*

"An ill night, lord," said the young warrior beside him, as if reading his thoughts.

"Aye," Cadwallon replied.

The small camp had overlooked the Afon Conui, nestled on the wooded slope that ran down to the marsh at the water's edge. The fire had been stamped out and not long ago either. Smoke still curled up from the ashes and the stones that surrounded it were warm. The corpses of the three sentries were warm too, but only barely.

"Poor Gusc," said the young warrior looking down at his slain comrades. "He owed me money."

"There wasn't much of a fight," said the second warrior, an older man whose name Cadwallon seemed to remember was Tathal. "Looks like they were come upon by surprise; Gusc here only had his sword halfway out of his scabbard before some bastard's knife cut his throat for him."

"Should we expect an attack?" asked the young warrior, a touch of fear creeping into his voice.

"I don't know." Cadwallon looked at the long reeds of the marsh below them. That dense foliage could easily conceal a band of warriors. So could the trees of the wooded slope upon which they stood for that matter. *Enemies could be everywhere.*

"Lord, return to the fortress," said Tathal. "We can deal with this. It's not safe for you to be here without an armed escort."

Cadwallon ignored him. Though he was right, of course. His presence wasn't strictly necessary and it was probably a little reckless for him to be there, but in truth he had welcomed a break from the side of his father's deathbed. News of three dead sentries and no sign of their attackers had drawn him from his father's chamber with eager haste.

It was the smell that got to him the most; the smell of death. Not the fast death of slaughter on the battlefield (and at thirty-five summers, Cadwallon had smelt enough of that), but the slow death of old age and sickness. The burning incense did little to mask the stink of sweat and shit, only contributing its own heavy fug to the mix. He had longed for the cool night air and salty tang of the sea. Now he wasn't so sure.

At their back, straddling twin hills connected by timber palisades, was Cair Dugannu, his father's fortress; the mighty royal seat of Venedotia. On fine days those twin hills afforded a wide view of seaweed-strewn mudflats, wavering marsh reeds and the deep blue of the ocean, its glassy surface broken only by the curve of the fishing weirs. Further along the coast, the earthworks of the old Roman fort could be seen shielding the port of Penlassoc; a snug little haven where vessels were beached on the mud to trade wine for fish and the fine pearls of the blue mussels that clustered at the mouth of the Afon Conui.

Such were the fine images of youth forever imprinted on Cadwallon's memory. But tonight it felt as if the darkness was pressing in on all sides, cutting him off from memories of sunshine and cawing gulls, obscuring his sight and threatening to overwhelm him.

He tried to shrug off his foolishness. He was no bard to wax poetic about doom and fate. The kingdom was on the verge of change; that was all. It was natural to feel some apprehension.

And yet … Here lie three dead sentries.

"What's your name, lad?" Cadwallon asked the young soldier.

"Gobrui, lord," he replied. "Son of Echel."

"How long have you been in my father's guard?"

"Six months, lord. My da was killed in that border dispute with Powys when I was nine. He always wanted me to be a warrior like him so I joined as soon as I was sixteen but …" his voice trailed off. Cadwallon smiled. He knew that the lad had been about to voice his shame that he had not yet made it beyond a night sentry but had thought better of complaining to his lord.

"I'm sure you will become a warrior to match your father's good name and make his shade very proud one day," he reassured him. "But take it from me, be careful wishing for war and glory. War is seldom glorious. Take these poor men here. They were come upon by surprise and left this world before they knew what was happening."

"Are we truly at war, then?" the lad asked.

"Difficult to say until we know who did this," said Tathal.

"Could've been robbers," offered Gobrui.

"Robbing sentries?" Tathal replied. "Our lads had precious little to steal apart from blades and leather and those were not taken." He looked at Cadwallon. "You don't reckon it was … *them* do you?" He jerked his head in a north-westerly direction.

"They haven't attacked in a decade," said Cadwallon. "Why would they now?"

Yes, why now? He thought. *Why tonight, of all nights?*

He gazed beyond the headland at the narrow straits that separated the mainland from the isle of Ynys Mon. That slim stretch of tidal water was all that stood between them and their age-old enemy. It had been ten years since they had returned. Gaels, *Scotti* in the Latin tongue; wolves from across the sea seeking land and plunder. Ynys Mon was theirs, ceded to them after years of bitter conflict. The Britons held one side of the straits while the Gaels held the other. He shivered and lied to himself that it was just the chilled night breeze from the river. To stare at death every day and trust their lives to the whim of the tides! Manawydan protect them!

"Remain with the bodies," he ordered, his voice suddenly more assertive. "I will send down a patrol to bring them back to the fortress."

"Will you send out troops to scour the woods and marshes?" Tathal asked.

"No. I want all our men within the palisades tonight. I won't risk ambush by sending out small patrols."

"My lord, there could be a warband lurking nearby. Shouldn't we at least …"

"No!" he didn't know why his voice had snapped

like that. Was it fear? As Gobrui had said, tonight was an ill night …

He left them then and headed up the slope towards the fortress.

Cair Dugannu had been fortified by his father after his grandfather's original holdfast on Ynys Mon had fallen to the Gaels. The return of the hounds of Erin had been a sore blow to the dynasty that had driven them into the sea a generation previously. After Rome had abandoned Albion, Venedotia, like the rest of the province, fell vulnerable to those who had never borne the yoke of the iron legions. Gaels plundered and settled in the west just as the Saeson did in the east and the Picts in the north. Facing barbarians on all sides, the Council of Britannia, an assembly which was hastily formed to administer their newfound independence, struggled to keep the old province together. Out of desperation, the Council's leader, Lord Vertigernus, had decided to fight fire with fire.

In the north dwelt a client tribe who had served as a buffer zone between Rome's northernmost border and the howling, blue-painted Picts that lived in the hills beyond it. Cunedag was their leader and a more ferocious warlord Albion had rarely seen. His standard was the red dragon, the origins of which lay in the carven standing stones of the Picts, for that people's blood flowed strongly in his line.

Cunedag was descended from Padarn Redcloak; a Pictish chieftain who had accepted a military rank from Rome and swapped barbarism for toga and trade. As Lord Vertigernus aped his Roman predecessors, so had Cunedag followed in his ancestor's footsteps. He and his sons took up the offer of butchery for pay and marched south to Venedotia.

Nine sons of Cunedag there were; Tybiaun, Etern, Ruman, Afloeg, Caradog, Osmael, Enniaun, Docmael and Dunaud. Together they brought fire and sword to the Gaels and forced them back in battle after bloody battle until only the island of Ynys Mon held out against them. That battle was the bloodiest. Tybiaun and Osmael fell but the Gaels were finally sent back across the sea whence they came.

The dragon standard was planted deep into the soil of Ynys Mon and the sons of Cunedag came to be known as the 'Dragons of the Isle' with Cunedag as their chief; the *Pendraig*. Before he died, he divided his kingdom between his surviving sons. To Etern went Eternion, to Ruman Rumaniog, to Afloeg Afloegion, Caradog Caradogion and Dunaud Dunauding. Meriaun – the son of Cunedag's fallen firstborn who had excelled himself by slaying the Gaelic chieftain Beli mac Benlli – was also given a portion; Meriauned.

The only son who did not receive a kingdom was Cunedag's seventh and favourite son Enniaun, known as 'Yrth', the impetuous. Cunedag had groomed Enniaun to rule as Pendraig after his passing. But when old Cunedag finally died and Enniaun succeeded him as High-king of Venedotia, the other rulers began to grumble at being subservient to their younger brother.

Envious eyes looked upon the dragon standard but the return of the Gaels had kept the Venedotian kings too busy to do anything about it. The wars were long. Ynys Mon was lost and the Dragons of the Isle grew old. One by one they died and were succeeded by their sons but family rivalries still burned deep. When King Afloeg died without an heir, Enniaun Yrth absorbed his kingdom on the Laigin Peninsula into his own lands, an act which caused further grumbling.

Although a fragile peace between Briton and Gael had reigned for many years now, the wars had turned Enniaun Yrth into a battle-hardened old warrior every bit as ferocious as Cunedag had been. None of the other kings dared act on their resentment while he still lived. Instead, they bided their time, knowing that one day a new king must be crowned Pendraig.

Cadwallon strode in through the west gate and made his way up the north hill where the Great Hall stood. He gave orders to a sergeant to dispatch a patrol to retrieve the slain sentries. A servant was relighting the torches that were sputtering low. All were still awake and about their duties. Few would sleep that night, least of all him.

The night was dark. The enemies innumerable. And in a chamber on the upper floor of the royal quarters, the Pendraig was dying.

The attack came before dawn. Enniaun had died in the small hours. Cadwallon was in the Great Hall, a horn of mead in his hand. He wasn't grieving. The old warhorse had been over sixty and had been a difficult man to like at the best of times. No, his thoughts dwelt on the immediate future.

To all intents and purposes, he was now the Pendraig, High-king of Venedotia. There would be a coronation ceremony of course and all the other kings

– his cousins and remaining uncle – would come to pay him homage. Some had already visited his father's deathbed when it became known that his time was near. Some had been conspicuously absent and their names had been noted.

His wife, Meddyf, entered the hall and joined him at the table.

"How are the boys?" he asked her.

"Sleeping, at last," she replied. "They were tired but they did their duty and paid their last respects to your father."

"How are they?"

She shrugged. "Maelcon acted like he didn't care which may be the truth for all I know. Guidno was upset but I think he was just scared. They weren't close to your father, after all."

"No," Cadwallon agreed. "Few were."

She poured him some more mead from the jug and took the horn from him, drawing a long sip herself before setting it down. "Will you be coming to bed soon?"

"No. I can't sleep."

"Thinking about the future?"

"I've been thinking about the future for many years now for all the good it did."

"Surely after so long you feel ready to be a king?"

He looked at her. "Do you feel ready to be a queen?"

She was silent for a while and then placed a hand on his arm. "We have known this day was coming for a long time," she said. "All is as it should be and that must be enough for us. Let us rest our heads in the lap of fate and be content."

He didn't answer her. As always, she sensed his mood and was trying to quell his concerns, good wife that she was. He couldn't hope for a better one and he needed her now. He wanted to tell her about the dead sentries. He wanted to tell her his deepest fears, not just about that night but about all the nights and days to come. But what sort of a husband would that make him, to burden her with his own troubles? *What sort of a king?*

The door to the Great Hall crashed open and Tathal staggered in. "My lord!" he wheezed, evidently having run up the north hill. "We are under attack!"

Cadwallon felt the warmth the mead had brought him suddenly drain from his face and a chill came over his heart. He slammed the horn down and stood up. "Bar the gates!" he said. "Man the palisades! Wake every warrior! Why do I not hear the warning bell?"

"The guards on the western palisade have been slain, lord. Nobody can get to the bell. They came upon us under cover of darkness and scaled the palisade with ropes and grappling hooks."

"Who, in the name of the gods?"

"The Gaels."

Cadwallon felt his stomach sink. What a fool he had been! They must have crossed the straits at the Lafan Sands at low tide earlier that day and waited in the marshes and woods. They had even slain his sentries and still he had not sent out patrols!

"They have us pinned on the north hill," Tathal went on. "The southern hill and the lower fortress fell but not before I sent a messenger out the east gate. With any luck he will make it through to Din Arth and get word to your brother."

Cadwallon turned to Meddyf. "Go and stay with the boys," he told her. "Bar the door."

"Where are you going?" she asked.

"I am the lord of this fortress now," he replied. "My place is on the palisades."

Tathal followed him out of the hall and they crossed the enclosure to the palisade that ringed the north hill. The gate was barred and every remaining warrior had marshalled on the rampart that faced south, overlooking the small valley between Dugannu's two hills. In that dip lay a cluster of roundhouses, pig runs and workshops. As Cadwallon climbed up to the rampart, he could see the Gaels ransacking and burning the homes of his people. On the other side of the dip the southern hill with its barracks and granary was already under Gaelic control.

"I've failed them …" he muttered. "May the gods forgive me, I've failed them!"

They could hear the screams of the fortress's inhabitants as glowing sparks whirled up into the night sky. *The sun has not yet risen on my reign and already I am defeated! How had they known? How had they known?*

The Gaels marshalled on the footpath that led up the side of the north hill. Cadwallon's men had a few bows between them and several arrows were sent down into the mob who quickly raised their shields and advanced on the gate.

The defence did not last long. A battering ram was brought forth and heaved against the gate by ten men, shields covering their heads. Cadwallon, Tathal and the remaining men on the palisades descended to ground level and formed a defensive line in front of the gradually splintering gate.

"You should go and be with your family, lord," said Tathal.

"No," Cadwallon replied. "I brought this upon us. My fate will be no different to yours. I should at least be able to die in battle."

The gate came down and the Gaels spilled in, falling upon the spears of the Britons with blood-curdling war cries. The line held for a moment but eventually, inevitably, the Britons were overwhelmed. The line broke and the fighting descended into the chaos of one-on-one combat.

Cadwallon roared as the pent-up shame and fear finally found an outlet and he reddened his sword in Gaelic blood. Tathal, loyal warrior that he was, kept himself ahead of his new king, hacking and slashing like a man twenty years younger.

The Gaels seemed to part as several of their warriors shouldered their way through to the front ranks. As soon as they saw them the Britons fell back in sheer terror. Cadwallon had never seen anything like these men. They were like nightmares from a mist-shrouded age. They were naked but for masks that concealed their features and those black, soulless eye sockets told him that these were masks fashioned from human skulls. They fought like demons, screeching and howling, all traces of humanity blasted from their minds by the battle fury.

"Gods, what are they?" Tathal uttered.

Focused solely on slaughter, the skull-faced warriors seemed impervious to pain, ignoring the wounds inflicted on their naked, woad-stained flesh as the Britons desperately tried to fight them off.

Cadwallon could see that it was hopeless. These monsters were driving a wedge between them while the rest of the Gaels flanked them on either side. They were as fish in a barrel. Tathal fell, his shoulder blade splintered by the axe of a skull-faced howler. The rest of Cadwallon's warriors rallied to him with cries of "To the Pendraig! To the Pendraig!"

He could have wept at their loyalty for there could be none among them who did not know that they would all be slaughtered within minutes. But the Gaels seemed to hold back, fresh spearmen pushing through the ranks to hold the Britons at a distance and, at the same time, drive back their own wild warriors.

"Which of you is Cadwallon mab Enniaun?" demanded a voice in British with a thick Gaelic accent.

All were silent but for the groans of the dying and the heaving breaths of the living. Cadwallon straightened and stepped forward. "I am he," he answered.

A large Gael wearing a tartan cloak and the torc of a chieftain shouldered his way forward. "I am Diugurnach mac Domhnall," he said. "Surrender this fortress and your remaining men will live."

"And what of my family?" Cadwallon asked.

"All will live if you throw down your weapons now. If you do not, all will die."

Cadwallon felt the eyes of his remaining men upon him. It had been selfish to think that he could die in battle. He had the lives of his people to think of. He tossed his bloodied sword to the mud. A heartbeat passed before all British blades and spears fell to the ground in unison.

The Gaels herded them into the Great Hall while the skull-faced warriors capered and foamed at the mouth amidst the blood and the entrails outside. All of the women, children and servants were roused from their quarters and marched into the hall. The chamber echoed with frightened weeping. Cadwallon looked for Meddyf and saw her clutching the hands of Maelcon and Guidno. She was visibly shaken yet her face remained brave and defiant.

The one called Diugurnach mounted the dais at the head of the hall and spoke to them. "I have taken this fortress and you are all my prisoners. Cadwallon mab Enniaun, step forward."

Cadwallon took a pace towards the dais, conscious of Meddyf, his sons, *everybody*, watching him. He must not fail them now. He was still their king. His courage must hold strong.

"Do you yield to me, princeling?"

"I yield this fortress to you to save what is left of my people," Cadwallon replied. "But I am no princeling. I am the Pendraig, the High-king of Venedotia. My uncle and my cousins all owe me allegiance. By tomorrow five-thousand British spears will be upon you and you will rue the day you set foot on Venedotian soil."

Diugurnach ignored the last and addressed the hall; "You all heard him! This fortress is mine! I offer food and plunder to any warrior who wishes to join me and pledge their allegiance. Step forward now!"

He knows he is vulnerable here, thought Cadwallon. *Otherwise he wouldn't recruit warriors from the enemy.*

Several of Cadwallon's warriors stepped forward

to the disapproving hiss and grumble of the assembly. Cadwallon saw young Gobrui among them but found that he could not begrudge the lad. They were all so frightened. One by one they knelt and kissed Diugurnach's sword before taking their places among the Gaels.

All warriors who did not pledge allegiance were taken outside where the skull-faced still howled. As Cadwallon and his family were escorted to their quarters, they heard the screams as they were butchered behind the Great Hall. *That they should remain loyal while I surrender*, he thought miserably. *That they should die and I should live!*

They were taken to the royal apartments at the rear of the fortress and left with their sorrows. The celebrations of the conquerors could be heard drifting through the thatch of the Great Hall and up through the open windows.

"Are they going to kill us, Da?" Guidno asked, his face as white as a sheet.

"Of course not," Maelcon snapped at his little brother. "Else why would they keep us alive now? We're far too important to kill."

Maelcon was ten and already showed much of the surliness of young manhood.

"Maelcon is right, Guidno," Cadwallon said. "We are royalty. They won't touch us. They won't dare." *Gods, I hope I'm right.*

"There are no guards outside our chamber," said Meddyf, peeping into the corridor beyond.

"Diugurnach can't spare the men," Cadwallon said. "They are needed on the palisades. He has enough warriors to seize Cair Dugannu but not enough to hold it."

"Or to keep its inhabitants from escaping …" Meddyf suggested.

"Escape?" he regarded her with surprise. "There is no need to be foolhardy. All we need do is sit tight and await the marshalling of the teulu. Once Tathal's messenger reaches Din Arth, my brother will have all Venedotia coming to our rescue. These Gaelic wolves don't know what they've done in attacking us."

The Teulu of the Red Dragon was the standing army of Venedotia. Formed by Cunedag in the old days, every king contributed warriors to its ranks. It was headquartered at Cair Cunor in the south and could reach the coast within two days.

"Someone is coming," Meddyf said.

The door opened and Gobrui entered. He was armed.

"Not drinking your king's mead in the Great Hall with your new friends, traitor?" Meddyf spat. "Or have your new masters already got you running errands?"

The boy blushed but he appeared to have something of import to say. "I know you have little reason to trust me, my lord, but I have prepared a way out, if you are willing."

"A way out?" said Cadwallon "Too risky. I'll not endanger my family on some reckless escape plan when all of Venedotia will be coming to our aid tomorrow."

"All of Venedotia?"

"Tathal was able to get a messenger out before the east gate fell. By midday tomorrow Owain and Cunor will be mustering the teulu."

"Begging your pardon, my lord, but the messenger did not get through. They led his horse back in with his carcass slung over its saddle not an hour ago."

"Damn!" Cadwallon cursed. "Damn these bastards!"

"There's more, my lord. Diugurnach did not act alone. He has support from somebody in Venedotia. My Gaelic isn't too good but they seem to be awaiting the arrival of somebody of great importance tomorrow. You are being kept alive for an audience with them. What your fate will be afterwards, I do not know."

"Diugurnach may have orders to keep you alive only long enough to be used as a pawn," said Meddyf. "Once you have served your purpose we may all be killed. Look what happened to those soldiers who remained loyal to you even after Diugurnach promised to spare everybody. I say we make a run for it. If we can reach Owain at Din Arth we will be safe, at least until the teulu can be mustered." She glanced at Gobrui. "How is it to be done?"

"It will have to be on foot," the youth replied. "Diugurnach has few warriors but we can't reach the stables without being seen. I have taken care of the guard at the east gate. The way is open but only for so long. If we are to leave then it must be now."

"Very well," said Cadwallon. "If you get us out of this, lad, you will be the hero of Venedotia. Come! Lead the way!"

They stepped out onto the gallery. Dawn was still a few hours away and the lamps burned low. Drunken singing could still be heard down in the Great Hall but all elsewhere was silent. Gobrui led them right along the gallery towards the west wall.

"Hold," said Cadwallon in a low whisper. "Wait here for me." He turned and Meddyf seized his arm.

"What are you doing?" she hissed.

"Just give me a moment," he replied, shaking himself free of her grip.

He hurried down the gallery and descended a couple of steps to the standard bearer's quarters. It was pitch black inside so he took one of the lamps from the gallery to light his way. Bronze and silver glinted in the darkness. He wove his way between the racks of spear shafts to the iron-bound chest at the back of the chamber. He opened it and took out what he wanted, bundling it under his arm before re-joining his family.

"What's that?" Meddyf demanded, her eyes on the bundle of red cloth under his arm.

"My father's dragon banner," he replied.

"You went back for that?" Her eyes blazed in the darkness.

"This is the very standard Cunedag brought with him from the lands of the Votadini over forty years ago," he said. "It is the symbol of our dynasty and I'll be damned if I'll leave it in the hands of the bastard Gaels."

"We're trying to escape with our lives and you tarry to collect a battle standard?"

"I am the Pendraig now. I am its custodian. Where I go, it goes. Else all is for naught."

"If you dare to suggest that a piece of brightly coloured cloth is equal to the lives of our sons I'll leave you right here in in this fortress!"

Cadwallon looked at the two frightened faces of

his boys. Maelcon looked upon his father with his mother's scathing eyes while Guidno seemed on the verge of weeping. *They don't understand,* he thought. *How could they? But they will someday. Maelcon especially if he is to succeed me …*

They headed to ground level and skirted the Great Hall. Gobrui pulled them into the shadows of the palisades as a drunken Gael stumbled out of the building and vomited under the eaves. They waited while he staggered to his feet and urinated before shambling back indoors, tying his breeches as he went.

They hurried over to the gate which had so recently been breached. Its shattered timbers lay all around. The corpses had been carried off but the ground was damp with the blood of the fallen.

"They leave no guard at the north gate?" Cadwallon asked.

"They see little need to," Gobrui replied. "They fear only attack from without and have all their guards on the palisades looking outwards."

As they descended the footpath they could see the ruins of the settlement between the two hills. Roundhouses still burned but the flames were low, licking at charred timbers which poked up from the ruins like blackened skeletons.

The east gate was closed and Cadwallon helped Gobrui heave it open just enough to allow them to slip out.

"How did you persuade the guard to leave his post?" Cadwallon asked him, looking up at the gatehouse.

Gobrui didn't answer but as soon as they left the

fortress they saw the guard's corpse impaled on the defensive spikes at the foot of the wall, his body pierced in at least three places.

Cadwallon was impressed but the need for haste was too great to bestow compliments. They had escaped the fortress but it was a long trek to Din Arth and when the Gaels realised their prisoners had escaped, they would be after them in hot pursuit.

They heaved the gate shut for the sake of appearances to buy themselves a little more time. Cadwallon scooped Guidno up into his arms and Meddyf led Maelcon by the hand. At the foot of the hill the treeline was a black haze that signified concealment and shelter. They hurried towards it; fleeting shadows in the pale light of dawn.

Owain

While Cair Dugannu was a moderate timber construction, Din Arth was a massive fortification with walls of quarried limestone piled three and a half meters high. It was a fort meant to inspire awe but, unlike Cair Dugannu, Din Arth was no royal seat despite its ruler's pretentions.

Owain mab Enniaun seethed as he rode through its gates, his ruddy complexion almost beet-red in his rage. In the warm spring afternoon, his great bearskin cloak made him swelter but he would not take it off until he was within his quarters. He wore it for effect; to bolster his already broad shoulders and suggest a bear-like temper which was no exaggeration. It was a theme he had built upon with the name of his fortress – which meant 'fort bear' in the British tongue – and his standard; a bear rampant on a blood-red field.

But Owain was no king. His brother Cadwallon was the heir to the Pendraig's crown. After years of pestering, their father had given Owain rulership of Rhos; a swathe of moorland between the Afon Conui and the Cluid Valley on the easternmost fringes of Venedotia. But the territory did not come with a royal title and Owain had soon set his sights higher. After all, had not their grandfather made all his sons kings during his lifetime?

"Would you have me appoint a king for every commote?" Enniaun Yrth had demanded. "There are already seven kings in Venedotia and that is six too many!"

On a clear day one could stand on the ramparts of Din Arth and see right across the Creudin Peninsula to the twin humps of Cair Dugannu. On that morning, the sky could have been no clearer and Owain had awoken to cries of alarm that smoke could be seen above Venedotia's royal seat.

Owain had ridden out with his best warriors but they had met refugees heading east from Penlassoc who warned them from riding too close to Cair Dugannu. The fort had fallen, they said, and Gaels were plundering Penlassoc for supplies. Roundhouses near to the fort had been put to the torch.

"What of my father?" Owain had demanded. "What of my brother and his family? Do they live?"

Few could give him any answers and he grew frantic, burning with shame for not having the courage to ride his troop within spear's range of Cair Dugannu to find out for himself.

It was a fisherman with an ear for Gaelic who had been down the Afon Conui that morning who provided Owain with some picture of what had happened.

"Your father is dead, lord, may God rest his soul." He touched the bone crucifix at his throat. "They say he died in the night before they attacked. Your brother, in his grief, wasn't ready for 'em, lord, but they do tell of his escape, so he must live, wherever he is."

"What?" Owain cried. "My brother escaped? How do you know this?"

"There was a great search party of mounted warriors and dogs too, set out from the fortress at the crack of dawn. Then the rest of them set on Penlassoc and looted it bare of meat and fish. Most folk are headed east to your fortress, my lord. I do hope you'll consider taking them in."

"Aye, they shall find refuge at Din Arth," Owain replied. "But my brother! Is he not among them?"

"Who can say, lord? He escaped before dawn so if he was headed in your direction, he should have reached you by now."

But he hadn't. Din Arth was the closest fort to Cair Dugannu and the obvious place to run to. So where was he?

Owain rode back to Din Arth, stopping to scour every baggage train and forlorn group of refugees for his brother's face. He did not find it. The refugees spoke of Gaelic hunting parties searching the woods and churning up the trackways. This fed Owain's hopes that his brother had not yet been found.

"If he did not make a crow's flight for Din Arth then he must have tried to lose his pursuers in the woods," his steward said once Owain was back at the fortress. His bear-skin cloak lay across the back of his chair in the Great Hall while he sipped cool wine in an effort to quench his temper.

"Gaels, for the love of Modron!" he cursed, invoking the name of the Great Mother. "They didn't waste any time, did they? My father's body was not yet cold before they struck. Don't you find that a bit timely?"

"I do, lord," the steward said. "They undoubtedly had word from someone within Cair Dugannu."

"If I ever find out who, I'll string him up by his own entrails!"

He had sent out patrols – all the mounted warriors he could spare – to find his brother. If they came into contact with the Gaels then there would be bloodshed but he didn't care. The Pendraig *had* to be found.

The thought had crossed his mind that if his brother and sons lay dead in a ditch somewhere then the throne might be within his own grasp. But it was a foolish thought, not to mention a callous one. His cousins would all have claims on the throne too and Rhos was not strong enough to fight them all. Indeed, his very position as ruler of Rhos rested on the Pendraig's support. If some cousin from one of the other kingdoms took the throne, Owain may very well find himself stripped of his territory. His brother *had* to survive.

He was pondering this when his wife, Elen, entered. The nurse followed her, carrying their baby son, Cunlas. Most of Cunedag's line were dark but Owain had inherited his mother's tawny locks which he kept closely cropped. His son, Cunlas, had followed suit and his small head looked as if it was wreathed in bushfire.

"Is it true, Husband?" Elen demanded, her voice trembling. "Has Cair Dugannu fallen to the Gaels?"

"It is true, my sweet," Owain replied. "They struck from Ynys Mon in the night. My father is dead and my brother's whereabouts unknown."

"Then we are ruined! The Gaels will turn to us next and butcher us all within these walls!"

Her cries upset Cunlas and he began to bawl. His nurse sat down with him and bounced him up and down, making cooing noises.

"Hush, Elen," Owain said. "Din Arth's walls are thick. We can hold out against them far longer than Cair Dugannu did. They were taken by surprise whereas we are forewarned."

"But what of your brother? Who now rules Venedotia?"

Aye, that was the question indeed, Owain thought calmly to himself as he sipped his wine. "Young Maelcon is the direct heir but if Cadwallon was slain then it is likely his sons were too. My uncle Etern thinks he has a claim as he is the last of the sons of Cunedag but he is old and foolish. Few would accept him on the throne."

"What of Meriaun?" Elen said. "He is Cunedag's eldest grandson and fought in the Gaelic wars himself."

"Aye, he has made much of his slaying of Beli mac Benlli and even goes so far as to say that it was that act which dealt the death blow to the Gaels a generation ago. He is a braggart and nothing more. If he presumes to stake his claim then he will have to use more than words. And then it would be civil war."

"*You* could stake your own claim," Elen said, her voice laced with proposition.

Owain smiled. *You'd like that, wouldn't you, my sweet? You'd like to place your pretty backside in my mother's chair at Cair Dugannu and wear finer dresses than I can afford as ruler of Rhos.* "I don't have the strength to take on all of the other kingdoms," he said, loathe to admit the fact, even to his wife.

"But as the Pendraig's second son, surely you have a stronger claim than anybody?"

"The Pendraig's *brother,*" he corrected her. "My father died before the Gaels attacked. Cadwallon was king for at least a few hours."

"Well? Son or brother? What's the difference?"

"A great deal and yet very little as it happens."

Owain's steward scuttled back in. "My lord! My lord!" he cried. "Your brother! The Pendraig! He's been found!"

Owain rose suddenly, overturning his wine cup. "Where is he?" he demanded.

"Here!" came a voice and the door to the Great Hall was heaved aside as Cadwallon strode in, his clothes muddy and his hair dishevelled. He was followed by his wife and sons as well as a young warrior Owain did not recognise.

"Brother!" Owain cried, coming forward to embrace Cadwallon. "We feared the worst!"

"Meddyf, my good sister!" said Elen, moving to embrace Cadwallon's wife, flinching a little when she saw her torn and muck-smeared clothes. "And my sweet nephews! Thank God you are all alive."

Is that disappointment I detect in her voice? Owain thought.

"It is through the efforts of Gobrui here that we live," said Cadwallon, indicating the youthful warrior at his side. "A more loyal follower I could not ask for. He got us out of Cair Dugannu right under the noses of the Gaels."

"The lad must be rewarded," said Owain. "But you must all be famished. Steward! Bring meat and mead for our guests!"

As the steward hurried off to see to the kitchen staff, the reunited family members sat at the table while Maelcon and Guidno lay down on the wolf skins by the hearth, exhausted.

"Tell me everything," Owain said to his brother.

Cadwallon related the events of the previous night, pausing only when the food arrived to tuck in ravenously. Owain and Elen waited patiently while their guests wolfed down braised mutton, dark brown bread, creamy white cheese and a clay flagon of mead.

"They can't possibly hope to keep Cair Dugannu," said Owain once Cadwallon was sopping up the meat juices with his crust. "They must know that we will strike back with all the power of the seven kingdoms."

Cadwallon gazed at the worn surface of the table. "There is something rotten at the centre of all of this," he said. "The Gaels are too bold, too reckless. What gives them that courage, I wonder?"

"They'll not be so bold once the Teulu of the Red Dragon is mustered and the combined might of Venedotia is marching on them," said Owain. "We must send word to Cair Cunor."

"Yes," said Cadwallon. "The teulu shall be mustered." He seemed to remember something and reached inside his tunica. He drew out a bungle of red cloth and placed it on the table between them. "The dragon banner," he said. "I brought it with us when we fled. Soon enough the Gaels will remember why they should fear the red dragon!"

Owain's steward re-entered the hall, his expression grave. "My lords," he announced. "There has come a messenger. A Gael. From Cair Dugannu."

Arthur

The heat of the morning sun beat down on the two boys as they circled each other in the training yard, their spears raised high, ready to strike. They peered over the rims of their shields at each other, their vision obscured by the sweat that rolled down their faces in great droplets. Both in their sixteenth year, one was heavier than the other and clearly the stronger of the two. The other could nearly be called skinny but what he lacked in strength he made up for in speed and agility.

The larger boy thrust out with his spear. His opponent parried quickly and counter-struck with his own weapon which slid off the first boy's shield with a rasping sound. There was a low murmur of approval from the small group of spectators who had gathered to watch. The larger boy tried again, lunging forward suddenly but he had overbalanced himself and stumbled forward. The skinny boy sidestepped and slammed his shield against his opponent's, knocking the boy to the ground with a heavy thud. He stood over him, victorious, his spear tip held close to his throat.

The crowd cheered and applauded the victor who helped the fallen boy to his feet.

"I keep telling you to mind your balance, Cei," he said, resting his spear and shield against the fence. "Your footwork is your downfall."

"A lucky win, Arthur," protested Cei. "Besides, I can't let you lose all the time." He took a playful swipe at Arthur with his spear butt and Arthur dodged nimbly, hurdling the fence.

Laughing, they walked over to a trough of water and Arthur scooped his hands in and splashed his face, washing the sweat and dirt away. Cei plunged his whole head in and emerged shaking droplets from himself like a dog that had just been for a swim.

A girl walked by carrying a loaf of bread wrapped in sackcloth under her arm. She was pretty and only slightly younger than the two boys.

"Morning, Rhan," Cei called out.

The girl threw him a brief glimpse and a small smile before turning crimson and scurrying off with her bread.

"She's a beauty, that one," Cei said to Arthur. "Too shy but I'm sure I can open her up like an oyster in time. You can see that she already fancies me."

"Really?" said Arthur. "Perhaps it's me she fancies."

Cei snorted. "You wouldn't know what to do with a girl if one fell into your lap." He splashed Arthur in the face before taking off at a run, guffawing. Arthur rubbed the water from his eyes and chased after him.

Cei seized a wooden shovel and struck out at Arthur's legs playfully. Arthur leapt out of the way and grabbed a length of timber to defend himself with. The wood clicked and clacked together as the two boys sparred back and forth, scattering some panicked chickens that scuttled out of the way, clucking angrily. Cei tossed aside his shovel and made for a sack of flour that was waiting in a cart outside the bakery. He heaved the sack up and swung it around, aiming for Arthur's head. The bottom of the sack split with a loud rip and the flour erupted from it. Arthur ducked as the gush of flour passed over his head.

"In the name of the Great Mother!" came a bellow.

Cei dropped the empty sack and bit down on a knuckle to stop the laughter that rose up in his chest. Peering from a mask of flour were the enraged eyes of Cadyreith, his father's steward, who had arrived on the scene just in time to catch the billowing white cloud full in the face.

"What on earth do you two think you're playing at?" Cadyreith raged, as he dusted and shook at his clothes in vain. "And wasting good flour too! If you lads were a year or so younger I would demand Lord Cunor take his sword belt to your hides. Maybe I will yet!"

"I'm sorry, Cadyreith," Arthur said, doing a better job of concealing his mirth than his foster-brother.

"Sorry doesn't clean my clothes, boy," the old man said gruffly. "Look at the state of me! And with the lords Owain and Cadwallon arrived just moments ago for a council with your father too!"

Cei forgot his amusement in an instant. "Owain and Cadwallon, here?" he cried.

"If you two had been paying attention to what was going on in the fortress this morning instead of acting like a pair of wild goats," said Cadyreith, "you would have learned that a messenger arrived last night ahead of King Cadwallon bearing grave news."

"*King* Cadwallon?" Arthur and Cei said in unison.

"Aye, king and Pendraig now. The High-king Enniaun died two nights ago, an event which preceded an attack on Cair Dugannu from Ynys Mon.

Venedotia's royal seat is in Gaelic hands now and King Cadwallon is in exile."

"What?" cried Cei. "Are we at war with the Gaels then?"

"That remains to be seen," said Cadyreith. "That's why a council has been called to discuss things. Your father has requested your presence. Arthur's too."

"Are we to sit in on the council?" Cei asked in excitement.

"I suppose so, although I must say that you both have a lot of growing up to do before you become worthy members of any council. Get yourselves dressed in something appropriate. There's no time for finery; we can't keep the Pendraig waiting."

They threw on their tunicas and belted them, ran their fingers through their damp hair and followed Cadyreith down the central range towards the large residence that had once been the praetorium.

Cair Cunor was an old Roman auxiliary fort, banked and ditched on a low shoulder of rock a mile west of the still waters of Lin Tegid. It was little changed since the days of the legions; its lines of barracks and official buildings an ideal home for an army come down from the north seeking new quarters.

Cunedag had chosen the fort and its surrounding commote as the base for his teulu for it lay at the very heart of Venedotia. Bordered by Meriauned, Dunauding, Rumaniog and Eternion, and at the crux of the Roman roads that led north-east and north-west through Venedotia, the teulu could be easily dispatched to any of the seven kingdoms should trouble arise. It was also close to the neighbouring territory of Powys – the old ancestral lands of Lord Vertigernus – whose descendants had never been too comfortable with a warrior dynasty with Pictish blood in their veins on their doorstep.

Cunor ruled from Cair Cunor independently, subject only to the Pendraig. He was the son of Cunedag's second son Osmael – the original penteulu – who had been slain by the Gaels on Ynys Mon. The title had passed to Cunor who had excelled himself in the wars with the Gaels and commanded the fortress from its crumbling praetorium.

As they walked down the central range, Arthur felt a sinking feeling in the pit of his stomach; a horrible feeling of loss that he couldn't quite account for. Everything was changing too fast. As they passed the colonnaded principia, he looked up at the lonely window that faced south. *Does she know?* he wondered.

The mosaic floor and plaster walls of the praetorium rang with excited chatter and wide-eyed faces. 'War' was the word on everybody's lips. It was a word Arthur and Cei had spoken gleefully since they had been old enough to hold a spear and while Cei bounded with enthusiasm, Arthur felt like he was on a high precipice, staring down into a black abyss.

Peace had reigned for over a decade and they had grown up in its comfortable embrace with the luxury of training for a battle that might never come. Now, in a single morning their youthful innocence had suddenly become something precarious that might vanish at any moment. This morning they had been boys fighting with blunted spears and wooden foils. Tomorrow they might be marching in to battle against the Gaels. Cadyreith was right, both he and

Cei had a lot of growing up to do.

The old dining room was filled with people many of whom Arthur did not recognise. He supposed they were mostly from Din Arth. At the head table sat the new Pendraig and his brother, Owain. To the side stood Cei's father, Cunor; a massive man with a fine, yellow beard.

"Ah, Cadyreith, you found my boys," said Cunor. He glanced at Cadyreith's flour-dusted tunic. "Has my faithful steward turned baker?"

"Apologies, my lord. These boys of yours were careless with a sack of flour."

Cunor glared at Arthur and Cei before introducing them. "My lords, this is my son, Cei, and my foster-son, Arthur."

Arthur felt the glances of Cadwallon and Owain pass over him like a cold breeze. If they remembered their illegitimate half-brother, they did not show it.

"Call the room to order," said Cadwallon.

Owain rose and hammered his fist down on the table several times. Everybody in the hall found seats and a hush descended. Cadwallon rose to address them.

"My friends, my loyal followers," he began. "You will have all heard by now that my father, the Pendraig Enniaun Yrth, has died. You may also have heard that Cair Dugannu was overrun by Gaels from Ynys Mon two nights past. These Gaels did not act on a whim. They knew my father was on his deathbed. They were informed by a traitor but this traitor was not from within the walls of Cair Dugannu as I had first thought. This traitor was from without.

"My family and I barely escaped with our lives and

we made, through a roundabout way, to the fortress of my dear brother here. Shortly after my arrival a rider from Cair Dugannu came to the gates bearing a message. The message was sent by King Meriaun of Meriauned."

There was a low rumbling in the hall at this. Heads turned and questioning faces tried to comprehend the Pendraig's words.

"Yes, it is my own cousin who is the traitor," Cadwallon continued. "As the firstborn of the eldest son of Cunedag, he has long cast envious eyes on my father's crown but he was too cowardly to act while he was still alive. He has bargained with the Gaels. What he promised them, I have no idea, but it must be a portion of the new kingdom he is planning to create. He sits now in Cair Dugannu, in my father's chair, and calls himself Pendraig! He would have all the kings of Venedotia bend the knee and pay him homage!"

The low rumble in the hall rose to an outcry so that Cadwallon had to raise his voice to be heard.

"I am cast out of my own home and denied my birth right by my own kin!"

"The Teulu of the Red Dragon must be marshalled!" said Owain, his deep voice carrying farther than his brother's. "We must strike while the iron is hot and oust Meriaun and his Gaelic hounds."

"I shall send out riders immediately, lord," said Cunor. "But much of the teulu comes from commotes ruled by your cousins. How do they stand in the matter?"

"Messengers must be sent to determine their allegiances," said Cadwallon. "King Mor of Rumaniog has long been a friend. I cannot believe he would support Meriaun against me."

"And Elnaw of Docmaeling can surely be counted on," said Owain. His territories lie even further east than my own. We stand between his lands and the Gaels. He has nothing to gain in supporting Meriaun, but if Rhos falls then his lands will be next."

"And of the others?" Cunor said. "As we sit here counting our allies, surely Meriaun sits at Cair Dugannu and counts his own. Who knows how many of them he has already coerced into supporting him?"

"Aye, we must send out our messengers without delay," said Cadwallon.

After some more discussion on logistics and accommodation for the gathering teulu, the meeting was adjourned and Arthur left Cei talking with his father. He exited the praetorium, crossed the central range and entered the principia through a side door.

As he climbed the stairs he passed a window and could see the dark green of the mountains to the south, dappled by the sunlight shining through drifting clouds. He often hoped that this view was some comfort to the woman who kept herself concealed from the world here in the upper story of the principia.

Her name was Eigyr and she had once been loved by a king. That love had died and her heart had been broken beyond repair. Some said that her mind had been broken too, although never within Arthur's hearing unless they wanted a bloodied nose. Few thought of her or even remembered her for she kept herself concealed from the world that had so ruined her. Although it was a self-imposed exile and though

Arthur visited her daily, he knew she was lonely.

She had some companions in the few other women who lived at Cair Cunor. They occasionally sat with her and helped on her tapestries. Weaving was how Eigyr passed her time and her chamber was hung with many extravagant tapestries in vibrant hues. She was weaving when Arthur opened the door and entered her chamber.

"Hello, Mother," he said.

Eigyr looked up from her loom and the woman who was currently keeping her company stood up to leave, out of respect for their privacy.

"Hello, Arthur."

He sat down in the vacated chair and drew it close to his mother's side. She continued with her tapestry and he watched her delicate fingers weave the coloured threads in and out of the warp. He could see the image of two peacocks drinking from a vase taking form, their vibrant colours creeping across the warp threads like the approaching tide of the sea. This motif, he knew, was symbolic of Christians drinking from the waters of eternal life.

The sons of Cunedag and their descendants worshiped the old gods but Eigyr, like most Britons, was a Christian. Arthur was undecided on which path he truly believed was his. He regularly attended mass with his mother in the small chapel by the banks of the river but he was used to Cei and the others swearing by the old gods and by Modron above all. He had seen warriors pour milk on the fields and wine on the floor at feasts in libation to the Great Mother. He had seen Cei's father bury the heart of a stag as an offering to the horned Lord of Beasts after a hunt. He had even seen a fine sword cast into Lin Tegid at the funeral of an old warrior so that it would be with him in the Otherworld. And at the spring festival of Calan Mai, when the bonfires of purification dotted the hills like fireflies, he had danced and drunk himself stupid with the others in an orgy of pagan passion.

"You have heard the news?" he asked her tentatively.

"Yes," said Eigyr, her brow furrowed as she concentrated. She looked up and sighed, as if remembering herself. Her brown eyes were suddenly full of sympathy. "I'm sorry, my son."

"Did you love him?"

It was a question he had often wanted to ask his mother but had never found the opportunity or courage. Now seemed as good a time as any.

"I loved him deeply once," she said. "And he loved me too, I have no doubt as to that, despite all the people who called me his whore."

Arthur winced. His mother's bitterness for her accusers far outweighed any bitterness she may have had for his father. It had been sixteen years since the High-king Enniaun Yrth had sent his pregnant mistress away. Arthur had suspected that he had promised to make her his queen although his mother had never admitted as much.

Eigyr was the daughter of Anblaud; a nobleman who had supported Vertigernus in the old days. When they had met, Enniaun had been in his forty-seventh year and Cadwallon and Owain's mother had been dead two years. Anblaud and his family were visiting the court of the Pendraig on Ynys Mon and few failed to notice the coy looks and idle chat that passed between the king and Anblaud's young daughter. Old Anblaud must have been giddy at the prospect of marrying his daughter to the king of Venedotia and Arthur imagined him encouraging the flirtations, giving his daughter tips on the best way to arouse an old man's cock.

Something blossomed between them – love, according to Eigyr but mere lust to everybody else – and Eigyr fell pregnant. She was already back in her father's lands in the south when it became known. Anblaud had accompanied her back to Ynys Mon, her belly swelling by the day, hoping that the impending scandal would hasten the marriage plans.

Enniaun did not make her his queen. He sent her to carry the babe to term in the farthest fringes of his domain. He had found another woman of higher stock and, although he would not deny the child was his, he would not acknowledge it either. It was an act of charity, many considered, to accommodate her at all but to Eigyr it was a cruel dismissal. She bore the insults with her head held high. People called her the king's whore but she knew that she had been the king's great love, denied a place at his side by mere circumstance while within her womb, royal blood quickened.

Arthur was born at Din Arth from whence he took his name. In his fifth year, Eigyr moved him to Cair Cunor where he was to be fostered and trained as a warrior in the Teulu of the Red Dragon as Arthur mab Eigyr. His very name left no ambiguity about his parentage. Such was the lot of a bastard.

Arthur had never been bothered by the fact that he

had no father. Life at Cair Cunor consisted of drills, lessons in sword and spear and horsemanship alongside hard-bitten veterans who cared less about a youth's ancestry than they did in his ability to fight and ride. And Arthur was good at both. He had always been aware of who his father was but it was something he had never dwelt on. In fact, he had thought more about his father today than he had in the past sixteen years.

His father was dead and it felt like a chapter of his life had been closed. Of course, he had never been formally recognised by him so thought of any inheritance had never occurred to him. But now that his father *could* never recognise him it felt, in a way, as if a great burden that had rested on his shoulders all his life had suddenly been lifted.

"What are you thinking?" his mother asked.

He shrugged. "I don't know. It's not as if I knew the man. I wasn't even a son to him."

"Don't ever believe that!" she snapped. "Bastard or no, you are as much his son as Owain and Cadwallon!"

He had forgotten his mother's fierce pride in her son's heritage; a pride that occasionally bordered on the delusional. "I didn't mean that," he said. "But you can't deny that he never acknowledged me. I was nothing to him."

"That doesn't matter," she persisted. "You have the blood of Cunedag in you. Nobody can take that away from you. Even if they abandon you, send you to live far away in some remote fortress like they did me and your sister Anna."

He was shocked. He had never heard his mother

talk of his long-lost half-sister Anna. She was several years older than him and, like him, she had been a bastard. But her pathway into this world had been nothing so innocent as a silly affair.

It happened just as Cunedag and his sons were celebrating their final victory over the Gaels. Meriaun, at the tender age of eighteen, had slain the Gaelic war-leader Beli mac Benlli in single combat and his followers had taken to their hide-covered boats and sailed back to Erin. Venedotia was won and the foundations of a dynasty were being laid.

The celebrations took place on Ynys Mon where Cunedag planned to build his *Lys* – his great court. Upon the island lived a community of priestesses, nine in number, who were called the Morgens – the *sea born*. They had worshiped the Great Mother since before the Romans had come, keeping to their sacred lakes and groves, custodians of the land's ancient knowledge.

The priestesses came to bless Venedotia's new rulers and rituals of kingship and sovereignty were carried out that were as ancient as the hills of Albion itself. What followed was an evening of drunken debauchery that shamed the house of Cunedag for a generation.

Enniaun was always a volatile and headstrong youth hence his nickname 'Yrth'; 'the impetuous'. At the age of twenty-eight he was a seasoned warrior and a virile one at that, renowned for brawling, drinking and womanising. On that night, one of the young priestesses caught his eye and, the drink and his own inflated sense of self-worth getting the better of him, he pursued this priestess into a secluded spot and raped her.

Such a thing was unheard of for the priestesses of the Great Mother were sacred in their own right. The Morgens cried their outrage and Cunedag roared at his insolent son for his blasphemous trespassing. The Morgens departed back to their dwellings in the wilderness and the sons of Cunedag were left to sober themselves in the cold light of dawn, wondering what they had done.

Nine months passed before the priestess came knocking at the door of Cunedag's Lys, which was little more than scaffolding in those early days. She bore a babe in her robes; a girl she claimed was the result of Enniaun's sacrilege. She had been cast out of her order for the Morgens valued maidenhood as essential to their service to the Great Mother. Feeling the eyes of his father and brothers upon him, Enniaun felt ashamed and took the woman and her child in.

The girl was named Anna and was placed in the care of wetnurses while her mother, who said that she could not abide to live in a fortress after spending all her life under the open sky, returned to the wilderness to live as a hermit.

By the time Anna had reached her twelfth year, old Cunedag had died and Enniaun ruled as Pendraig. He soon found a use for his bastard daughter. Since Cunedag and his sons had left their old seat at Din Eidyn in the far north, the wild Pictish tribes had united under their king, Talorc mab Aniel and had taken the lands of the Votadini. A lord from the south called Leudon had fought hard to drive the Picts back north and had succeeded in recapturing

Din Eidyn. To secure his claim over the area, he wished to marry into the line of Cunedag whose ancestral home he now ruled. The young Anna presented such a chance.

Anna, at twelve years old, was sent north to become King Leudon's queen and all thought it a good way to rid themselves of the embarrassment caused by Enniaun's drunkenness on that fateful night. But Anna was a reluctant bride and she ran away no less than a week after the wedding, to die in the wild heather and peat bogs of her new kingdom.

Another unwitting casualty of the family he had been born into, Arthur reflected bitterly. But he did not care for such trivial things as family, at least not in the sense of blood relations. Cei was as good as a brother to him and Cunor, distant yet kind, was the only father he had ever needed. Let his mother pine for what might have been. His family was the teulu and war was coming.

Meddyf

They waited in the dining hall of the praetorium while the messenger approached. Meddyf glanced at her husband sitting at the head of the hall. His face was impassive, exuding strength but also fairness. He looked every inch the king and a far better one than his father had been. *If only he could see himself the way others do*, she mused. *If only he could overcome his doubts.*

It wasn't the brewing war that had kept him awake every night since they had arrived at Cair Cunor. Cadwallon was a veteran of the Gaelic Wars and was no coward in the face of battle. But he was no longer a young prince seeking glory, he was a king; a king of kings. And all Venedotia looked to him for leadership. That was the task which occupied his mind as they lay in each other's arms until the small hours. That, and the unnameable horror that had been unleashed upon them at Cair Dugannu.

He had forbidden them all from mentioning the skull-faced warriors, who had made such short work of his men, to anybody at Cair Cunor. It would damage morale, he said, and he was absolutely right. She shuddered to think of those mad, howling things and knew she was not alone in suspecting that some pagan sorcery had been at work. It was best not to incite gossip until allies had been procured and the teulu was strong.

The messenger had been one of six dispatched to all the sub-kings of Venedotia. All but one of them had borne Cadwallon's plea to support him against Meriaun the Usurper. The messenger to Meriaun had merely carried Cadwallon's terms of surrender.

Being the closest kingdom, Eternion had been the first to yield its answer and it was an answer that did not please the gathered bannermen in the hall of Cair Cunor.

"King Etern, having received the address of the lord Cadwallon mab Enniaun relating to his cousin Meriaun mab Tybiaun, has sought fit to return this answer," said Cadyreith, reading from a scroll, its wax seal broken and dangling precariously. "That he chooses to decline to enter into an alliance with Cadwallon. That he does not find the grounds sufficient to induce him to remove Meriaun from the throne which would have passed to his father had not Tybiaun mab Cunedag fallen before his time."

Cadyreith lowered the scroll and the messenger looked up at Cadwallon, nervously awaiting his reaction.

"He refuses!" cried Owain in a fit of indignation. "Our own uncle chooses that … that *swineherd* over you!"

"Aye, our own uncle," said Cadwallon. "But then, our uncle is the last of the generation who begrudged our father the throne. It does not surprise me that he chooses to support Meriaun merely to spite me."

"Have any other messengers returned, lord?" asked a bannerman from Rhos.

"No, none," Cadwallon replied. "It is still early. We must not let ourselves be disheartened. Etern was always going to be the first to answer and his answer does not surprise me overmuch. Others will rally to our cause, I have no doubt of it."

Good! Thought Meddyf. Good, husband. Show no fear. Save your fear for the dark nights when I can hold you and we can fight your worries together.

"Others may rally," said Cunor, "but this fortress has always been within easy striking distance of Eternion. Etern could take it in a day if his loyalty to Meriaun stretched that far."

"We do not know if he would go so far as to enter into hostilities against me," said Cadwallon.

"If he does then we do not have enough spears to defend ourselves. The teulu is only as strong as the number of warriors provided by each kingdom. And none have arrived …"

"They will come," Cadwallon said. "They will come."

The council dispersed and Meddyf went out to the gardens. It was a generous term for the rough vegetable plots that had been dug over the old Roman flower beds and ornamental bushes of the fort commander's residence. Lord Cunor put little stock in such things as flowers. Instead the ground was given up to the growing of turnips, peas and cabbages. Even herbs were considered a waste of space it seemed, for there was none of the thyme, mint and celery seed that grew in the kitchen gardens at Cair Dugannu or Din Arth. Cair Cunor was a military fortification and everything within its walls was geared to the feeding and quartering of a warband.

She found Elen sunning herself on a stone bench as a nurse dandled little Cunlas between her knees. Guidno played at little wooden soldiers on the cracked paving while Maelcon looked on, bored. He was sulking after having been admonished for getting into a fight with the baker's son. Meddyf didn't know what the scuffle had been about but it had ended with a bloody-nose for the baker's son who had been too frightened to strike the young prince. Cadwallon had given Maelcon a stern lecture on the importance of humility.

"I thought you would be making a name for yourself in the training yard, Maelcon," she said. "I'm sure Cair Cunor boasts the best martial tutors in all Venedotia."

"What's the point?" Maelcon answered with a surly frown. "Father would never let me ride with him anyway. Why bother getting myself sweaty and dusty for no good reason?"

Maelcon had never shown much interest in the martial arts. He learned his lessons as was demanded of him but his instructors often despaired at his lack of interest. He would much rather spend his time reading old texts. Guidno on the other hand, showed more promise but he was still very young. *Gods, they are both still so young,* she thought. *That war should come now, before they are ready!*

"Your son is right to be bored, Meddyf," said Elen. "It is so dreadfully dull here. While our husbands talk endlessly of war, we are doomed to tedium in this ghastly place. Do you know, they started training right outside our window before the sun was up this morning? I couldn't sleep a wink. And we are all squeezed into these awful Roman lodgings where there is a constant draught through the cracked plaster. Not to mention the food!"

"This is the teulu's headquarters, Elen," said Meddyf. "They have little room for luxuries here." She resisted the urge to roll her eyes. Elen had done nothing but complain since they had arrived at Cair

Cunor. It wasn't as if any of them had a choice. Just as Meddyf's own home at Cair Dugannu was now occupied by Meriaun and his Gaels, so too was Din Arth. They had managed to get away before the Gaels fell on them, narrowly avoiding a siege. They were now a family without a home, moving from fort to fort, one pace ahead of the enemy.

Meddyf was struggling to keep her own spirits up. She did not like forts and drills and turnip stew any more than Elen did. She had been born beneath open skies on the wide moors where grassy expanses circled the shores of Lin Conui. It was from that lake that the Afon Conui flowed north to the sea, and it was that river's current that had carried Meddyf when she had been little more than a girl, ferried by her family's ambitions, into the arms of Cadwallon.

Her father, Maeldaf, was a bannerman who had held a commote for Enniaun Yrth. It had been a match the like of which a minor noble could only dream of and Meddyf had been happy with it too for her part. The young prince was handsome, true, but he was also kind and intelligent and nothing at all like his father, who was a blustering old bear of a man, rarely out of his cups.

Cadwallon was occupied with his lords for most of the afternoon and Meddyf did not see him until it was nearly time to take their seats in the praetorium for meat. He was in a rage when she found him in the colonnaded atrium.

"Someone's been talking!" he grumbled.

"Who's been talking?" It wasn't just rage in his voice. She detected a fear there too.

"There are mutterings in the teulu that we face otherworldly enemies. That the dead march against us. I specifically forbade you all from talking about what we saw the night of the attack."

Meddyf suppressed a flashback to those skull-faced monstrosities who had known neither fear nor pain in their mad slaughter. "Does Owain know?"

"Yes, I told him because he is my brother and I trust him. And you needn't think it was his big mouth for it was he who brought me news of this tongue-wagging about the fort."

"Well, don't look at me, husband. I have respected your wishes and agree with their necessity. The last thing we need is fear demoralising the warriors."

"Somebody doesn't share your discretion. Besides you, Owain and the boys, only young Gobrui knows and I am loath to upbraid the one who aided our escape."

They entered the dining hall together, and once the meal was over, Cadwallon called in a series of warriors who had been overheard talking about dead Gaels marching to war. Each of them was grilled separately and finally, by following the line of whispers like a hunter tracking the spoor of a deer, the source of the rumours was revealed.

It was the young son of the baker who had come running to his father with gruesome tales. The baker, having no more sense than an empty bucket or so Cadwallon admonished him, had gone on to tell the fish trader's wife who had told a blacksmith's apprentice and so the rumour had spread. And who,

Cadwallon demanded of the trembling baker's boy, had given *him* such wild flights of fancy?

Some adults would not have told Cadwallon the truth for fear of being accused of insolence but children have no such inhibitions when the truth is demanded of them and the baker's boy spoke the name of Cadwallon's eldest son.

Maelcon, resentful of the ticking off he had received for bloodying the baker's son's nose, had taken his revenge by filling his head with the most frightening images he could think of; of rotting corpses, their skulls pecked clean of flesh and gleaming white in the moonlight, lurching and shambling across the straits. These dead men, Maelcon had claimed, were in league with King Meriaun and were hell-bent on devouring everybody within Cair Cunor's walls.

All were dismissed and Cadwallon summoned his son, his face a mask of controlled rage. Meddyf left with the others, recognising the need for a father and son to be alone together. She hoped Cadwallon wouldn't beat the boy. He wasn't a particularly strict father but he had every right to be enraged. With so many enemies and so few allies, the last thing they needed was rumour spreading like wildfire.

She passed Maelcon on his way into the hall. He looked frightened, knowing that he was for it, whatever he had done, but still held his head high and proud, every bit the prince. Despite his foolishness, Meddyf's heart soared with love for him.

Later, when Maelcon had been sent to bed, Meddyf sat with Cadwallon at the head table. The servants had finished clearing away and were laying down fresh rushes on the floor.

"I hope you weren't too hard on him," she said.

"How could I be?" he replied, shrugging his shoulders in exasperation. "He is only ten, after all. And the things he saw …"

"A child's imagination soon runs away with him."

"But that's just the problem. It wasn't his imagination, was it? He disobeyed my orders in opening his mouth, but those things he told the baker's boy were no fantasies. They were real."

"Embellished to a good degree."

"True, but we do face the dead. By all the Gods, I don't know how it is possible, but somehow Meriaun has raised the very dead against me!"

It was the first time he had spoken it aloud and Meddyf could see that it was something of a relief to him. Excepting Maelcon, they had all kept silent on the matter. It was as if giving voice to their thoughts would somehow make them more real, and they had enough facing them without dealing with the dead arisen just yet. So those fears had been relegated to the dark, primal part of their minds, not forgotten, just placed to one side to be dealt with at a later time.

"We don't know what those things were," she said at length.

"You didn't see them up close," he said. "You didn't face them in battle."

It was true, she had only caught a glimpse of them as they had been escorted back to their quarters. She had seen white bone and deathly pale bodies smeared with blood and woad, slick and glistening in the moonlight. The warriors who had refused to betray their lord had been led out, and she had been glad that the edge of the hall had blocked their vision and prevented her and her children from seeing what those monsters had done to the prisoners.

Monsters they were, that was beyond a doubt. But the dead given life anew? She knew the native tales of Albion were full of such things but she had been raised a Christian, despite her marriage to a pagan. She had never objected to the rituals and superstitions of the family she had married into, keeping her own mass in the chapel at Penlassoc, but she had never really contemplated that there was any truth behind the old tales. Her husband clearly believed in them for she knew what nightmares rode roughshod through his dreams at night, making him toss and turn. It wasn't just the shame of losing Cair Dugannu. It was the fear that ate away at his confidence; the raw, primal fear of the dark and what it might hold.

When she retired to her chamber that night, she prayed to God for guidance and aid in the days to come.

Arthur

The dragon standard fluttered high over Cair Cunor; a rallying point to all who would oppose Meriaun the Usurper. So far, only King Mor had answered the call. Warriors from Rumaniog and the commotes of Rhos arrived in a steady stream by the day and the fort grew full to bursting.

Arthur and Cei were charged with overseeing accommodation for the newcomers. Several of Cair Cunor's barracks had been disused for over a decade and needed a thorough cleaning out of bracken and sparrows' nests. Even the old bathhouse, which had fallen into disrepair long ago, was converted into sleeping quarters. When they ran out of room in the fortress, further accommodation was found in the abandoned settlement on its south-eastern wall.

The warriors were in high spirits; many of whom, like Arthur and Cei, were young and had been waiting for a battle all their lives. They were swarthy, moustachioed youths with bright tunicas and shields painted with the black raven of Rumaniog, the bear of Rhos and the various sigils of a myriad commotes.

One figure arrived at Cair Cunor's gates alone. He rode a grey mare and wore a green tunica under a hooded cloak that had once been white but was now grey, stained and blackened at the hem from travel. He had an old, lined face burned brown by the sun. It still looked capable of a smile if the mood took him. His once black hair and beard were now streaked with grey.

"Menw!" said Arthur with excitement. "The Pendraig's bard!"

Menw had not been seen for many months. A bard was not expected to spend all his time reciting the tales of ancient heroes and extolling the merits of his lord to mead-soaked audiences. A good bard, many lords maintained, was one who travelled the realm extensively, learning new tales and keeping his finger on the pulse of the people to best advise his lord. Arthur had only seen Menw a couple of times in his life when the bard had passed through Cair Cunor on his travels. He mostly remembered Menw's songs and the strumming of his long fingers on the harp he carried in his crane-skin satchel.

"What's his business here?" said Cei. "We need warriors, not bards."

"Nobody has known of his whereabouts for a long time now," said Arthur. "He disappeared before the Pendraig grew sick. Who knows what he has been up to or what news he brings?"

When Cadwallon learned that his father's old bard had returned, he immediately called another council. Arthur and Cei, glad of a break from arguing with warriors about bunks, the digging of latrines and the finding of fodder for the horses, eagerly washed up and made their way to the praetorium.

"What news from the commotes?" Cadwallon asked Menw as a cup of mead and a platter of bread and chicken were placed before the weary bard.

Menw drank deeply and bit off a hunk of the bread. All in the chamber waited patiently as the old man chewed it and washed it down with mead before starting on the chicken thigh. He had an appetite that suggested that his fare of late had been meagre.

"Fear sweeps Venedotia like a plague," he said at

last, licking meat juices from his fingers. "In every commote from the Laigin Peninsula to the farms beneath Cair Legion's walls people burn bright fires into the night and sleep with doors bolted."

"When I have marshalled my teulu I shall drive these Gaels back into the sea," said Cadwallon. "The people will have nothing more to fear once this war is over."

"Gaels is one thing," said Menw, gnawing on the chicken bone. "What the people fear comes not from Erin nor is it easily dispatched with swords and spears."

"What are you getting at?" Cadwallon asked, his eyes narrowing.

"Tell me, my king, when the Gaels took Cair Dugannu, were they accompanied by any … *others*?"

"Others?"

"Were there any in their number who did not seem of this world?"

"What is this?" Owain asked, his voice testy. "My brother was forced from his ancestral home by Gaels allied to our cousin Meriaun. What do you mean by *others*?"

Cadwallon was silent and Menw's eyes remained fixed on him as if waiting for something. Everybody in the chamber turned to look at their king.

"What I am about to say," Cadwallon said slowly, "does not go beyond this chamber. Is that quite clear?"

Arthur found himself voicing his assent along with the others.

"You have all heard the rumours, I am sure," Cadwallon continued. "The truth of the matter is that there *were* some others that night. I have tried to stamp out those rumours for I feared to see the same loss of hope in the eyes of my teulu as I saw in my father's men on the walls of Cair Dugannu." He paused to pour himself some mead and his hands shook a little, spilling some over the rim of his horn. He gulped deeply and set down the horn firmly. "I don't know what they were, gods help me. They wore masks, of that much I am certain. Masks made from skulls. They were naked and their flesh was pale. I am not even sure that they were entirely … *alive*."

"Not alive?" asked Cunor. "What are you getting at?"

"I fought close to them. I smelt their stench, saw their black, lifeless eyes. I saw blows dealt to them that would have killed you or I and yet not one of them fell."

"Did these men call out any battle cries or curses?" said Menw.

"Not that I could make out. They screeched and yelled a good deal."

"Did you hear any words pass their lips at all?"

"No, none."

"Then it is as I suspected. The *Cauldron-born*."

"Cauldron-born?" asked Cunor.

"Do you not remember your nursery tales, Cunor mab Osmael? Do you not remember Bran and the Cauldron of Rebirth?"

"Nursery tales, aye," Cunor replied. "And I left them in the nursery where they belong."

"The simplest story told to a child often holds a kernel of truth," said Menw. "And believe me, the Cauldron of Rebirth is as real as this table." He knocked the rough oak with his knuckle.

"A tale, surely! A tale of heroes and battles that never happened!"

"Are not the warriors and battles of one generation the heroes and legends of the next?"

"Cauldron-born!" Owain scoffed. "We are here to plan our campaign, bard. If you've nothing of use to tell us then …"

"Owain," cautioned Cadwallon. "Menw was our father's bard long before we were given our first spears. His kind are the keepers of this land's knowledge; knowledge which block-headed warriors would do well to heed." He turned his eyes back to Menw. "What do you know?"

"It has been many years since I journeyed to Ynys Mon," the bard continued. "A British bard receives a poor welcome there these days. There are fishermen and traders who occasionally cross the straits – those the Gaels allow – and I have spoken with several of them. They say that the Morgens have acquired a great treasure."

"The Morgens?" Owain asked. "Surely the Gaels have raped and murdered the nine sisters by now. We have not heard from them in over a decade."

"You forget that the Gaels once shared our veneration of the Great Mother," said Menw. "Those who have not converted to the worship of the Christ Messiah still follow the old ways. And this Diugurnach is a pagan of the staunchest stock by all accounts. No, the Morgens are alive and have been secretly brewing a recipe of ancient fear. It is my belief that they have found a treasure so ancient and powerful that they have cowed even the Gaels into their thrall through fear alone."

"Are you telling us that the Morgens have found the Cauldron of Rebirth and are cooking up the dead to send against us?" Cunor demanded.

Menw said nothing. There was a frightened stillness in the chamber that was broken only by Owain's outraged protestations.

"Why should the Morgens support the Gaels against us?" said Cadwallon. "And how does Meriaun fit into all of this?"

"That remains to be discovered," said Menw. "There is a triumvirate here somewhere; an alliance that connects Meriaun to the Gaels and the Morgens but how and why are questions I do not have the answers to. Yet."

"We must seek out these answers," said Cadwallon.

"You're not taking all this seriously?" said Owain.

Cadwallon turned sharply to his brother. "I saw them, Owain! You did not! You did not see how they tore through the men at Cair Dugannu, how they chilled their hearts to stone with fear, how they turned seasoned warriors into meek lambs for the slaughter. I was there. I saw them. There are forces at work too terrible to be ignored and I will not charge blindly into a war without knowing what it is that I face. Tell me, Menw, what must we do?"

Menw sat back in his chair and folded his hands in his lap as if he had been waiting for precisely this question.

"We must journey to Ynys Mon under cover of night and without the enemy knowing it. We must steal the cauldron. Only then can the power of the

Cauldron-born be shattered. You have only to pick the men for the job and I will lead them myself."

"We are on the cusp of a war the like of which Venedotia has not seen since Cunedag's day," said Owain in defiance. "And you ask us to send a band of warriors chasing after some nursery tale which will likely get them all killed?"

"How many men do you need?" Cadwallon asked Menw.

"Seven should do it," said Menw. "Seven is a good number. Seven returned from Erin when Bran set out to rescue his sister Branwen. Seven were victorious against the cauldron before."

"Seven out of Bran's entire teulu!" said Owain. "Oh yes, I have not forgotten the tales. And how many of our warriors will return from Ynys Mon? None? While we face all the might of Meriauned and their allies. Brother, you must see that this is folly!"

"Seven men we can spare," Cadwallon replied. "Seven to uncover the enemy's plot. Seven to bring hope to thousands. Menw, you shall have your men. Cunor, I would discuss this with you in private. This council is ended."

Owain threw his hands up in despair as the chamber emptied itself. Arthur and Cei followed the older men out into the shade of the colonnades.

"Damn fool, coming here and stirring things up," said Cei, as they watched Menw from across the atrium. The bard was talking to some young warriors who were pestering him for news, their faces full of hope and excitement. They had not been at the council. They did not know what they all faced. "I wish he'd kept well away from here. We are outnumbered and outmanoeuvred as it is. Cadwallon had the right of it, keeping silent about those damned wild men. The last thing we need is ghost stories scaring the men."

"So you think it's all woodsmoke and old wives' tales?" Arthur demanded. He didn't know why but he was irritated by Cei's scepticism.

Cei turned to him. "What do you think? The *Cauldron-born*? The Morgens stirring up mists of sorcery against us? Of course it is!"

"Cadwallon doesn't think so," said Arthur. "Didn't you hear the fear in his voice? Didn't you see how he listened to Menw while Owain and your father scoffed at him?" He felt angry. Cei had begun to get on his nerves over the last few days but he could not quite put his finger on why.

Menw had finished speaking with the warriors and had made his way over to them.

"Young Cei mab Cunor," said the bard, bowing his head just a little to indicate a portion of the respect usually reserved for royalty. "And Arthur mab Eigyr, I believe?" he gave Arthur the same, short bow.

Arthur was taken aback, as much by the bow as by the bard's recognition of him.

"Yes, I can see Enniaun Yrth's eyes in your face, boy," said Menw. "My condolences."

It took a while for Arthur to understand what the bard was referring to but then he grasped it. His father had died. It was a natural thing to say out of politeness, perhaps even to a bastard who had never known his father. And then a second thing occurred to him. Aside from his mother, Menw was the first person since his father's death to offer their condolences. Not even Cei, who was as a brother to him, had made even the slightest acknowledgement of it. And the source of his irritation for his foster-brother over the past few days was finally revealed to him.

"Thank you," Arthur said. "Your coming is welcome. But, please, there is one thing I do not understand about what you have told us."

The bard cocked his head expectantly.

"The cauldron was destroyed by one of Bran's warriors, so the tales go," said Arthur. "If the tales are true, then how is it that the cauldron still exists?"

Menw smiled. "Objects can pass in and out of Annun just as we mortals do. They are reborn, so to speak, as we are, and can live many lives."

Annun was one of the names for the Otherworld and meant the 'Deep Place'. Ynys Aballach was another; the 'Isle of Apples'.

"Cei! Arthur!" called Cunor from across the courtyard. "Get over here!"

Menw accompanied them back into the dining room. It was empty but for Cadwallon, Owain and Cunor.

"Sit down, both of you," said Cunor. No such command was given to Menw who required none and took his seat alongside them.

"This mission to Ynys Mon," Cunor began. "How does it sit with you?"

"A wild goose chase, father," said Cei. "An unnecessary expenditure when we need every spear here to repel Etern's forces should he decide to march on us."

"And you, Arthur? You know that you have always been free to speak your mind to me, just as Cei is."

"I do not agree with Cei, my lord," Arthur replied. "If Menw believes that this is a worthwhile mission that can improve our knowledge of our enemies' plans whilst simultaneously undermining them, then I can only agree with him."

He saw Menw smiling at him and avoided the scowl he knew would be smeared across Cei's face. He could see something of that scowl on the face of Owain for he was of a like mind to Cei but Cadwallon remained impassive, watching Arthur closely.

"I'm glad you agree to it, Arthur," said Cunor, "for, although I share some of Cei's misgivings, it has been decided that this mission will set out immediately and you are both to lead it."

There was a heavy silence as this sank in.

"Us?" Cei exclaimed. "We are to go on this foolhardy mission behind enemy lines? Do you think so little of us, Father, that you would send us away upon the eve of war?"

"Do not be petulant, Cei!" Cunor snapped. "Did it not cross your mind that it is because I think so *highly* of you both that I have agreed to send you on this mission, this mission which has been sanctioned by our Pendraig himself?"

Cei lapsed into a sullen silence, not wanting to argue further with his father in front of Cadwallon and Owain.

"Menw will be guiding you on this journey," said Cadwallon, "and your father will pick four of his best warriors to accompany you."

"You are to leave this afternoon," said Cunor,

"and make for the Afon Conui. Under cover of darkness you will travel to the coast and pass right under the noses of the enemy at Cair Dugannu. From there you will cross the straits and make landfall upon the shores of Ynys Mon before dawn. I have already sent Beduir and Gualchmei ahead to procure a fishing boat for your purposes."

Cei's face brightened a little at this. Beduir was known to them, older and well-liked. He had already had his first taste of combat in a Powysian raid and had the scars to prove it. Gualchmei was Arthur's cousin, cunning and wily, who made up for his short stature with cat-like nimbleness.

"I suggest you go down to the armoury now and select what gear you want to take," said Cunor. "I will have the remaining two members of the party ready in front of the stables and will see you off from there."

As Arthur and Cei rose, Cadwallon stood up and extended his arm to them. "I do not take your bravery lightly," he said, "and you will forever have my deepest gratitude. I wish the three of you luck and look forward to your return."

"I just can't believe it!" Cei said to Arthur as they walked down the central range towards the armoury. "We've waited all our lives for a war and now that one has come, my father sends us as far away from it as possible."

"We may yet see some fighting," said Arthur. "Ynys Mon is probably infested with Gaels."

"If they haven't all crossed to the mainland with Diugurnach."

"They wouldn't leave their lands unguarded. I think you are wrong to assume that this will be an easy reconnaissance mission."

"Come on, Arthur! My father is sending us there so we will not risk our lives in the battle to come. After all our training he still sees us as children. He's trying to protect us or perhaps he doesn't trust us not to shame him in battle."

In the armoury they began selecting weapons from the great racks of shields, swords, spears and axes. They needed to travel light so they avoided the heavy mail and scale coats for rough-spun tunicas and short cloaks. Cei chose a round buckler that had once been painted green but now much of the wood showed through while Arthur chose a blue one studded with iron nails. They took spears and the long Roman swords known as spathas.

Cei went to the stables to see to their horses while Arthur headed to the principia. As he climbed the stairs, he wondered when, if ever, he would climb those stairs again. Who knew what might happen while he was away?

"Mother," he said, as he entered the chamber at the top. "I am going away."

She looked up sharply at him, concern crossing her face.

"Cei and I will be riding out before dusk on orders from Lord Cunor."

"So," she said slowly, "you have finally become a warrior. You know, in ancient times, it was traditional for the mother to determine when her son was ready for battle by presenting him with his first spear."

Arthur smiled. "But if it was left up to you, I would be grey in the beard before I received my spear."

Eigyr forced a smile. "You are all I have, Arthur. I could not bear to lose you on some muddy battlefield."

"You won't," he replied, full of a confidence he wished that he truly felt. "It is a simple reconnaissance mission. If there is to be a battle, I doubt we shall even see any of it."

"And that disappoints you, I can tell," replied his mother. "You are keen for battle like all unproven warriors. Just take care of yourself, Arthur. You have a destiny far greater than that of a simple soldier. One day your brothers will realise this and accept you as their equal."

Arthur didn't bother to argue. He had long ago come to terms with his mother's irrational pride in him. But being cooped up in this tower, he was her only contact with the outside world, her only reason for living. He leant forward to kiss her on the forehead. She patted his beardless cheek softly in return and he could see the faintest sign of tears in her eyes as he got up to leave.

Outside, the chaos of the fortress hit him like a wall of noise. Warriors were training in the yard by the barracks, men saddled horses and captains roared orders, all to the clink of hammer upon anvil as weapons and armour were forged and repaired.

Cunor was by the stables, talking to Menw. Two warriors stood nearby. One of them had a beautiful peregrine falcon on his gloved wrist, a hood pulled down over its eyes. Arthur saw Cei approaching down the central range.

"Boys," said Cunor. "I want you to meet Cundelig and Guihir. Cundelig is a scout trained in the Roman fashion. The eyes of his bird, Hebog, can spot enemy troop movements miles away. Guihir is famed for his mastery of tongues. He is fluent in as many languages as I can count and some say that he can even speak to beasts."

Guihir smiled proudly at Cei and Arthur. Cei rolled his eyes.

"Father," said Cei, "I think it would have been better if I had chosen from the men myself."

"No," replied Cunor sternly. "This is your first mission and I decide who goes with you."

"At least give me a few men who can actually fight!"

"Do not argue with me, Cei. Your mission requires stealth, not blunt force. The men I have chosen have the right skills to get the job done. And if it comes to a fight, I'll wager they are worthier than you give them credit."

It was futile to argue. As Menw, Cundelig and Guihir mounted their horses, Cei mumbled under his breath to Arthur; "An old teller of tales, a soldier who uses his tongue more than his spear and a man with a bird. I only hope we *do* encounter a party of Gaels, just so my father will see how misguided he was to send these fools with us."

Arthur nodded silently as they swung themselves up into their saddles. Two servants would ride with them to the Afon Conui and then return with the horses. Cadwallon appeared just as they were preparing to set out. He smiled at them and threw out a salute as a Roman general might have done from his tribune on the parade ground in the old days as a legion marched out to battle. But they were not a legion. They were five men – soon to be seven – heading beyond enemy lines with no idea of what might be waiting for them.

Cunor did not embrace them or waste words on sentimentality. They were on duty and were no longer his sons, but his warriors. They had a mission to fulfil. The gates of Cair Cunor were heaved open, and beyond the rays of the slowly sinking sun turned the mountains to gold. Cei led them out with Arthur at his side and Menw, Cundelig and Guihir behind, the waning light glinting off their iron helms. Arthur turned his head to glance at the window on the upper story of the principia. He wondered if his mother was watching him from that window, her cheeks wet with tears. He set his face, turned in his saddle and focused on the road ahead.

PART II

"And Arthur called Menw the son of Teirgwaedd, in order that if they went into a savage country, he might cast a charm and an illusion over them, so that none might see them whilst they could see every one."

- Culhwch and Olwen

The Afon Conui wound north and gradually widened as the moorland sloped down into a wooded vale. They rode through the shimmering tributaries and, as darkness fell, the hooves of their horses sent up the gushing waters in glittering diamonds.

Arthur and Cei breathed the cool night air deeply. Despite the seeming triviality of their mission, this was what they had been waiting for; to ride out over the land with the wind in their hair, free from Cair Cunor, free from fortress life with only their own counsel to keep. This is what they had been born for and for the first time in their lives, they felt like men.

Cundelig let Hebog take wing and the peregrine followed the group at a distance, wheeling above the treetops at such a distance that he looked frozen in the air before swooping down suddenly, only to rise once more.

"How long have you had that bird?" Cei asked Cundelig.

"Raised him from a hatchling," Cundelig said with pride. "It was my father who taught me how to train him. He was chief falconer at the royal court of Rheged."

"That's where you hail from, is it? Rheged?"

"Aye, my father's father settled there after Constantine's rebellion fell apart in Gaul. He was an *explorator* – a scout – in the rebel general's army. He was from Albion originally and he fled back home after Constantine's execution. We come from a long line of Roman army scouts. My grandfather taught my father all he knew and my father passed that knowledge on to his sons."

"How did you wind up at Cair Cunor?"

"When my father died, my older brother took his place as Rheged's falconer. I took Hebog with me and sought employment in the various teulus of the west." He held out his wrist and Hebog descended to land gracefully upon the thick leather gauntlet, clutching at it with his impressive talons. Cundelig fed him a dead mouse as a treat and the peregrine gulped it down whole.

"What about you?" Cei said, turning in his saddle to address Guihir. "What's your story?"

"Another cursed second son, I'm afraid," the interpreter said with a shrug. "My father was a minor Powysian noble and my brother and I received the usual martial training as befitting the sons of nobility. But it was my brother who would inherit the land and I was given over to the church. I've always been good with languages and took to my lessons well. Our abbot made me his interpreter on his trip to Rome. Latin is one thing but there aren't half a lot of funny languages spoken between Albion and the Holy City. Gaulish, Frankish, Vandal. Once you know a few universal basics, you can pick up most other languages without too much hard work."

"You've been to Rome?" Arthur asked, far more in awe of Guihir's travels than his mastery of tongues.

"Oh yes. And it's as magnificent as they say. But the church was no life for me and so I left the cloisters, seeking honest pay and the sins of a life well-lived. You know what I mean!" He threw a wink at Arthur. "The life of a monk doesn't exactly provide many opportunities for meeting the fairer sex."

Cundelig snorted at this. "You renounced your vows just to chase women? Have you no honour?"

"Oh, I am as pious as the next Christian," said Guihir a little defensively. "If there is one thing spending a few years in the cloisters can tell you, it is that few Christians are as holy as they make out. I just decided to be a little more honest about it. So I wandered, brawled and whored my way around the west before the need for decent coin drew me to old King Enniaun's teulu. Five years I've been with it and I haven't looked back since. There's always call for a man good with his tongue. The ladies think so too." He winked at them. Cundelig rolled his eyes in derision.

The trickling river seemed all the louder in the lull of evening. Less than twenty miles from the coast the river opened into Conui's tidal estuary and the west bank grew thickly wooded. A clapper bridge of mossy stone slabs forded the river and they could see the faint glow of a campfire in the trees on the other side. They dismounted and led their horses across the bridge. As they approached the fire, they could see two figures seated by it. Low voices murmured in the confines of the wood.

Cei whistled out a birdcall. The two figures rose and approached them, silhouetted against the flames.

"Beduir!" said Cei, striding forward to greet the larger of the two men.

Beduir was tall, broad in the chest and had jet-black hair that fell almost to his waist which he kept bound in a single tail, tied in two places. "Finally convinced your old da to let you out of the house, Cei?" Beduir said. "About bloody time!"

Arthur recognised his cousin loitering in the shadows. Gualchmei was short with a touch of the feral about him. He carried a flat composite bow in the Persian style and a quiver of arrows with red fletching was slung over his shoulder. Arthur went forward to embrace him.

Arthur had often felt sorry for his grandfather Anblaud who had been unfortunate enough to see two grandsons who would never bear their fathers' names. Eigyr had had a younger sister – Guiar – whose belly had begun to swell before their father had found her an advantageous match. No amount of threats or beatings had loosened her tongue on the father's identity and she had been dismissed to some lonely retreat to bear her child in shame. The child – Gualchmei – was torn from his mother's arms at a young age and sent away to be fostered. Young Gualchmei eventually made his way to Cair Cunor where he had joined the teulu alongside his cousin. There was always room for fatherless bastards in the teulu, it was jovially maintained.

The servants led the horses back across the bridge and began the trip back to Cair Cunor, while the rest of the party joined their new comrades by the fire and ate of the meat that was slowly roasting.

"It is a little over an hour until the tide will be right," said Beduir, "so we can rest awhile before we head downriver."

Through the trees, Arthur could see the mast and rigging of a sturdy fishing barge leaning at a slant as it rested on the mud. He wondered if Beduir and his cousin had bought or stolen it.

They talked a while and conversation inevitably

turned to the dangers facing them and the rumoured Cauldron-born.

"Can it be true?" Gualchmei asked, his eyes wide by the light of the flickering fire. "Can the Morgens be sending the dead against us?"

"It's all nonsense, lad," said Cei. "The Morgens can no more summon the dead than I can summon a big-titted wench right here in this forest. It's all woodsmoke and whispers. If there is a cauldron then we'll take the damned thing and haul it back south to destroy it before Meriaun's teulu. That'll show them that we are no bedwetting pups to fear whatever alliance they've made with those toothless old crones on Ynys Mon."

"I'd be wary of that tongue of yours, Cei," said Menw. "You may feel brave twenty miles from the coast but once you're on their island, you may find a tad more respect for the Morgens. They are not women to be insulted lightly."

Cei scoffed but knew better than to argue with a bard. Beduir tried to break the uneasy stillness that had fallen over the group. "Menw, how about a song? Something to lighten the mood?"

"Lighten the mood?" said the bard, as he chewed on a piece of meat, his lined features deepened by the flickering flames. "You lads don't need idle songs of war to fill your empty heads. You need wisdom. You think it's just Gaels we'll be facing come the dawn when the straits are behind us? Pah! I'll sing you a song, one you've all heard before but seem to have forgotten. Listen."

He reached into his satchel and drew out his harp. It was a fine thing, carven with a leaf motif of blackened wood that told of a great age. His fingers began to wander over its strings, gathering speed as a runner will break into a jog until they began to dance. Then, he began his tale.

Back when Albion was young there was a fair and mighty king called Bran who was loved by all. As is true today, there was much hostility between the Britons and the Gaels. Peace was long sought after and eventually found when Bran's sister, Branwen, was married to Matholuch, the High-King of Erin.

Thirteen ships arrived bearing treasure and gifts that were to be Branwen's dowry and nine days of feasting ensued. The druids performed the sacred rights of marriage and as Branwen and Matholuch looked into each other's eyes, both found happiness there.

The whole kingdom rejoiced except one. Bran and Branwen had two half-brothers. Their names were Nisien and Efnisien. Nisien had grown to be loving and gentle but his brother Efnisien was a spiteful and hateful youth who wanted nothing more than war with the Gaels. For this reason, he was not invited to the wedding.

Efnisien was enraged when he found out that his half-sister had been married to the King of the Gaels and further outraged that he had not been invited to the wedding. And so, while the Britons and the Gaels drank themselves into a stupor, Efnisien sneaked into the stables where King Matholuch's horses were kept. In a fury, he mutilated them with his knife so that they were no longer of use to anybody and had to be put out of their misery.

Matholuch was enraged by this act and took it as a grave insult. Fearing that all efforts for peace had been lost, Bran offered many gifts as recompense including a magnificent cauldron so large and heavy that four servants were required to carry it.

'This cauldron,' explained Bran, 'has a magical property that a dead man may be thrown into it today and tomorrow he will arise as good as he ever was, robbed of nothing but his speech.'

Matholuch stared at the caldron, his eyes glinting with the thought of its potential. With such a cauldron, there would not be an enemy who would dare stand against him. And so it was that peace was re-forged between Erin and Albion. The work of Efnisien was undone and the following morning Matholuch returned to Erin with his new bride.

The peace between the two realms lasted for many years and Branwen was very happy as Matholuch's queen. They had a son whom they called Guern and he was sent to be fostered in the best house in the land. But, after a while, word reached Matholuch's ears that his people thought he had been too lenient with the Britons after he had been so insulted at his wedding feast. They mocked the king behind his back and called him weak. This enraged Matholuch so much that he began to resent his wife and started to treat her very badly.

Branwen was sent to work in the kitchens where she performed menial and humiliating tasks and was often beaten. Matholuch stopped all ships to Albion so her brother would not hear of her situation and would think that all was well.

Three years passed and Branwen's situation did not improve. But one day, she came across an injured starling and she placed it on the edge of her kneading-trough. Day by day she nursed it back to health and in so doing, learned its language. She told the small bird of her plight and how to recognise her brother, King Bran of Albion.

The little bird flew off and made its way to Bran's court where it landed on the king's shoulder and whispered into his ear of the suffering of his sister. Bran was enraged and called all his warriors to his side. A massive army was prepared to invade Erin. The huge fleet of the Britons crossed the sea and the masts of the ships were so numerous that the watchers on the coast of Erin swore that a whole forest approached them. In a panic, King Matholuch sent emissaries to King Bran promising that he would surrender his kingdom to Guern, Bran's nephew. This was not good enough for Bran who wanted to rule Erin for himself and so he told the messengers to come back with a better offer.

Matholuch invited Bran and his warriors to a feast in his great hall to discuss terms. The Britons and the Gaels entered the hall and arranged themselves opposite each other. Bran called his nephew over so that he might examine him. And the boy went from warrior to warrior, greeting them all individually but stayed well clear of his troublesome uncle, Efnisien. Angered by this slight, the trickster rose up and grabbed the boy and hurled him into the fire pit. Branwen screamed and made to dive in after her burning son but was restrained by Bran.

Such a commotion ensued that all hopes for peace were destroyed and the Britons and the Gaels waged war upon each other once more. The fighting was hard and fierce and many sons of Erin fell. It was then that Matholuch decided to use the magical cauldron and he ordered the dead bodies that lay strewn across the battlefield be boiled inside it. And so, the ranks of the Gaels were swollen with the warriors of the dead – the Cauldron-born – their souls returned from the Otherworld to work the vengeance of their master.

The Britons were overwhelmed by the Cauldron-born and Efnisien, seeing the horrors his actions had brought upon his people, felt a rare pang of guilt. That night, he crept into the enemy camp and hid himself among the corpses. When two Gaels threw Efnisien into the cauldron, he stretched himself out, straining against the sides of the vessel. The cauldron burst apart and vanished back to Annun, killing Efnisien in the process.

All across the battlefield, the Cauldron-born fell in their paces, dead once more, and the Britons were able to beat the Gaels. Thanks to Efnisien's self-sacrifice, Bran slew Matholuch and returned home with his sister Branwen.

Cei was the first to break the silence that hung in the wake of Menw's tale. "It's a fine story," he said, "but you still can't convince me that the dead walk on Ynys Mon."

"Cei, for once in your life, know when to shut up," said Arthur.

Cei glared at him. Arthur felt haunted by the tale of Bran and the cauldron. He had felt haunted ever since the Cauldron-born had been mentioned in the Pendraig's council.

"See now?" Cei said. "You've even got my brave foster-brother quaking in his breeches and jumping at shadows. That's all your tales do for people."

Beduir stood up and peered through the trees. The mast of the fishing barge was no longer at an angle but stood straight as a flame, the vessel beneath it buoyed by the returned tide.

"We must be moving," he said, "if we are to make the straits by dawn."

They piled into the barge and stowed their weapons in the fish hold. Gualchmei untied the mooring rope and hopped on board as Beduir shoved off. They made good time, and as the coast approached they unfurled the sail and caught the wind that would carry them out into the straits. The twin humps of Cair Dugannu could be seen on their right, dark against the paling sky, the torches of the sentries winking in the blackness.

"Get under cover," said Beduir. "Gualchmei and I will see us past the coastline."

Arthur and the others scrambled into the fish hold and Gualchmei secured the canvas over their heads. From a distance the vessel would look no more suspicious than a two-manned fishing boat heading out for the early morning's catch.

Down in the darkness Arthur felt the current pick up as the river washed out into the straits and the boat began to rock violently. He had never suffered from seasickness, but down there in the hold with no visibility and no idea if they had been spotted from the coastline, he felt the panic rising in his gut and tried to quell it. Nobody spoke.

The canvas was suddenly pulled off and they looked up at Gualchmei's head and shoulders, a black silhouette against the starry sky.

"The danger is past!" he said. "We made it!"

They clambered out of the fish hold and watched the coastline receding behind them. The sky was paling in the east and to their west flowed the strong currents of the straits.

The tides washed around Ynys Mon at different speeds, meeting in the centre at a point known locally as the 'Swellies'. At high tide this confluence of whirlpools and surges was extremely treacherous and was avoided by all sailors with any sense in their heads.

They cut northwards and the dark mound of Ynys Mon reared up before them, mysterious and foreboding.

"The last stronghold of the druids," said Menw, following Arthur's gaze. "A great evil was done there long ago and the island does not forget."

"The Romans?" Arthur asked. He had heard of the massacre which had put an end to the druidic order several centuries ago.

"The druids inspired the greatest resistance to the iron legions and the new governor of Albion knew he had to suppress them if he was to maintain control over the tribes. Ynys Mon became a refuge for druids and other fugitives who sought sanctuary with the Morgens. The governor led an army across these straits to wipe out druid and priestess alike.

"The druids met them on the shores and called upon the fury of all the gods while the Morgens, dressed in black, ran back and forth, screeching curses. But the gods of Albion forsook the old orders on that day. The Romans struck them down, slaughtered their captives and burned down their sacred groves. It was a great evil that scarred the island and the island remembers."

"How is it that the Morgens survived?" Arthur asked, feeling a chill that the warm summer night did not warrant.

"In the same manner that an acorn from a fallen oak might sprout in harsh soil. The Romans may have wiped them out but the order grew anew and continued its practises in defiance of Albion's new masters. As for the druids, their order was driven underground. The great councils were no more and they lost contact with one another. They were no longer members of an organised religion but wanderers, tale-tellers and spiritual guides. We bards are the inheritors of the druids, their successors, keepers of the land's history and custodians of its secrets."

The wind carried them around the eastern side of the island and they made for a small, secluded cove banked by grassy slopes. They beached the boat and pulled it up onto the sand as far as they were able. They were exhausted, none of them having slept in many hours, and dawn was already breaking.

"We shall rest here awhile and continue when it gets fully light," said Cei. "No fire though. We can't risk being seen."

They made themselves comfortable, with their backs to a rock that kept them out of the wind, and broke into their rations of dried mutton and hard bread. Sleep came easily, despite their rough surroundings, and Beduir kept watch as the day broke over the island.

Arthur woke to the cawing of gulls and the rolling of the waves across the dark sand. A few of the others were already up and preparing to set out.

"The Morgens dwell on the shores of a lake on the western side of the island," said Menw. "We can make the journey in a day as long as we encounter no obstacles."

Nobody wanted to comment on what those obstacles might be, so they set out in determined silence, crossing low hills that rippled with ferns and yellow gorse. They occasionally saw cattle grazing but nothing in the way of settlements or habitation, just the endless brackish hills dotted by wind-blasted and leafless trees. There weren't even any trackways. Arthur had never seen anywhere so bleak and haunted.

A little after midday the hills dipped into a shallow basin and they entered a forest of tall pines and dense fern. They had still not encountered a soul and their spirits had begun to rise, thinking their mission easier than it had at first seemed.

"We are more or less in the centre of the island now," said Menw. "These woods reach all the way to the old Roman fort on the south-eastern point. We must sharpen eastwards and meet the Afon Crigil at its source. Beyond that river lies the marshy area where the Morgens dwell."

The mention of the sea-born dampened their spirits a little, and the knowledge that their ultimate goal – and its guardians – was near, chilled their hearts like a cold wind.

Cundelig scouted ahead with Hebog who hovered above the treetops. It was not long before he came hurrying back with the peregrine on his gauntlet. "There is a group of warriors moving in a north-easterly direction less than a league from here."

"How many?" Cei asked, unslinging his shield from his back.

"I don't know but Hebog circled them, indicating that they have horses."

"Gaels?" asked Gualchmei.

Cundelig gave him a withering look. "Hebog can tell me where the enemy is, in which direction they are travelling and if they are mounted or not. He can't tell me what language they speak or which gods they pray to."

"If they are heading north-east then we wait here and avoid them," said Menw.

"And risk have them doubling back and falling on our rear?" Cei said. "I don't know about you, bard, but I'm keen to rid this island of every Gael I can."

"We don't even know if they are Gaels," said Arthur. "Maybe they're locals."

"Can't take the chance," Cei replied. "Let's see if we can't get a look at them."

He hurried off, sword in hand and the others followed, drawing their own weapons.

They crested a small, leafy rise and peered down into a dip. Voices could be heard in the muffled stillness of the forest. Arthur tried to make out the words but they were too far off and the dialect too thick.

"Gaels," Guihir confirmed grimly.

"Can you make out what they're saying?" Beduir asked.

"Nothing of much interest. Something crude about a woman in the harbour settlement further south."

They could see movement through the trees and threw themselves flat on their bellies along the rise. As the party of Gaels passed, they could make out three warriors on horseback and four on foot.

"We can take them!" said Cei. "Seven against seven!"

"Not good odds at the best of times," warned Menw. "And three of them are mounted."

"But we have surprise on our side. Gualchmei, let's see how good you are with that bow. Sneak along the rise and see if you can't pick a couple of them off. As soon as your arrows start to fly, we'll charge their rear."

“Wait a minute,” said Arthur. “That will leave Gualchmei completely exposed on the ridge. One of us at least should go with him.”

“I need as many of us as possible to attack them,” said Cei. “They’ll be too occupied dealing with us to pursue Gualchmei. Besides, he will have the high ground and a ranged weapon. He’ll be fine.”

“Cei, we should think this through …” said Beduir.

“No time!” said Cei. “They are moving away from us. Gualchmei, get going!”

The young bowman nodded and took off at a crouched run, drawing an arrow from his quiver as he went.

“You’re using my cousin as bait,” Arthur said to Cei.

“He’s a warrior under my command first, your cousin second,” Cei replied. “He knew the risks when he agreed to join this expedition.”

Gualchmei had vanished behind the rise as it curved around to the north. The party of Gaels was almost obscured by the trees and Arthur knew he couldn’t be the only one who was worried that they wouldn’t have much time to catch up to them once Gualchmei’s position was exposed.

A shaggy head poked up from the rise and they saw the flat Persian bow bend and loose, sending its black shaft down into the scouting party.

“Now!” Cei hissed and, as one, they rose and descended the slope in a slither of needles and sandy earth.

Cries could be heard up ahead, and Arthur hoped that Gualchmei’s first arrow had at least evened the odds a little. As they came upon the Gaels they could see that it had, for one warrior hung slack in his saddle, a red-fletched shaft sticking out of his neck.

The footmen heard them approaching and turned to meet them. Shields slammed against shields and spear tips jabbed and thrusted. Arthur took the defensive, letting his opponent's spear slide and scrape against the boss of his shield. Menw, Cundelig and Guihir flanked the party and pressed in with their spears, fencing the Gaels in on three sides. The two mounted Gaels brought up the rear and pressed their own warriors forward, shouldering them against the Britons with the flanks of their horses, out of reach of the Britons' spear tips.

Cei was the first to draw blood, and a Gael went down with a skewered throat, gurgling a cry from blooded lips.

Beduir sliced through a spear shaft with his sword and slammed the rim of his shield into the face of his opponent. As the man stumbled backwards, clutching at his shattered nose and broken teeth, Beduir slid his blade in through his ribs.

An arrow sailed down from the rise and struck one of the riders between the shoulder blades. He roared an oath in Gaelic as his companion turned and urged his mount up the rise to where Gualchmei was frantically trying to nock another arrow to his bowstring.

Arthur saw the danger and battered his opponent's spear away with his shield before thrusting with his own. It lodged in the man's groin and held fast. He caught the Gael's mad counter-jab on his shield and let go of his spear to draw his sword. A chop to the unguarded neck nearly severed the man's head and he went down fast.

Arthur broke from the skirmish and took off after the horseman. Discarding his shield as he scrambled up the rise, he could see the rider bearing down on his cousin.

Gualchmei cried out as the Gael speared him in the shoulder and pinned him down like a harpooned fish. Arthur bellowed and swung his blade at the horse's thigh, hamstringing it.

The horse screamed and went down, bringing its rider with it. The Gael rolled past Arthur's feet and tried to rise but Arthur brought his sword down on the man's head.

The blade cut through the helm and lodged deep in the skull beneath. The man grunted and blood cascaded from under the rim of his helm. Arthur ripped his blade free and the helm clung to it, rattling on the slick, red steel. He shook it free and stepped over the fallen Gael to reach Gualchmei's side.

The spear had been wrenched free by the rider's fall and the wound bled profusely. Gualchmei was white with fear and his face contorted by pain. Arthur clasped his hand over the wound and bellowed for Menw.

In the dip beyond the rise the skirmish was over. Cei and the others had finished off the last Gael; they were cleaning their weapons and securing the horses which were wild with panic. Menw hurried up to see to the wounded Gualchmei.

"It is not serious but he needs treatment," said the bard after inspecting the wound. He began binding it with clean cloth from his satchel before bending the arm at the elbow and tying it in place at the shoulder. "Give him water."

Gualchmei had been on the verge of losing consciousness but spluttered a little to life as a trickle from Beduir's waterskin passed his lips.

"The wound may be infected," said Menw. "We need a fire so I can boil the herbs required to prevent a fever."

"Not here," said Cei, climbing up to them. "There may be other patrols about. And this lot will soon be missed."

Arthur could not contain his rage any longer. He got up and shoved Cei roughly, sending him sprawling. "What was the point of this?" he demanded. "We could have sneaked past them and Gualchmei wouldn't be lying here wounded. But you had to take on all of Erin within a day of setting out, didn't you? You had to prove yourself! But it was Gualchmei who paid the price. It was Gualchmei who took the greatest risk in your mad plan!"

Cei scrambled to his feet, his face red with either rage or embarrassment. A vein bulged in his neck. "We were always going to have to fight them! If not today then tomorrow, or the day after!"

"We could have avoided them!"

"And fight them on the way back to the boat? They're dead, Arthur. They're dead and we're alive and to my mind that makes it a victory."

He shouldered his way past Arthur and began instructing the others to collect spears to replace the ones they had damaged or lost. Nobody interfered in the altercation. All knew that though Cei was their captain, Arthur was as his brother, and none would take it upon themselves to stand in the way of a brothers' quarrel.

They continued south-west in silence. Beduir and Guihir took turns in supporting Gualchmei when he needed it. He was in a lot of pain but did his best to hide it. Arthur still seethed at Cei's recklessness. His first command had clearly gone to his head, and he was more interested in proving himself when they should be exercising the utmost caution.

Cei sent Cundelig farther afield to scout for other patrols. After a time, he came running back with word that a large party had made camp between them and the river.

"This is no scouting party," he said. "They are at least twenty strong with horses too. They carry chests of grain on a wain."

"Tax collectors," said Cei. "They must be making the rounds of the island. Is there any way to skirt them?"

"They have the ford," Cundelig said. "And the river looks too swollen by the spring melt to hope for another crossing point downriver."

"Then we *must* wait this time," said Beduir. "They'll soon move on and the crossing will be clear."

"They'll be wondering what happened to their scouting party," said Arthur. "And will undoubtedly send out another. They may not be moving on any time soon once they find the bodies of seven of their comrades."

"And I don't like the look of Gualchmei," said Menw. "We need to get a fire going so I can clean and re-dress that wound."

"I'm fine," protested Gualchmei in a distant voice.

His face looked pale and clammy.

They debated whether they should make an inconspicuous camp in some gully that might conceal the smoke of a small campfire, or if they should turn back, then the decision was made for them. It was Cundelig's sharp ears that first heard the approaching noises.

"Dogs," he said. "Those bloody great wolfhounds of Erin. I saw some of them with the camp."

They could all hear them now; the baying and yelping of hounds begging to be let loose from their leashes. There were horns blowing too and men shouting to each other over wide distances.

"They're heading straight for us," said Cei.

"Must have seen Hebog," Cundelig muttered. "He hovered a good while over their camp."

"The bird gave us away?" Guihir exclaimed. "I thought he was supposed to help us not lead the enemy to us!"

Cundelig scowled at him but remained silent.

"We must run," said Menw. "And make for moving water to throw the dogs off our scent."

They turned tail and headed back the way they had come, skirting the vale where they had slaughtered the scouting party. As the forest petered out around them, Menw led them north. None questioned him for he knew the island better than they did, but they were in open country now and could hear the hunt growing closer behind them. Arthur knew that if they did not reach cover soon, they would be ridden down by mounted warriors or torn apart by baying hounds.

Gualchmei was fading fast. He fell to the back of the column and Beduir doubled back to support him.

Menw showed no mercy and kept up a brutal pace that Arthur thought was well past a man of his years.

They pushed on as the sun vanished behind them and those brown, brackish hills dulled to grey beneath a darkening sky. The sweat chilled on Arthur's back and it seemed to him that the ground flew beneath his feet, the hills streaking past him while the wind sang in his ears. He kept his eyes on the ground in front of him as they ran on and on, never daring to look about them or at each other, for fear that they might not spot a treacherous hummock or grassy hole that would trip them and break an ankle.

Eventually Menw slowed and they all took full advantage of the breather, resting their hands on their knees and gasping for breath. The bard raised a hand to his wild eyes and peered into the distance behind them. "We have not lost them," he said.

By squinting, Arthur could see the dim dots of mounted men and dogs in the distance, crossing the hills in their direction.

Menw turned and continued. All the others could do was share exhausted looks of desperation before falling in line and following him.

"Spineless worm!" raged Owain. "He means to wait it out to see which bear is worth betting on!"

A messenger had arrived from the southernmost sub-kingdom of Venedotia. King Usai of Caradogion's position was one of neutrality. That far-flung outpost of Cunedag's legacy had always been the outsider and least involved of Venedotia's disputes.

Cadwallon had never had much hope in Usai's support; only a desperate hope that a shared heritage would breed some loyalty. Another messenger had arrived the day before proclaiming King Elnaw of Docmaeling's support for Meriaun. That made two kingdoms in support of the enemy against Cadwallon's single ally; Mor of Rumaniog. Only one king had not yet given his answer; Efiaun of Dunauding.

Mor cleared his throat and ruffled the white streaks in his black hair. "It is Dunauding that should concern us the most," he said. "If Efiaun joins Meriaun we will have enemies to the east and west of us. Our passage to Cair Dugannu will be a narrow one."

"Cair Dugannu!" said Owain. "If only it were as simple as retaking the royal seat. Not only are we far outnumbered by Gaels and traitors, we'd never hold the fortress against our cousins for long, even if we did take it."

"Not since the lords of the Laigin Peninsula threw their support behind Meriaun," said Cunor gloomily. "I had hoped that they would recognise a usurper when they saw one and put their petty resentment of your father behind them just this once."

The Laigin Peninsula was named after the Gaelic tribe – one of the five great tribes of Erin – who had settled it before Cunedag's coming. Despite the wars that had driven the Gaels from the peninsula, the name had stuck and it had fallen to King Afloeg to rule it. When he died without an heir, Enniaun Yrth's absorption of Afloegion into his own kingdom had been greatly resented by Afloeg's bannermen. They had never truly accepted Enniaun as their king and apparently accepted his son even less so.

"Why does Efiaun delay in sending his reply?" said Cadwallon in frustration. "Surely he cannot mean to wait out the war in his fortress as Usai does? Dunauding is central to Venedotia's strength as a kingdom. If he bars our way to the Pass of Kings, then we are truly stuck here with Etern gnashing at our heels."

The Pass of Kings was a steep-sided valley between the mountain known as the Giant's Cairn and the Heaps; a rocky range of mountains that walled its eastern side. Widely considered the gateway to the coast, the Pass of Kings had been hotly contested during Cunedag's wars with the Gaels. Cadwallon hoped to avoid such a contest with his cousin.

Once the council was adjourned, Cadwallon strolled out onto the sunny central range and made his way towards the north-eastern gate. He passed the training yard and stopped to watch his sons at their lessons. Guidno was sparring with his tutor but Maelcon sat in the shade of a thatched overhang, a codex in his lap. It looked to be an expensive Christian text and Cadwallon wondered where he had got it from.

"Good, Guidno!" he cheered, as he crossed the yard. "Keep your spear tip up like Brochmael shows you!"

He stepped into the shade of the overhang and Maelcon looked up at him from beneath his dark brows.

"What's that?" Cadwallon asked, indicating the codex.

"A copy of Saint Jerome's translation of the New Testament," Maelcon replied. "Deacon Arminius lent it to me to practice my Latin."

Cadwallon pursed his lips but said nothing. Meddyf had been ecstatic to learn that Cair Cunor had its very own deacon who lived within its walls and preached his sermons in the small church in the nearby settlement. Cair Dugannu had no such thing, most of its inhabitants being followers of the old faith.

It had been Meddyf who had suggested that Maelcon take lessons from Deacon Arminius. The boy craved learning, not warfare, she had said. She may have been right, but he hadn't been fooled. Who could blame her for wanting to share her faith with her son? It must be lonely being a Christian queen in a predominantly pagan corner of Albion. He knew that she secretly wanted to raise their sons as Christians and Cadwallon couldn't bring himself to protest overmuch. He had drawn the line at baptism and always ensured they attended the religious rites of the old faith whenever required. But really, what was one more god when there were already so many to pay one's devotions to?

Neither was Cadwallon against the idea of his eldest son learning to read and write. In fact, it could prove useful for a future king. He didn't even particularly mind the Christian subject matter. No, Cadwallon's fear was that Maelcon would spend too much time reading old scriptures, learning tales of Christ and his followers, that his martial obligations would be neglected. If they could win this damnable war, Maelcon would be the next Pendraig, and what good was a Pendraig who could not hold his own in single combat or lead his teulu to victory on the battlefield?

He glanced at Guidno who was so young and already doing so well under his tutor's instructions. It was not unheard of for a king to pass his kingdom to his second son in favour of his first. It was a king's duty to do what was best for his kingdom. But he had always had Maelcon in mind for the throne and it felt like a betrayal to even think otherwise. "Maelcon, I want you to put that thing away and join your brother in the training yard."

Maelcon glanced up at him. "But Da ..." he protested.

"No arguments! We all have to do things we don't particularly want to on occasion, and we *are* at war. It is time you recognised that. Come on now, you have your duties just as I have mine."

Maelcon sulked and closed the codex before ambling off towards Guidno and Brochmael. Cadwallon sighed and continued onwards, exiting the fort through the north-eastern gate.

The nearby church was a small oblong structure of timber and whitewashed plaster. As Cadwallon arrived, Cair Cunor's small Christian congregation were dispersing after hearing Mass. He found Meddyf with Owain's wife, Elen.

"A king to escort us home!" said Meddyf with one of her wry smiles. "How honoured we are!"

"I have just come from the council chamber and needed some air," he replied.

"That bad? What is to be your decision?"

"We stay put for the time being," he said, noticing a look of disappointment cross Elen's face, which she quickly tried to hide and failed. "I will not march until we have every possible ally under the dragon banner," he assured her.

"I have been praying for my father," Meddyf said. "Has there been any news from him?"

"No, I am sorry. The last we heard from the Conui Valley was that your father is rounding up every bannerman he can. He will be joining us here as soon as he is able and with riders too. I await his coming as eagerly as you do, Meddyf."

"But the Gaels," Meddyf insisted. "How much further down the valley will they travel?"

"As far as they can without engaging your father and his friends," Cadwallon said with as encouraging a smile as he could muster. The truth of it was that Maeldaf and a rag-tag army of bannermen could not hope to stand against Diugurnach's Gaels if they passed down the Conui en masse. Just as his wife prayed to her Christ for Maeldaf's safety, Cadwallon prayed to Modron that his father-in-law would have the sense to ride south before it was too late to escape the enemy's advance.

"I saw our boys at their lessons in the training yard on my way over here," he said in an effort to change the subject. "Guidno improves all the time but Maelcon would rather read. I understand Deacon Arminius is lending him Christian texts now."

"Arminius says that his comprehension of Latin is exceptional for his age."

"While his martial skills are far from exceptional."

"He's just not a warrior, husband."

"And he never will be if you keep encouraging him to shirk his lessons."

"I must have a word with that Eigyr," said Elen abruptly, keen to leave the king and his queen to discuss familial matters in private. "She always seems so terribly alone." They watched Elen hurry off to speak with the curious lady who dwelt in the upper chambers of the principia only venturing out for Mass.

"You coddle the boy, Meddyf," Cadwallon said, returning to the topic in hand.

"Oh, don't be such a brute," she replied. "I know all young princes must learn the art of sword and spear but I just don't have the heart to force him to do things that he is clearly not cut out for."

"He will be a man in a few years. It is time he started to grow up. He needs to focus on his duties. One day he might have to ride into battle. What good will his Christian teachings be then?"

Meddyf was silent and he knew she had a good retort on the tip of her tongue but had bitten down on it. They crossed the remaining distance to the gate of the fort in silence. When they reached the praetorium they were confronted by Cunor who seemed greatly agitated.

"My lord," he said, "a rider came just after you left, one of our watchmen from the eastern border of the commote."

"What news?" Cadwallon asked, knowing full well what might cause a border watchman to gallop to Cair Cunor as fast as he could.

"Eternion is mustered," said Cunor. "King Etern marches on us as we speak. They will be here by tomorrow morning."

The chase continued as the sun went down. The sky grew bruised and the breeze chilled. They eventually crested a hill and saw the glittering streak of a river below them. Menw urged them on and they plunged down into its icy waters. The hunt was close now; almost upon the rise above them. The companions scooted down river on their haunches, clawing their way past mossy rocks; keeping as much to the shadows of the overhanging roots and earthy banks as possible.

Arthur felt chilled to the bone by the time Menw scrambled out of the water and climbed the bank on the opposite side. Here they were shaded by a knot of fir trees and they huddled together in the dimness, the chattering of their teeth loud in their ears.

The sound of the hunt was distant now and it drew farther away. They waited until the last of the dogs' yelps was a memory on the wind before they rose, clothes clinging to their aching joints. It was pitch black and the moon struggled to be seen behind shifting clouds.

"We must head north," said Menw. "To the coast. To Cunedag's old Lys. There we can hide for a while and Gualchmei can be healed while we discuss what our next plan is."

"That old place?" Cei said. "It must be a ruin by now. Surely there are some settlements closer where we can buy or steal ourselves some warmth and food."

"And hope that nobody runs to the enemy with information of our whereabouts?" the bard replied.

"No, the Lys is deserted and will suit our needs admirably. It is not far but we must move now before Gualchmei grows any worse."

Beduir had to carry their wounded comrade the rest of the journey, for as they all shivered in their wet clothes under the night sky, Gualchmei burned with a fever.

After some time they could see the thatched roofs of a settlement atop a bald hill. Beyond it lay the cliffs and the booming surf. They had reached the north-eastern tip of the island. It was a walled place but its defences were in poor repair. The thatch of the buildings was black with mould and fallen in in some parts while weeds and long grass pawed at the cracked whitewash.

They waded through the thick grass and entered the largest of the buildings; an oblong hall with tall rectangular windows. The roof was supported by timbers which had once been painted vibrant colours but were now faded and greenish with moss. The thatch had sunk in and the gaping hole had let in the rainwater which had pooled on the stone flags at the far end.

Arthur gazed around at the moonlit chamber. This had been Cunedag's Lys; his original court after he and his sons had expelled the Gaels nearly forty years ago. Now, the Gaels had returned and this once magnificent building was home only to ghosts and rats, the memories of laughter and cheer as distant as the winds of last winter.

"Who goes there?" called a voice from without. The companions jumped and unslung their weapons. In the light of the doorway the figure of a man could be seen peering in. He stepped closer, a stout cudgel gripped in his hands. As the light fell on his face, Arthur saw his eyes widen at the sight of them. He had evidently thought to come upon a lone intruder or perhaps a pair of rogues, easily sent on their way with a few blows of his cudgel. Seven armed warriors were more than he had anticipated.

"We mean you no harm, friend," said Cei, "so long as you mean us none."

"Well, you are no Gaels, so that counts in your favour," replied the man. "Who are you?"

"I am Cei mab Cunor, son to the Penteulu of Venedotia. These are my followers. I am frank with you for you do not seem to bear the Gaels any allegiance."

"Aye, you are right in that. What is your business here?"

"We have been sent by the Pendraig on a mission of vital importance. We ran into some of our mutual enemies and my companion here was sorely wounded. We thought to find shelter here."

"I am a mere servant," said the man. "I would gladly offer you shelter but it is not my place to do so. You must speak to the master."

"A master of this old ruin?" Menw said. "I was under the impression all associated with it fled when Ynys Mon fell to the Gaels. I myself was in Powys on business when the last defences fell …"

"The old Lys is something of a sacred place for those still loyal to the Dragons of the Isle," said the servant. "Come, I will take you to my master."

He led them from the crumbling Lys and across the enclosure to what had been the steward's quarters in days past. The light of a hearth fire could be seen through one of the windows and smoke drifted from the hole in the thatch, which was in a better state than that of the other buildings. He opened the door and led them into an antechamber.

"Leave your weapons here," he said.

The companions looked at one another. It could be a trap but what other choice did they have? The propped their spears and shields against the wall and unbuckled their sword belts. Arthur helped Beduir with Gualchmei who was in a stumbling, mumbling state of delirium.

It was then that they noticed the two women looking at them. They stood in the doorway to the inner hall with its hide apron parted just enough to reveal their frightened but resolute faces down the end of the spear they gripped between them. One of them looked to be the same age as Cei and Arthur while the other was somewhat younger.

"Steady …" said Cei, frozen in the act of setting his sword down.

"Who are these people, Cadfan?" one of the girls asked. She had tawny hair that spilled down over the shoulders of a shabby tunica, and from her pale face green eyes burned with the defiance of youth.

"Fellow Britons," said the servant named Cadfan. "Warriors from the court of Venedotia. I saw movement in the Lys and thought some bandits were on the prowl. They say they are sent by the Pendraig."

The women did not lower their spear. "What interest has the son of Cunedag in sending his warriors to us now?" asked the tawny-haired one.

"The son of Cunedag is dead," replied Arthur.

"There is a new Pendraig; Cadwallon mab Enniaun."

"It's all the same to us," said the girl. "And you have not answered my question."

"Must we be interrogated at spearpoint?" Cei demanded. "We have already told your servant our business and that our comrade is sorely wounded. Surely you can see that we mean you no harm."

"What is it, girls?" came a voice from within.

"Warriors, Father," called back the tawny-haired girl over her shoulder. "Britons."

"Britons?" came the reply. "And you keep our countrymen waiting on our doorstep? Show them in!"

The girls lowered the spear slowly but the tawny-haired one kept her unblinking, semi-hostile gaze on them.

They filed into the hall where a hearth fire was crackling merrily. A man with lank, greying hair sat nearby, a blanket over him. "You have wounded," he said upon seeing Gualchmei hanging between the arms of Arthur and Beduir. "Set him down on the table. Girls, clear some space."

"I can see to him," said Menw. "I require only water to be boiled and clean linen if you have it."

The seated man regarded Menw curiously for a moment before remembering himself and sending his daughters to fetch what was needed. "I am Gogfran," he said. "Steward of this place. These are my daughters, Guenhuifar and Guenhuifach."

"Steward?" Menw said, as Guenhuifach set the water to boil. "Of Cunedag's old Lys?"

"Steward of weeds and rubble," said Gogfran with a sad smile. "Custodian of ghosts and memories."

"I seem to remember a Gogfran who was King

Enniaun's steward years ago, before the Gaels returned," the bard went on.

"Aye, that was me," said Gogfran. "And you are Menw the bard. I knew I recognised your face as soon as you stepped across my threshold."

"Gods, man, what have you been doing here all these years?" Menw exclaimed. "I had assumed you had been killed or dismissed when the island fell."

"When Enniaun Yrth led his teulu back across the straits, some of us stayed. I was born on this island, you see. My family have dwelt here since the days of the druids. It may only be an outpost to the sons of Cunedag, but I could never abandon it. We took shelter with some villagers, my wife and I. The girls were but babes. They were bad times. The Gaels take what they want and kill any who deny them. We went hungry more than one winter. But we survived. It's what we do, us islanders."

"But to live here, in this old ruin …" said Cei.

"*This old ruin*, Cei mab Cunor," Menw interrupted, "was built by your grandfather."

"Cunor's son?" Gogfran said, his eyes passing from Menw to Cei. "Aye, Osmael, the first penteulu built the first fort here. It was said he was to receive Ynys Mon as his own just as his brothers received other portions of Venedotia as their kingdoms, but his death put an end to that. So, the son of Cunor mab Osmael has returned to us!" He sucked his teeth in amusement.

"Gaels have plagued us for years," said the tawny-haired sister who was called Guenhuifar. "And Venedotia sends the son of its penteulu and six warriors to us." Her face told them that she was far from impressed.

"The teulu is occupied in the south," said Arthur. "You may not have heard, but King Meriaun has allied himself with the Gaels and is waging war for the crown of Venedotia."

"We could hardly be so ignorant," Guenhuifar replied, "with Gaels looting every store and granary to feed the war effort. There isn't a family on the island who has not been robbed or brutalised by their roving gangs. Times are harder than ever and the mighty Pendraig sends seven warriors to aid us!"

"Hush, girl!" said Gogfran, embarrassed by his daughter's animosity to their guests.

The water had begun to boil and Guenhuifach, a quiet, doe-eyed girl, swung the pot away from the flames and carried it over to the unconscious Gualchmei. She had made a neat pile of linen rags at the head of the table.

"You have treated the wounded before," Menw observed, as he joined her at the table.

The girl blushed, avoiding his eyes and bustled off to attend to the fire.

"She is her mother's daughter, and no mistake," said Gogfran. "My wife taught her to care for the sick and elderly as best she could. It was how we earned our keep in the old days before it was safe to return to the Lys. And she has tended to me these past few months. Could a father wish for more than two such daughters? Even if Guenhuifar here takes more after me than her mother, though age has not dulled her tongue nor softened her temper as it has mine!"

Guenhuifar sat by the fire; the light of which made her hair seem aflame itself. She rolled her eyes. "You do talk some nonsense, Da," she muttered.

"What is it that ails you, Gogfran?" Menw asked him, as he unwrapped the blood-soaked cloth that bound the wound. Gualchmei squirmed and moaned softly.

"Coughing fever, curse it. Can't seem to rid myself of it."

"Have you tried celandine boiled with nettle leaves?" Menw asked Guenhuifach.

"Yes, but so little of it grows around here," she replied in a quiet voice. "We have used all there is and I fear to stray too far in search of more."

"I've told you a thousand times that I would go and fetch all your herbs and plants if you only told me what to look for," said Guenhuifar.

"And have you come back with mint instead of mugwort?" said Guenhuifach. She smiled at Menw. "My sister's knowledge of herbology is somewhat lacking, I'm afraid."

Guenhuifar grunted and stoked the fire.

"I have something in my satchel that may help him," said Menw. "Just let me see to this young man first."

He dipped a rag in the hot water and bathed the wound, squeezing and prodding to make sure there were no slivers of metal still within. Gualchmei gasped with pain.

"Be still, son," said the bard. "This will soon be on the mend."

He washed the wound with the contents of a small bottle of vinegar and sewed it up with a sharp bone needle and fine thread. Then he boiled up a poultice of herbs which he mashed in a small mortar and pestle and applied to Gualchmei's shoulder.

"He needs rest now," Menw said at last. "As do we all. I apologise for keeping you good people from your beds. Dawn cannot be far off."

"Not at all," said Gogfran. "Any warrior of the Pendraig's is welcome here. But sleep is far from my mind now. I would hear of your business here and all the news you have from the mainland."

Menw glanced at Cei who indicated that there was no need for secrecy. As the tired warriors sat by the fire, the steam coming off their damp clothes in thin wisps, Menw told their hosts all.

Meddyf

The teulu had been marching all morning and for much of the previous day. The Roman road that led northwest from Cair Cunor through the mountains towards Din Emrys was in poor repair. Long grass grew through the stones and where the road crossed the boggy ground of the moors, it vanished completely. Cunedag may have chosen Cair Cunor as the fortress of his teulu for its place in the Roman road network but nobody had maintained those roads since the legions had departed.

Meddyf climbed down from the caravan and ordered what baggage they had brought with them be unloaded to lighten the weight. The caravan's wheel was well and truly stuck in the sludge. With much cursing, the men put their shoulders to it and heaved it up out of the rut it had wedged itself into.

Meddyf felt her apprehension rising. They were making slow progress and a warm welcome at their destination was no certain thing. Of all the sub-kings of Venedotia, only King Mor of Rumaniog had answered the call and he rode at the head of the column with her husband under the dragon standard. *Two kings under the banner when there should be six marching against a traitor!* That alone spoke of the crumbling of the line of Cunedag and the end of an era. That kings like Usai should claim neutrality as if they were not all bonded by blood!

It beggared belief that Etern was so foolish as to march on the Pendraig's position. He had always hated Enniaun Yrth, his younger brother who had inherited Cunedag's crown. To Etern's mind, that crown was rightfully his. But he had few winters left to him and no sons. He could not possibly think that Meriaun would ever let him sit on the throne at Cair Dugannu. Why support one nephew over another? What was there to gain? Nobody knew the answer and could only guess that an old man's jealousy had spoken instead of his honour or his reason.

Cair Cunor had been emptied within a morning and the caravan of horses, equipment, food and supplies wound its way westwards into the mountains. They would make for Din Emrys and hope for the hospitality of King Efiaun of Dunauding. It was the only place left to go and was renowned for its impenetrable defences. Cadwallon had sent riders north to call Maeldaf to meet them en route. Whatever forces he had mustered in the Conui Valley, it was time to call them to the dragon standard.

Elen had been as insufferable as ever at being forced to move once more. She had been in a state of panic ever since news had reached them that the Gaels were marching down the Conui Valley, burning and looting as they went. When the rider from the eastern border had arrived with reports of King Etern mustering his teulu, she had been near inconsolable.

Meddyf tried to comfort her by telling her that the Gaels' advance would be slowed by their lust for plunder and that they had a day's march on Etern's teulu. But still, Elen wept and Meddyf soon lost her patience with her. It wasn't Elen's people who were being burned out of their homes in the Conui Valley. It wasn't Elen's father who faced them alone.

She prayed every day to the Virgin Mary to watch over her father and uncle. Her uncle Drustan was a mere stripling who had seen only fourteen winters. Meddyf's mother had been of Pictish stock; one of the many children of Talorc mab Cuch, a chieftain who had held lands in the thick forests of Caledonia. Talorc had been a virile old goat to the end and Meddyf had lost count of the number of uncles and aunts she had up there. One of them – Drustan – was sixteen years her junior and had been sent to be fostered in her father's household. She looked on him more as a little brother than an uncle. Whatever danger her father faced in the Conui Valley, young Drustan faced it also and she longed for them to join the relative safety of the teulu.

Of all the women, Meddyf had come to like Eigyr best, though she was distant and somewhat frail. She had little to do with anybody but it was not a shyness that kept her apart, nor aloofness. She was pleasant and intelligent but seemed to suffer from an invisible wound or phantom burden. Meddyf learnt that she had spent much of the last fifteen years in her rooms at Cair Cunor seeing nobody and rarely venturing outside. When Cadwallon had given the order for Cair Cunor to be emptied, they had had to prise her from her rooms like a limpet off a rock, all the while protesting that she had to remain in case Arthur came back to her.

Arthur, Meddyf later found out, was Eigyr's son who had accompanied the band of warriors Cadwallon had dispatched to Ynys Mon. Meddyf sighed, Eigyr would be lucky to see her son again just as Cunor would be to see his. Like Owain, Meddyf had thought the expedition a foolish waste. Few outside her husband's council knew the purpose of it but Cadwallon had told her, as he told her most things. *Cauldron of Rebirth? Pah!* Although Meddyf did not know in truth what they faced, she often despaired at the pagan superstitions of the people that surrounded her.

The men eventually got the caravan's wheel up out of the rut and the baggage was loaded once more before the column took up its slow slither through the hills.

They camped in a gully that night and the riders Cadwallon had sent north returned before dark. They reported that Maeldaf and his forces were trapped in the Conui Valley.

"At first light we march north to relieve him," said Cadwallon. "Make sure everybody is ready. I will waste no time in reaching my wife's father."

But, before they set out, the scouts from the south returned with grave faces. "Meriauned is mustered," they said. "Even with their king at Cair Dugannu, his son, Prince Cadwaldr has marshalled the teulu and crossed the Afon Maudach to the south of us. They could cut us off from Din Emrys if we do not reach it in time."

"Then we must march at once," said Owain.

"And what of my father?" Meddyf asked.

"My lady," Cunor said, his face giving that forced apologetic smile Meddyf hated in the faces of men who sought to patronise her. "We are vulnerable on the road. Meriauned's teulu could reach Din Emrys before we do or they could cut east and fall upon us here. Either would be our doom. We must make for Din Emrys with all haste."

"And leave my father in the valley to face the

Gaels alone?"

Cunor turned to Cadwallon in desperation.

"Loyalty is hard to find these days," Cadwallon said. "And what sort of a Pendraig would I be if I left my people at the mercy of the Gaels?" He planted his fists on the map table and breathed deeply as if summoning the courage to say what he had to say.

Meddyf could see that he had decided upon something, that his mind was resolute, but he feared to speak it. He feared the judgement of his followers.

"I will send out all the cavalry we have to clear Maeldaf's way to us while we head southwest to break the advance of Meriauned before they reach Din Emrys."

There was a murmuring at this. "You would split the teulu?" Cunor asked, "And meet Prince Cadwaldr with no cavalry?"

"I have no choice," said Cadwallon. "I cannot leave my father-in-law, and whatever bannermen he has mustered to face the Gaels alone in my name, without sending him some aid. And I have no desire to sit out a siege at Din Emrys. The teulu of Meriauned is without its king. If we can come upon them by surprise, we might just win out. It's a desperate gamble, but make no mistake, my lords, we *are* desperate."

Well done! Meddyf thought, barely able to stop her face cracking into a smile. She had never been so proud of her husband, nor had she loved him more than she did in that moment.

"It's a risky plan," said Cunor, examining the crude but colourful map spread on the table. "But the terrain is in our favour. If we march south we should meet them passing through the forests here. The trees will conceal our advance and we will not be hindered by cavalry which they will be. Forests are no places for cavalry charges."

"And our cavalry will be put to better use in the Conui Valley," Cadwallon said. "The Gaels have no horse and will be trapped with nowhere to run but back north."

"Am I to lead the cavalry, lord?" Cunor asked.

"No, I shall have need of your strategic mind in defeating our enemies to the south."

"Then Caradog shall lead the mounted expedition. Where are you, Caradog?"

"Here, sir," spoke a burly but elderly warrior. Caradog was one of Cunor's captains.

"Brother, let me go with Caradog and our cavalry," said Owain. "Some of those who have been burned out of their homes are known to me. It would do them good to see the bear of Rhos fluttering above the relief force."

"Very well," said Cadwallon. "Once you have secured my father-in-law and his bannermen, head directly for Din Emrys. We shall meet you there when we can. If its gates are barred to you, do not try and force your way in. Leave the diplomacy to me."

"You don't trust my diplomatic skills?" Owain said, with mock hurt.

"I don't know, I've never seen them," Cadwallon replied, and the tent bellowed with laughter.

Meddyf allowed herself a small smile. It never failed to surprise her how a joke was always on the lips of men about to risk all in battle. She supposed they needed something to laugh at, something to distract their minds from the danger they were in. And the danger was very real this time. All rode on the outcome of her husband's gamble. But she knew that even if he had made a wrong decision from a military point of view, for her it was the only right decision to make.

Arthur planted his shovel in the earth and rested on the handle to catch his breath. The sweat stood out on his bare torso, and his hands, although well calloused from years of sword and spear practise, burned raw.

Three days had passed since they had arrived at the Lys. Gualchmei's wound had improved and his fever had died down. Gogfran too had shown improvement and Menw, having used all the celandine in his satchel, had ventured farther afield to find more.

It surprised Arthur that Guenhuifar also ventured far from her father's hearth, dressed in a man's breeches and tunica, and always with a bow and quiver of arrows across her back, her auburn hair tied back in a neat plait. She was usually gone for a day at a time and often returned with a rabbit for the pot.

"With no men about the place and my father sick, I don't have much choice," she said a little defensively, when she once caught Arthur watching her as she gutted and skinned a rabbit, the sleeves of her tunica rolled up to her elbows. "Meat is hard to come by. Sometimes I take the skins to trade for flour and salt in the nearest settlements."

"Aren't you worried about the Gaels?"

She glared at him. "They leave us alone and we leave them alone. But I suppose you and your friends are here to change all that."

"Surely you aren't content with the Gaels ruling this island?"

"I didn't say that. But I don't think kicking the

hornets' nest is a good idea either. Not unless you are planning to finish the job. When will you be leaving us, anyway?"

"Depends on Cei," Arthur said with a shrug.

"You and he don't seem to get along."

"You noticed?"

"Hard not to."

"He is as a brother to me, truly, but … we quarreled recently. He has a rather pig-headed way of going about things. It was because of him that Gualchmei was injured."

"Perhaps he's not the best choice to lead your expedition then."

"He is the penteulu's son."

Cei had set them to work repairing and reinforcing the Lys's fortifications. The Gaels would be looking for them and were probably ransacking every settlement for trace of them. It wouldn't be long before it occurred to them to check the old Lys in the north-eastern corner of the island and Cei wanted to be ready for them when they did.

Arthur had pointed out that seven warriors – and one of them sorely wounded – could not hold out against all the Gaels on the island, no matter how well they dug in behind refortified walls. It would be better to continue with their mission than remain sitting ducks in a poorly defended fort, but Cei insisted that they could not set out until Gualchmei was able to draw a bow once more. They would need to be at full strength to steal the cauldron from the Morgens and, for the time being, they had to stay put and hope for the best.

Arthur detected a little reluctance on Cei's part to

set out once more. No longer was he the gung-ho glory seeker he had been when they had crossed the straits. Their first skirmish with their enemy had humbled him and dulled his keenness for action. It wasn't cowardice that held him back – Cei was anything but a coward – but he clearly felt some shame in his recklessness that had seen Gualchmei wounded. He had even come close to apologising to Arthur on one occasion which would have been staggeringly out of character for him.

The outer earthworks were almost finished and Cei and Beduir had started working on the gate, replacing its rotten portions with fresh wood and strengthening it with crossbeams. Cundelig and Guihir emerged from the woods bearing a long, freshly cut timber between them.

"Perfect!" said Beduir. "Put it down here. Cut off the smaller branches and we'll shape it to size."

Within the hour they had a perfectly usable bolt for the gate. Guenhuifar brought out water to them and they slaked their thirst in grateful gulps for the sun was blazing and the air warm.

"My father wishes to thank you for restoring the defenses," she said, although it seemed a little forced on her part, as if she had been told to say it.

"No need to thank us," said Cei. "We're all in this together if the Gaels come here looking for us."

"I would think that you might consider moving on," she said, "and remove the danger you hold over our heads. We have held no interest for the Gaels so far and they have left us alone for many years."

"Their time is at its end," said Cei. "We have been sent here to deal the death blow to their alliance with the Morgens. Soon the Pendraig will come to drive the Gaels back to Erin."

"As his grandfather did?" Guenhuifar replied through lips that curled in a sneer. "How long did that last? It was a mere generation before they returned and Enniaun Yrth abandoned us to their rule. The sons of Cunedag care little for us, they never have. They took more cattle than refugees across the straits when they left. That shows you how much they value the loyalty of men like my father."

"Your father stayed of his own accord," Cei pointed out.

"Yes. Because he believed that one day the Pendraig would return and the dragon banner would fly over the Lys once more. Even I believed it as a child but we have waited too long. I have seen my father grow old and sick and still he does not relinquish his hope. He clings to it for it is all he has left but it is killing him. Day by day, I see it. And now you come here bringing him false hope …"

"False hope?" said Arthur. "You believe that we will fail?"

She shrugged. "Fail or succeed, it will make little difference to us. This cauldron you speak of, *if* you manage to steal it you plan to take it back to the mainland, no?"

"That is the idea," said Cei.

"And that will be the last we'll see of you, I know it. The Gaels will remain, you will win your war and will celebrate with your precious cauldron at Cair Dugannu while, for us, life will go on unchanged. The Pendraig will not return to Ynys Mon. I gave up on that dream a long time ago. I only wish my father might be able to before he dies."

She turned from them and headed back indoors where they could see Gualchmei emerging from the hall, his arm still in its sling.

"By Modron's tits, she's a bitter one," said Cei, watching Guenhuifar's hips sway under her tunica as she walked away from them. "But so fair on the outside!"

That night, as usual, they ate their evening meal by the hearth in the hall with Gogfran and his daughters.

"Guenhuifar tells me that the gate is repaired," said Gogfran. "I can't thank you enough."

"It is we who should thank you," said Arthur. "Without your kind hospitality we may have lost Gualchmei to his poisoned wound."

"And I may not have lived to see the autumn leaves fall," Gogfran replied, "without your bard's medicine."

"It is the least I could do," said Menw. "But time marches on and I fear that we must soon march with it. The gods alone know what is happening on the mainland. Perhaps war has already broken out for the crown of Venedotia. Every day we tarry here is a day that may be the death of many a comrade."

"I wish I could be of more help to you," said Gogfran. "But you go up against ancient sorceries. The Morgens have lived on the western part of the island since before the Romans came. They allow few to witness what goes on around their sacred lake."

"On our second night here," said Menw, "you said that there has been a spate of grave robberies in these parts."

"All over the island," said Guenhuifar. "I have

seen those desecrated plots myself."

"No doubt the handiwork of the Gaels," said Gogfran. "Digging up corpses for the Morgens to use in their dark rites. More dead for their army, if the legends about the cauldron are true." He repressed a shudder which set him off in a coughing fit. He recovered slowly and took a sip of the hot drink of Menw's herbs that Guenhuifach held to his lips, wincing at the taste as he swallowed.

"Where has the largest concentration of these grave robberies taken place?" Menw asked.

"The burial mounds have been largely left alone," said Guenhuifar. "They are sacred to the Morgens and the Gaels have a fear of them. There's a Christian graveyard at the church of Saint Padraig on the northernmost tip of the island not eight miles from here. There are many graves there that have been unearthed."

"Padraig founded the church after he was shipwrecked here on his way to Erin to convert the Gaels to Christianity," said Gogfran.

"Did he have much success?" Cei asked.

"Some. But the Gaels are a hard-headed lot and sticklers for tradition, especially the tradition of bloodletting. Most of the raiders who came to these shores aren't about to let the word of a new god stay their hands when there is rape and plunder to be enjoyed."

"Their war leader is named Diugurnach, we are told," Beduir said.

"Aye, he's chief among them on this island. Part of some great clan that rules at Tara. I think he plans to make himself a king in Albion."

"And he may do just that through his alliance with King Meriaun," said Menw. "Do you know anything about that?"

Gogfran shook his head. "The Gaels are concentrated on the western side of the island and are closer to the Morgens than one might credit their bravery."

Menw sucked his teeth thoughtfully. "I think I'll take a look at this Christian cemetery," he said.

He disappeared the following morning and did not return for two days. In the meantime, the companions made several other improvements to the Lys's defences. The tips of the palisade timbers, long since dulled by moss and weathering, were re-sharpened leaving them gleaming white in contrast to their blackened posts. They dug a ditch just inside the entrance of the compound and fitted it with spikes before covering it with as much brush and bracken as they could forage.

Menw returned on the morning of their sixth day and his face was grave. "The Gaels are indeed looking for us and have narrowed in on this corner of the island. It will not be long before they come knocking."

"Then we should leave," said Arthur. "We have endangered these good people for long enough."

"No sense in that, lad," said Menw. "We are cornered and even I cannot guide us past their lines. They have cast their net wide and are strong in number."

"So we must dig in here," said Cei. "Bar the gates. I want watches kept through the night and every one of us sleeps in his war gear."

There was talk of Cundelig sending up Hebog to see from which direction the enemy was approaching but Cundelig would have none of it. "He is known to them," he said. "It was on account of spotting him in the sky that they came after us in the first place. Why alert them to our presence now? Besides, I won't risk him being shot down by one of their arrows."

"Aye, they'll find us soon enough as it is," said Menw. "We must prepare to weather the storm."

They came a little before noon on the following day; a long line of warriors numbering about twenty. Cadfan sounded the alarm and the companions assembled on the palisade.

"Do any of them look like the Cauldron-born to you?" Cei asked Menw.

"Not that I can see from this distance," the bard replied. "But they are fierce warriors nonetheless."

"Rabble!" Gogfran said, and he hawked a glob of phlegm over the spiked palisade. "Without Diugurnach to lead them they are just a mob made up of those not chosen to join the war on the mainland. The runts of the litter! If only I was at my full strength …" He began to cough and hack and Guenhuifach took him indoors.

Cadfan had run down to the courtyard and returned wearing a battered iron helm and gripping a shield and spear.

"Can you fight?" Cei asked the servant.

"As well as any man will when faced with imminent death," Cadfan replied.

"Good enough." Cei turned to Gualchmei and Guenhuifar. "Go inside. Bar the doors. They won't get past us, but if they do …"

"If they do," said Guenhuifar, "then we'll finish off your leavings."

"I share Gogfran's shame," said Gualchmei. "My shoulder is not healed enough to bend my bow but if we could just strap a shield to my weak arm and place a spear in my other hand …"

"No," said Cei. "We cannot afford to have any weakness in our defences. Better a man short than a weak link. Go inside with our hosts."

Gualchmei's face reddened and it looked as if tears were beginning to form in his eyes.

"Cei does not mean any insult, cousin," Arthur told him. "We need at least one warrior within the hall to protect Gogfran and the women should we fail to hold them back. You shall have your shield and spear. I will arm you myself."

Guenhuifar overheard this and, as they entered the hall, she cast a rare smile at Arthur that made his face flush.

The Gaels approached and their chieftain – one of Diugurnach's lieutenants – sat astride his horse and whirled an axe around by its leather thong while he bellowed war cries. Spears and blades hammered against shields and the Britons on the ramparts began to mutter prayers. Menw, Cei and Cadfan prayed to Modron while the others asked the virgin mother of Christ for protection. Arthur remained silent although he hoped that somebody was listening. Perhaps they would have need of many gods to overcome these odds.

The Gaels began their offensive up the hill. The Britons kept low behind the palisade for already the occasional stone from a sling ricocheted off the timbers. Gogfran had been right, they were a disorganised rabble. They carried no battering ram and had no strategy other than to stumble through the ditch and break upon the gates like a weak tide.

"Now!" Cei cried and the companions stood up and cast spears, rocks and chunks of masonry down on the Gaels.

Men screamed as limbs were broken and skulls were caved in while spears nailed men to the ground. Shields were upraised and rocks bounced off them, tumbling into the ditch. The call for retreat was given and they fell back to the trees, carrying their wounded beneath their shields.

The Britons whooped and cheered. The first round had been won but it was only the opening act. The drubbing the Gaels had received sharpened their wits and made them more resolute and cautious.

It was midday when the smoke of braziers could be seen at the treeline. Bowmen emerged with arrows wound with oil-soaked rags. They lit these in the braziers and loosed them at the gates. Most were extinguished in their flight and those that lodged in the wood were hastily doused by the Britons who hurried along the ramparts with pails of water.

The Gaels kept up their offensive for most of the afternoon and grew more effective at it. Arthur and his companions were so occupied dousing the fires that the enemy was able to creep closer which only improved their aim and decreased the number of arrows extinguished mid-flight.

"We can't keep this up!" Beduir said, as he heaved the contents of a pail over the palisade. "Too many bloody arrows!"

Flames were creeping up the timbers and spreading all the quicker in the charred spots that had already been scorched. Guenhuifar and Guenhuifach had emerged to help carry water from the spring to the men on the ramparts and everybody was sore, tired and raw-eyed from the smoke.

"We need only hold them until it seems natural for us to fall back," said Cei. "Then we let them come upon our second line of defence."

It was a risky plan but they were outnumbered and had to resort to trickery if they were to win out. As Arthur passed pail after pail to Beduir, his arms screaming with fatigue, he tried to count the number of Gaels he had seen fall in their initial attack. *How many were left?*

The smoke grew thicker and caught in their throats. They could no longer see the ground or the enemy and the heat was unbearable.

"It's gone!" Cei cried. "Fall back! There is nothing more we can do to save the gate. Fall back!"

They scrambled down the ladders and hurried towards their agreed positions Cei had mapped out for them the night before. Arthur, Cei and Beduir took cover behind a barricade of thorn bushes before the doors to the hall, taking up their spears and shields. Cundelig and Guihir hid themselves in the ruined Lys where the shadows concealed them. Menw remained where he was and called out to the gods for aid.

The flames licked up the palisades and smoke rolled out from under the gate, engulfing it in a black cloud. Soon the whole thing was a sheet of roaring flame, its crackling drowning out Menw's words.

The time came and the gates, their supports eaten through, tumbled down sending forth a billowing gust of fire and smoke that whirled around Menw like a sea mist. Arthur cleared his eyes and looked up to see the Gaels making their way through the ruined gate, stepping over the burning timbers and leaping through the smoke like demons from hell.

Wait … thought Arthur. *Wait for it* …

The Gaels looked about as if expecting a full garrison to assault them at any minute. Menw walked towards them; a single old man against fifteen-odd warriors. The Gaels laughed and roared insults at the bard. He stopped walking and stretched out his arms as if inviting them.

The Gaels advanced in a line, three men deep. They stepped on the bracken-covered trench and the first line disappeared into the earth. Screams of outrage and agony drifted up from the pit and the other two lines fell back in alarm.

"Now!" Cei cried and they leapt up and charged the enemy with spears lowered.

Incapacitated by sharpened stakes which pierced thighs, feet and calves, the first five Gaels were sitting ducks for the Britons who reddened their spears in their guts. The rest of the Gaels, having overcome their initial surprise, marshalled themselves and flanked the Britons on either side of the pit.

Arthur discarded his spear and drew his sword as a Gael came at him. He dodged a swipe and cut in low only to be deflected by a ringing blow that reverberated through his arm. An arrow sailed out of nowhere and struck the Gael in the chest. Arthur whirled around.

From the thatched roof of the hall he could see Gualchmei's flatbow bending as a second arrow was drawn. But it was not Gualchmei who drew it. The flame-red hair of Guenhuifar billowed in the wind like a pennant and she let the arrow fly. It struck a Gael's shield but distracted him long enough for Cei to cut his legs out from under him.

"That's a bit of a bonus," Cei said, as he thrust his sword tip down into the fallen Gael's gullet. "The lass can shoot!"

The Gaels were unsure of themselves now. The trench was filled with their dead and several more lay about the compound. Their chieftain bellowed them on before dismounting to stride forth and mete out some violence himself.

"Fall back!" Cei cried. "Fall back to the Lys!"

They had been prepared for this; the final part of their plan. Disengaging from the enemy, they turned tail and fled into the shadows of the ruined building. Guenhuifar loosed arrow after arrow at the pursuing Gaels, and Arthur began to worry that some of them might break off and torch the thatch of the hall to rid themselves of her, but there was nothing for it now but to see their plan through to its end.

Their footsteps echoed in the cool darkness of the Lys and the mirror of stagnant water sent ripples of light across the walls at the far end as they sought refuge in the shadows.

The Gaels slipped in between the broken doors, not noticing Cundelig and Guihir on either side of the doorway. Once half of the Gaels were inside the building, they both swung high, double-handed blows at the next pair to enter. The two men went down with a clatter and a splash of blood from shattered noses and cloven faces. Those who had already entered spun around to face Cundelig and Guihir, snarling their anger at being ambushed.

And then Cei, Arthur and Beduir charged them.

It was three against four but surprise gave them the edge they needed. Within seconds the stone flags were awash with blood, and the last screams of the dying sang in the echoing chamber while Cundelig and Guihir held off the remaining enemies at the doors as they desperately tried to aid their companions.

Cei led the charge, forcing them back out into the compound. Only the chieftain and two of his warriors were left and they were keeping well out of Guenhuifar's range. The chieftain called a retreat and they turned and fled, not even stopping to recover their dead.

The Britons roared in their exaltation. Guenhuifar slid down from the thatch and walked over to them, beaming. Arthur thought a smile vastly improved her already attractive face.

"Where did you learn to shoot like that, lass?" Cei asked her. "Has Gualchmei been giving you lessons behind our backs?"

"Shooting Gaels is no different to shooting rabbits," she said. "Only infinitely more satisfying."

Arthur could see through her bravado. He could see the way her hands were shaking and knew the reason why, for his own still shook a little whenever he thought too much about the events of the past few days. *She's never killed a man before.*

"Truly, I have never shot a bow as fine as this."

She stroked the smooth wood and ivory tips with appreciation.

"You do the art proud," said Gualchmei from the doorway, his shield still strapped to his injured arm and his spear propped up against the wall. "I spy my fletching sticking out of at least two Gaelic dogs."

"Well, we gave those whoresons a thing or two to think about, eh?" said Beduir, slapping Cei and Arthur on the shoulders. He grinned at Guenhuifar. "Has your da got anything better than ale to drink about the place? Killing Gaels works up a thirst!"

"We shall all drink the Pendraig's mead tonight!" said Gogfran, emerging behind Gualchmei. "There are still a few casks in the cellars. I was saving them for his return but we have a victory to celebrate and a new Pendraig to drink to!"

"I must beg that we drink moderately," said Menw. "We have won a victory but our quest still lies before us and I have a plan that may see it to its fruition. Come, I could do with a cup of the old inspiration myself and I will tell you what I learned at the church of Saint Padraig."

Cadwallon

The wood was still and sombre as if watchful of the army that passed through its leafy realm. The gushing of the Afon Elan drowned most noise but still the teulu proceeded with caution. Bridles were muffled by gloved fists and voices kept to a low whisper. It was not just the desire to come upon the enemy without warning that stilled the men's tongues. This wood was old and the dim light filtered through the greenery above played upon the superstitions of those who trod its soft loam.

Further south the river joined the Afon Maudach before it swept westwards, forming the border between Dunauding and Meriauned. The teulu of Meriauned had crossed the Maudach several days ago and were now somewhere in this wood, marching northward.

The scouts Cadwallon had sent out came back with bloodied blades.

"They march blind, lord," said one. "We encountered several of their own scouts and made sure that they did not make it back to report."

"That alone may alert them to our presence," said Cadwallon.

"They'll be upon us before the absence of their scouts is noticed. They are but three leagues south-west from here."

"How many?"

"Three-hundred foot. A hundred cavalry."

Cadwallon cursed. "And us with no cavalry of our own. I only hope I haven't wasted those riders I sent with my brother."

"We should meet them at the ford before the Black Falls, lord," said Cunor. "The ground is uneven and the cover is good. We have bowmen. Use them. Riddle them with shafts before they know what they've wandered into. That will soften them up enough for our charge. I advise we send every mounted man we have left to cross the Afon Camlan upriver where it runs off the moors and enters the forest. Once we have engaged the enemy at the ford, signal them to charge their left flank. Our riders will be no match for the enemy cavalry but our arrows and spearmen should be able to break apart their ranks, loosening them up for us."

"I trust your council, old friend," said Cadwallon. "You will ride with our mounted troops, such as they are?"

"I would lead them myself, lord."

"I will send King Mor and his household troops with you."

The riders broke off from the teulu almost immediately, heading west at all speed to cross the river before the enemy reached the ford. The rest of the teulu continued southwest and it was not long before the distant roar of the Black Falls could be heard.

The woods were thick and the ground rocky. There was no way through for the caravans and food wains. Cadwallon dismounted and led his horse to the rear of the column. Meddyf poked her head out from behind the caravan curtain. Inside Maelcon and Guidno could be seen, peering out.

"This is where we part," he told her. "The river lies ahead and that is where we will make our stand. I have instructed thirty warriors to escort you and the baggage train to the high ridge yonder."

"Take your warriors," said Meddyf. "They are no good to us."

"I will not leave my family and the families of every man under my standard vulnerable."

"If you fail to break their lines," Meddyf said slowly, "thirty warriors won't save us from rape and murder. Take them, husband. You need every spear you can get."

Cadwallon saw her logic, characteristically cold as it was. He recalled the thirty warriors and sent them back to the ranks.

There were tears and frightened voices as the caravans were urged up to the ridge. Cadwallon was haunted by the terrified faces of the women and children under his protection. He had to win this battle for their sakes. He kissed Meddyf and his sons goodbye and prayed to every god he could think of that it would not be the last time he did so. He rode back to the head of the teulu and gave orders for the bowmen to move out and conceal themselves in the trees that lined the high ground west of the ford.

They crept upon the gushing river which flowed over mossy black rocks towards the falls. The bubbling ford was swollen by the spring runoff and crossing would be slow going. *Let the bastards come to us*, Cadwallon thought. *Let them flounder while we hold the high ground.*

They kept to the green shadows of the woods; a long defensive line of spearmen ready to charge the shallows at a signal from their lord. Through the trees ahead, Cadwallon could see his bowmen squatting on the high rocks of the cascades, arrows nocked to bowstrings.

The cawing of birds to the south rose, first one group, then another, until the woods seemed to resound with screeching and flapping of birds taking wing, so that even the distant falls were drowned out.

"They are coming," Cadwallon said to the men at his side.

The enemy emerged tentatively in small groups from the woods on the other side of the river. Mail and iron helms glinted in the filtered light. As the first of them tested the depth of the rushing waters with the shaft of his spear, the mass of cavalry materialised from the green gloom, a thick body of chestnut and dun mares, interspersed by the occasional bay or blue roan. As they started to cross, the men on the rocks drew their bows.

Cadwallon waited until the footmen were halfway across the river, its waters lapping around their middles, and the first of the horses were wetting their fetlocks in the icy current before he gave his horn blower the word.

The long, low blast of the aurochs horn rippled through the forest and seemed to turn all to stone. The men in the river froze and looked about, terrified by the sound. They knew what it meant.

The bowmen loosed and the volley of arrows fell upon the enemy like hail. Men howled and horses screamed as the deadly darts tore into them and bodies rolled and bucked in the tumbling current.

Cadwallon drew his sword. He hoped Cunor and Mor had heard the horn blast. They had to be well within hearing distance if they were to win this battle.

He waited until the second volley of arrows had settled before he gave the order to charge, his voice hoarse and his sword hilt slippery in his sweaty palm.

It was a mad, savage dash down to the water's edge. They kept running until the freezing torrent of the river slowed their assault and dragged at their limbs as if they were of lead. The river ran red now and was clogged with corpses. There were some survivors who struggled to double back and outrun their attackers but Cadwallon and his men cut them down from behind.

Cadwallon had slaughtered Gaels in the wars for Ynys Mon and had grown accustomed to the screaming of the wounded and the gibbering, desperate prayers of those who knew they were on death's threshold. But these men who fell beneath his blade and went down on his orders were his countrymen; men who had pledged allegiance to his father once upon a time. These same men would have been his were it not for one man's greed so now they must die without a voice in the matter. *Gods, is there anything more awful and unnatural than civil war?*

They made the far bank and faced the enemy which had retreated from the range of the bowmen and marshalled themselves deeper in the woods. Cadwallon ordered all his spearmen to form a defensive barrier, the dragon standard protected by a single row of bristling points. The enemy, its courage bolstered by the knowledge that they faced mere footmen, made to charge.

"Hold steady!" Cadwallon yelled at his men. He could smell piss as somebody near him urinated in his terror. *A man should never have to face a cavalry charge with only a spear in his hands.*

The cavalry broke upon them and the shockwave rippled through the ranks. Horses tumbled end over end, their breasts pierced, tossing their riders like rag dolls, landing on Cadwallon's men, crushing them.

Cadwallon screamed and hewed at an outthrust arm, dodging the spear tip, and hacking the limb off at the elbow. All around him men died, trampled under hoof, run through by spears, heads cloven by swinging blades. *Is this it? Is this the pitiful end to my short reign?*

Suddenly the rear ranks of the enemy erupted into chaos. Men were hurled this way and that as some unstoppable force thundered into their left flank. Cadwallon could see the raven banner of Rumaniog wavering about through the trees and knew Cunor and Mor had heard his call.

"Push forward!" he yelled. "King Mor is with us! Rumaniog is with us!"

His shattered force heeded the call and pushed onwards, more out of mad desperation than anything else. It was fight or die, most likely both, so what did they have to lose? All along the line, warriors clustered together in small groups and charged the enemy. Long spears and tight formations won out and the enemy was driven deeper into the woods – against the press of Cunor and King Mor's mounted troops.

Cadwallon lost track of time and place. All he knew was the clamour and flurry of battle; the splintering of shields, the slither and rasp of steel, the screams of the stricken. War cries sounded from every part of the forest and the thrumming of hooves on soft loam pounded like drums as the enemy mustered and charged, and mustered and charged again, each time growing a little smaller, a little weaker.

We are winning, he thought and then wished he hadn't. It did not do to be overly confident. What did he know anyway? Numbers were like water (*or blood*) flowing around him as if from an infinite source.

And then it was over. Groups of war-weary men threw down their arms and knelt, pleading for mercy. There were no more cavalry charges and already Cadwallon's men were putting down the screaming horses with spear thrusts. The wounded men were not so lucky. It was considered near blasphemous to leave a wounded horse to suffer but a wounded man might be healed and held for ransom.

Cunor rode towards Cadwallon, his shield red with gore and his helm dented. His face beamed like a dog in the midst of play. "We have overcome them, my lord!" he said.

"Thanks to your charge," Cadwallon replied. "By Modron's tits, we had a bad few moments after we crossed the river. I feared you might not make it in time!"

Prisoners were jostled about between the riders and pushed to the front for Cadwallon's inspection.

"What of Cadwaldr," he asked. "Is he here?"

"Answer him!" Cunor barked, pointing his sword tip at a kneeling prisoner with an ugly gash in his forehead. "Who is in command here?"

"Meriauned's penteulu," said the man. "We saw him fall …"

"And Meriaun's son? Where is Cadwaldr?"

"In Meriauned. Keeping his father's throne warm."

"The runt never had the stomach for battle," Cunor sneered.

"Does Meriauned have many more warriors?" Cadwallon asked the prisoner. "Will they attack again?"

The man's eyes looked at the earth in shame. "No. We are Meriaun's entire teulu."

"Could be lying," said King Mor.

"No," said Cunor, looking around at the slain and the captives. "He tells the truth. Meriauned has no more left to send against us. Just their damned allies and mercenaries in the north."

Cadwallon left his teulu to mop up the mess and returned across the river with a few of his household guard. Upon the ridge Meddyf waited for him with his sons and he wanted to embrace them all and give thanks to Modron before they started the long march north to Din Emrys.

PART III

"The Cauldron of Dyrnwch the Giant: if meat for a coward were put in it to boil, it would never boil; but if meat for a brave man were put in it, it would boil quickly."
- The Thirteen Treasures of the Island of Britain

The sky was a small patch of blue, vibrant as a bird's egg through the press of corpses that weighed down on Arthur. Every breath was a strain, both from the weight of the dead and the stink of old sweat and leather. He could barely move his arms and every minute was a fight against claustrophobia. He wished Menw had let them lie on top of the corpses in the cart instead of beneath them but the bard had insisted that this was the only way.

Somewhere in the hot tangle of limbs and matted hair, Cei breathed heavily and Arthur took comfort in his close proximity. Despite their quarrel and fraught relationship over the past few days, he would not have liked to have anybody but Cei at his side when the odds were stacked so heavily against them.

Menw's plan had required only two of them to ride in the cart and play dead while Guihir drove it. 'Efnisien's trick', was what Menw had called it. Arthur and Cei had stripped to their breeches and donned the blood-soaked tunicas and cloaks of two of the Gaels they had slain. Guihir also dressed in the garb of the enemy. As only he could speak with any Gaels they might encounter and convince them that he was one of their own, it was his job to get them into the lair of the Morgens. Menw, Beduir, Gualchmei and Cundelig would follow the cart at a distance. Then, once darkness had fallen, Arthur and Cei would steal the cauldron from under the nose of the enemy while the others created a distraction.

There were so many things that could go wrong with the plan that Arthur dared not dwell on them for too long. They didn't know exactly what happened to the dead the Gaels brought to the Morgens. Guihir could easily pass for a Gael but would that be enough? What if the Gaels who were sent out to rob graves were all known to the Morgens?

Guihir kept them updated on the progress of the journey, leaning back to talk to them through the pile of bodies. "We've just passed the western edge of Lin Alaw," he said, referring to the great lake in the centre of Ynys Mon. "I can see the forest to the south; nothing but gorse and heath up ahead."

They had skirted the large lake on its northern side and planned to follow the Afon Alaw which emptied into the sea north of the sacred lake of the Morgens. At some point they would cut south but when that would be, Arthur could only guess. All he could see of their journey was a glimpse of the vast blue sky above.

"We've got company," said Guihir after a time. "Riders. Five of them. Hunters by the looks of it for they've got a deer between them."

The cart slowed to a halt and Arthur could hear the baying of the shaggy hounds and the pattering of their paws in the mud as they circled the cart. He also heard the snort of horses and the jingle of harnesses. Guihir struck up conversation with the hunters in Gaelic, his well-trained tongue rattling out the speech of Erin, of which Arthur could only pick out some compliments referring to the hunt.

The Gaels replied with cheerful voices and there was mirth at some jest. It seemed to be going well and, as the wheels of the cart creaked off once more with the hunters riding alongside, Arthur guessed that they now had an armed escort. This was either a good thing or a very bad thing. An escort into the lair of the Morgens was preferable to Guihir turning up on his own but what if their new friends insisted on unloading the cart themselves? Once again, he cursed Menw and his reckless plan. Anything could happen once they were among the enemy and now it was too late to turn back.

The sky began to darken and the ground grew rougher causing all the corpses in the cart to bounce up and down on top of Arthur sickeningly. Guihir reined his horse in and the cart ground to a halt.

Voices.

Many Gaelic voices.

Arthur gripped the hilt of his sword, trying not to cause the bodies on top of him to move. He knew that Cei would be doing the same thing. If it came to it, they may have to fight their way out.

They heard Guihir jump down from the cart and his squelching footsteps disappeared. The voices died down and vanished, leaving Arthur feeling that he and Cei were suddenly alone. The plan was to wait until dark when the others would make their distraction. Guihir was supposed to maintain his guise as one of the Gaels until it was safe for him to make his escape after Arthur and Cei had located the cauldron and stolen it.

It seemed like the unloading of the bodies from the cart was not a priority which suited Arthur just fine. The thought of playing dead while his limp body was manhandled and tossed about was too much for him. They would surely loot him of his sword too and then where would he be?

The wait for the oncoming darkness was the worst of it. The sun seemed to take forever to sink, and all the while Arthur and Cei had to lie among the stinking dead, scarcely daring to breathe, not knowing if the Gaels would suddenly think to unload the cart.

The sky above turned black and the taste of the night air grew tantalisingly chill and fresh from within the tangle of corpses. Arthur longed to be free and to breathe the cool air deeply but there was no sign of Menw's promised distraction. At last, Cei stirred and spoke.

"We should make a move. We can't wait all night to be discovered. The gods know where Menw and the others have got to."

"I'd rather fight all the Gaels on the island than spend another minute among their dead," said Arthur.

Getting free of the corpses was a struggle in itself after having lain still for so long. Arthur's own limbs felt as dead as the ones that had been sprawled over him all day. They clambered down from the cart and stretched and gulped down fresh air in an attempt to dispel the stink of death from their nostrils. They squatted by the cart and looked about.

They were within a stone enclosure. Thatched roundhouses dotted the compound and the lights of fires could be seen between them, silhouetting distant figures that wandered about. The place looked little different to the other villages on the island.

"I don't see any lake, sacred or otherwise," said Cei. "Do you?"

"No," Arthur replied. "Perhaps beyond the roofs of the roundhouses?"

"Looks like it's just trees over there. I don't think this is the lair of the Morgens. I think this is just some Gaelic settlement."

"Shit! What do we do now?"

"I would say cut and run for the woods, but we can't leave Guihir supping mead with the enemy."

"Or we could see the plan through," said Arthur. "These corpses are undoubtedly headed for the Morgens. This may just be a brief stop on the way." He shuddered involuntarily at the thought of climbing back in among the dead. He would much rather abandon the plan and think of another. They were within a stone's throw of the wall but Cei was right, Guihir was still risking his life for the sake of the plan. Could they really do any less? "Aye, let's find him and get out of here."

They had to be cautious. They may be dressed as Gaels but their blood-soaked tunics would arouse suspicion, and besides, this settlement was scarcely large enough to allow for anonymity. They were strangers and would be challenged by the first warrior who set eyes on them. That Guihir had not already been killed was undoubtedly due to some claim of his that he was from a different settlement, but their lack of Gaelic would give them away the minute they were questioned.

They followed the perimeter wall, keeping to the shadows. Guihir could be in any of the huts and Arthur had no idea how they were to find him. They hadn't got far when something bright and fast sailed through the night air above them. At first, Arthur thought it was a shooting star but it landed in the muddy compound and sizzled before going out.

Another streak of flame followed it, but this one landed on the roof of a roundhouse and began to burn brighter as the thatch caught.

Somebody else had spotted it and gave up a cry. By the time the third fire arrow landed – this time in the wattle wall of an outbuilding where it flamed and kindled the overhanging thatch – warriors had begun to emerge from the dwellings, some of them tying their breeches, others taking up their spears. All around the settlement was a growing sense of panic and a mustering to defend themselves against their unseen attackers.

"Looks like Gualchmei's shoulder is better," Cei whispered to Arthur.

"Right time, wrong place," said Arthur. "But I suppose he knows that. They must be trying to give us an opportunity to escape. Come on!"

They drew their swords and hurried towards the roundhouses. There was little need for subtlety now. The settlement was in so much of an uproar that nobody would stop to question them. Two roundhouses were blazing and the villagers were forming bucket lines from the spring in a desperate attempt to douse the flames. Warriors ran towards the north-eastern wall of the compound and formed a defensive line at its gate. Hounds yelped and bayed as they were whipped into action, and small parties made to leave the compound to flush out the attackers, but they hesitated in the face of the darkness and the woods. They did not know how many enemies were out there.

Arthur and Cei tensed for a fight as a figure ran towards them but relaxed their guard when they saw it was Guihir.

"Get out of sight, you fools!" he yelled at them. "You stick out like sore thumbs, the pair of you!"

They made for the western wall and clambered over it, rolling across its turf surfacing to land in the mud on the other side. Somebody within the compound yelled and they knew that their escape had been noticed.

They cut a bee-line for the woods but by the sound of the hounds giving chase behind them they were being hotly pursued. Branches snapped at them like whips and ferns and roots tried to trip them as they plunged into the earthy blackness of the woods. The moon was shielded by the wavering pines above and the dank darkness of the forest consumed them.

On and on they pushed, the sound of the chase behind them reminding Arthur of that awful day they had been pursued across the breadth of the island by the same enemy. That had led them to Cunedag's Lys (*and to Guenhuifar*). Where would this chase lead them?

The forest grew thicker and running became impossible. It wasn't just the terrifying feeling of not knowing what lay three feet in front of them but the tangles of thorns and dense foliage seemed like an impenetrable wall that was intent on keeping them out. They had to push through it or face the hounds and warriors that pursued them.

"Where are Menw and the others?" Cei panted over Arthur's shoulder. The muffled density of the forest made them feel like they were breathing into each other's ears.

"Way behind us," said Arthur. "Or retreated to safety with any luck."

"Then why did we head into this?" Cei demanded, batting a branch away with his sword.

"It's the only cover," said Guihir. "Better in here than running across open fields."

"Have you any idea where we are going?"

"No. I wish Cundelig were with us."

It didn't matter to Arthur where they were going, only forward; away from their pursuers. They would press on until it was dawn and then they would have a better idea of where they were. They were on an island. This forest could only be so big.

They found a stony glade which provided them with a respite from the cloying claustrophobia of the woods and gave them a window to the starry sky above, encircled by the gently swaying tips of the pine trees. The air was cool and refreshing. They had long given up running, the thick foliage forcing them to walk for over an hour now, yet Arthur felt the desperate need to stop and breathe.

"Well, I think we can safely say that the plan has gone sideways," said Cei. "You led us into the Gael's bloody camp, not the sacred lake of the Morgens!"

"I hardly had a choice," said Guihir. "When those hunters spotted us, they insisted on escorting me to their village."

"Did they ask you about the cartload of corpses you were driving?"

"Of course they bloody did! That settlement we escaped from is the closest settlement to the lake of the Morgens. Those villagers provide the nine sisters with the bulk of the corpses and they wanted to know who I was. I had a hard time of it convincing them that I had been sent from a settlement on the eastern side of the island. I told them that the Morgens were branching out as there were more graves on that side. They seemed to believe that readily enough."

"Did they say what they are using the corpses for?" Cei asked.

"No. They have no idea. This lot are farmers, fishermen and craftsmen. Only a few of have any contact with the Morgens; the ones who deliver the corpses for their necromancy but even they don't know much about it."

"Necromancy?" Arthur asked. "That's what they said?"

"Well, the Gaelic word is close enough. They're a superstitious lot and believe whatever the Morgens tell them. They only rob Christian graves. The graves of pagans and the ancient mounds are to be left well alone and that suits the Gaels well enough. They're mostly pagans themselves and are only too happy to desecrate the graves of Christians."

"A grave is a grave and should be bloody well left alone," said Cei. "Pagan or otherwise."

"Can't disagree with you there," Guihir said.

"How long until dawn?" Arthur asked.

"Difficult to say with nothing but trees around us," said Guihir, "but my guess is that it's a good four hours off."

"Let's keep walking south," Arthur said. "If the lake of the Morgens is beyond this forest then maybe Menw will lead the others to it and we can meet up there and plan what to do next."

They plodded on, single file. Cei led the way, hacking a path through the thorns and low branches with his sword. The ground rose up and down in a series of hills and dips, carpeted with pine needles which muffled their footfalls as well as those of anybody who might be following them.

The moonlight was filtered by the piney branches and little of it reached the forest floor. Cei pushed through to a low sweep of ground and his sword arm was granted a respite. It was then that they heard it; a distant crackling of somebody or something moving through the woods to their right, a little behind them.

"Are we being pursued?" Arthur whispered.

"They're being bloody quiet about it if we are," said Cei.

They stood stock still and looked behind them. There, where the small rise dipped away to their right, something was causing the branches to waver. There was a snapping of twigs.

They hurried down the slope at a quiet jog, stumbling and sliding before the density of the trees thickened once more and they pushed on blindly. Arthur was in front now and he could feel Cei's hot breath on his neck, farther back the frightened panting of Guihir.

Thoughts ran through his mind of what pursued them. He knew that it had to be the Gaels from the village they had escaped from, but the moonlit trees and the blackness that filled the gaps between them, coupled with the island's dark history, made phantoms leap and caper in his mind. He thought of the druids, butchered by the Romans an age past, their spirits haunting the forests and moors of Ynys Mon. He thought of the Morgens and their dark sorcery, of the dead risen from their cauldron.

He was so thirsty. They had not carried any water

with them in the cart. It had been sometime that morning when he had last drunk anything and now thirst burned in his throat, making every swallow a dry and painful exercise. He focused on putting one foot in front of the other, every pace through the forest fought for with his sword as if he were on the battlefield, fighting for quarter against innumerable hosts.

The forest grew thicker and thicker and as the ground rose up into another hill, Arthur slipped and scrabbled for a foothold on the mossy rocks. There was no way through. They would have to turn back and find a way around and hope they didn't run into their pursuers.

There was no sign of Cei and Guihir. A feeling of deep fear crawled up out of his gut with the realisation that he was totally alone. Where had they gone? *When* had they gone? How long had he blundered onwards, oblivious that he was wandering away from his companions?

He retraced the last few minutes in his mind. He had definitely heard Cei treading behind him recently so they couldn't have been separated for very long. They were probably nearby, looking for him. He wanted to call out but fear held a check on his voice; fear that the *others* would hear.

He squinted into the blackness. It was hopeless. Cei and Guihir might only be a few paces away and he wouldn't see them for the silver trunks, tangled briar and impenetrable darkness. If only he could call out to them …

But there! A crackle of branches to his left. A dim movement. They were nearby after all! They had just lost sight of each other for a moment. No need to panic.

"Cei!" he hissed. There was no answer. "Cei!"

The movement and the snapping of twigs continued. Cei *had* to hear him at this close distance. Why wasn't he answering? "Cei!" he said, louder this time.

The movement stopped. The branches shivered in the wake of whoever had brushed past them and then were still. Nothing.

Something struck Arthur on the left side of his face. A blinding white light filled his vision and his head was seized by an agonising pain. He felt the forest floor under his right cheek – pine needles sticking to his sweaty face. And then he felt nothing at all.

Voices.

Woodsmoke.

Pain.

Daylight.

Daylight? How long had he been asleep?

And then he realised that he had not been sleeping. The daylight that streamed in through the smoke hole above and peeped in from behind the hide apron, bluish and blinding, was not the light of morning shining through his Roman arch window at Cair Cunor. The bracken beneath him was not the straw of his bunk in the praetorium. Where the hell was he?

The events of the last few days shuffled

themselves into some sort of order in his mind. Menw. The cauldron. The Gaels. The village. The forest and … *here.* Smoke hole. Thatched roof. Daylight. Pain. Gods, the pain! The left side of his face felt twice as big as the right. His left eyebrow sagged, partially obscuring his vision. He reached up and touched it gingerly. It was swollen and several bristly things brushed his fingertips. *Stitches?*

He sat up and the walls swirled nauseatingly. He was in a roundhouse. It was morning. He could hear people outside. Birds. Wind.

The hide apron was swept suddenly aside and Arthur shielded his eyes from the blinding light. A figure crawled in and squatted beside him. A wooden ladle was pressed to his lips and Arthur drank, cautiously at first and then, upon realising that it was fresh water, gulped and slurped thirstily, unable to stop much of it running down his chin to soak the front of his tunica.

His carer moved back and Arthur got a better look at him. He was old, impossibly old, with wispy bits of white hair sprouting from the sides of a bald pate which was peeling and liver spotted. The old man grinned at Arthur and there were no teeth in that grin.

"You're drinking the Goddess's waters, lad," he said. "Sacred water."

The Goddesses waters? Then it occurred to Arthur where he might be. "The lake? The lake of the Morgens?"

The toothless old man gurned at him and scuttled off. Arthur tried to get up off his pallet but his leg was restrained by something. He then found the manacle that attached his right leg to one of the roundhouse's supports by a length of chain. He tugged at it but both chain and support were strong. He knew that if he dug deep enough into the hard-packed earthen floor he would be able to free himself but he had a feeling his attendant would not leave him alone for long.

As he suspected, the old man was soon back, this time bearing a wooden bowl of stew which was thin and watery. Lumps of unidentifiable meat floated in it which, upon tasting, Arthur could deduce that they came from some sort of bird.

"Eat," urged the old man. "Be strong. You will need your strength." He smiled.

"What for?" Arthur asked him.

The toothless grin widened. "The Nine wish to question you."

Arthur felt a deep, primal fear rising in his gut. It was the same fear he had felt ever since they had set out form Cair Cunor, but now that somebody was here to give voice to it, the fear threatened to choke him.

The Nine. The Sea-born.

Here he was then. At the goal of their quest, alone, injured and – now it occurred to him – completely unarmed.

The old man left him with his stew and Arthur ate slowly, reluctantly giving in to his hunger knowing that he was being fed for a purpose. He was being kept alive for questioning.

He was left alone for much of the day and all he could do was lie on his pallet and listen to the sounds outside. Many different voices passed back and forth beyond the hide apron of his prison. He guessed that he was in some sort of settlement built to support the Morgens. Its inhabitants, like the old man, were probably their servants.

He wondered what had happened to Cei and Guihir. Had they been killed? Had they wandered off after losing sight of him, to meet up with Menw and the others, abandoning him to an unknown fate in the forest? Or had they been captured too? The thought of them being held in separate huts somewhere nearby kindled a dim hope in him. If they could somehow work together, they might just be able to escape.

The old man returned as the light outside was starting to bronze with the onset of dusk. He was not alone this time. Two youths were with him. One was strong and broad in the chest while the other was thin and had the look of an idiot about him. Both were shaven-headed. "It is time," the old man said to Arthur, and produced a pair of pliers.

At first, Arthur thought he was going to be tortured on the spot, but the old man used the pliers to remove the pin from his leg manacle. As soon as he was free, the two youths pounced on him and began to bind his arms behind his back. Arthur tensed, his body wanting to lash out, to defend himself, but he knew it would be fruitless. The old man had brought along help for a reason.

He was hauled to his feet and pulled out of the roundhouse. The sun was setting, turning the ocean to a disc of fire in the west. He was near the coast on marshy land where the reeds danced in the wind. The settlement was clustered around the shores of a small lake, the surface of which shimmered in the breeze.

Simple folk in rough spun garments stared at him as he was led off.

He was taken to the shores of the lake and led around its reedy edge to an area set apart from the settlement. There was no fence or enclosure although a lone portal of timbers had been constructed through which Arthur was led. Its lintel was crowned by a raven carved in age-blackened wood, and the wooden posts that supported it contained cavities into which human skulls had been set, their idiot grins laughing at him.

A large roundhouse occupied the area and, at a glance, it was markedly different to the other roundhouses clustered around the lake. It was decorated with many twisted feathers, skulls and bones – both animal and human – and woven figurines that dangled and turned in the wind.

Several cookfires radiated heat nearby and the steam from three or four bubbling cauldrons drifted on the wind. But none of these charred old things could possibly be the cauldron of legend they were pursuing. They were little more than cookpots although what boiled within Arthur could only guess at. The stench was foul, and as they passed he was able to peer over the rim of one. He saw bones, white and glistening, turning over and over in the milky depths.

As he was brought up to the doorway of the roundhouse, the hide apron twitched and was pulled aside. Figures began to emerge, and the sight of them made Arthur cringe in fear, for he felt as if he had entered the darkest and most nightmarish parts of the pagan Otherworld.

They wore black robes which concealed their forms and he did not know if they were fat, thin or even man or woman beneath them. All had long hair; straggly, greasy tendrils into which had been woven many ornaments of bone and bronze. Their faces had been smeared with some sort of greasy white substance and their eyes circled in charcoal which made them look like spectres. The paint was cracked and peeling as if it had been applied a long time ago and never washed off, only slathered with new layers. Despite the lack of any concrete evidence, Arthur got the impression that they were women. They seemed to be very old although it was difficult to tell beneath the caked cosmetics. They were nine in number.

"Welcome," said one of them, who seemed to be both the least decrepit and the senior in command. "Are you feeling rested?"

"My companions," said Arthur in a voice weak more with fear than anything else. "What have you done with them?"

"You alone were brought to us," said the woman. "We are aware of the other two intruders but they eluded our agents in the woods. You were the only one they were able to apprehend."

Arthur closed his eyes. So Cei and Guihir were safe. He was glad of that, yet now he knew he was alone.

"It was foolish of you to try and meddle with our operations," the whitened lips went on. "And now, we would like to know if you are one of the Britons who slaughtered a party of Gaels at the old Lys on the north-eastern tip of the island."

Arthur saw no point in lying. He was most likely

due a slow and unpleasant death anyway so why bother? "Aye, that was us," he replied.

"So. And that leads us to our next question."

Arthur didn't like the way the way there seemed to be a hive mind in effect with one voice speaking for nine.

"What brings warriors from Albion to Ynys Mon?"

"Ynys Mon is *part* of Albion," said Arthur, feeling a curious sense of indignation at any implication that it was otherwise. "It always has been. And so have you. Even if you have thrown your lot in with the Gaels of late."

The chief Morgen sucked her breath in between her teeth at his boldness. "You are a simple warrior and are naive," she said. "Gaels and Britons; it makes little difference. We all walk this earth, do we not? Beli casts his light on all of us, does it not? We are all subject to the ever-turning wheel of the year and to the whim of Modron. Rulers come and go but only Modron knows who is fit to sit upon the thrones of the world."

Arthur gritted his teeth. "Cunedag and his sons wrenched this land away from the Gaels. You yourselves blessed his victory and the beginning of his dynasty. How can you now turn your backs on that dynasty by helping the Gaels?"

"The Gaels are a means to an end. They are tools, crude but useful."

"Meriaun then. Why help him instead of Cadwallon, the rightful king?"

"The only rightful king is the one Modron choses. As I said, rulers come and rulers go and now Albion is on the cusp of a great change. We can feel it in the water, in the land and in the trees. All whisper Modron's message to us. But I sense something in you; an anger that surpasses more than a simple warrior's thirst for battle. What is that, I wonder?"

Arthur realised that she was right. He *was* angry. More angry than any of his companions, because inexplicably the quest meant more to him than it did to them. He had shied away from the truth for it was a truth he had ignored all his life. He was now forced to face it, forced by these nine women, by their lone speaker. The truth was that he *did* care about his lineage. He cared about Cunedag's dynasty and the crown of the Pendraig. He cared because, bastard or no, he was bound to it all as a thorn is to a rose.

The Morgens were supposed to aid the Pendraig, not meddle in his affairs. They were priestesses, nothing more. How dare they take it upon themselves to try and change things?

"The Pendraig is my brother," he said, feeling more pride in his ancestry than he had ever felt before. *His mother's pride.* "I am the son of the old Pendraig. My blood is their blood."

The chief Morgen narrowed her eyes at him as if stripping him down to the bone to find a kernel of truth in his words. "The son of the old Pendraig," she repeated slowly. "And who, I wonder, does that make you?"

Arthur noticed that for the first time the head Morgen had spoken of herself in the first person. There was no 'we' asking *this* question.

"I am the bastard son of Enniaun Yrth," said Arthur.

"And your mother?"

"My mother was the daughter of a minor lord. She loved my father but was discarded by him. I was raised in the teulu and never knew my father."

The Morgen stared at him for a long time. Then, she turned to the other eight of her order. "Leave us. I wish to question him alone."

Without a word, the other Morgens shambled off and returned to their roundhouse. Arthur was struck by how much older they seemed than the one who appeared to be their high-priestess.

"Unbind him," she said to the three men at Arthur's side.

If there was any hesitation Arthur did not see it and his captors said not a word as they dutifully obeyed her orders. They too were dismissed and Arthur found himself alone with the high-priestess.

"You may stand," she said to him. "We shall walk together a little. Come."

They wandered down to the shores of the lake, the reeds brushing their thighs. "Aren't you afraid that I will try to run?" Arthur asked.

"No. Because you have as many questions as I do." Her white lips curled up into a smile. Now that he was closer to her, he could see that she was definitely not as old as the other Morgens. He wouldn't put her age beyond thirty-five. She was short and, by what little he could see of her hair that wasn't covered by her hood, it was dark brown. He wondered if she was pretty beneath all that cracked makeup.

"What is your name?"

"Arthur."

"Well, *Arthur*. I know why you are here. You have come seeking the truth to your existence."

"No. I came seeking a way to destroy your alliance with the Gaels."

"Come, now. Haven't you always wondered about your place in the world? Hasn't there always been that niggling feeling that you were destined to be something greater than the unwanted side effect of a sordid night's pleasure? We bastards inherit nothing. We must forge our own way in the world if we are to share in anything."

"We?"

"Yes, I too was unwanted by my father. My mother too for that matter but that is no concern of yours. I knew my father only a little and I was his shame, even more than you were. You see, you were born of passion. I was born of rape."

Arthur was silent as he took in the implication of her words. She sensed his dawning realisation. "Yes, we share the same father, Arthur."

"Anna!"

"So, they still whisper my name in our family, do they? I had wondered if I had faded from memory altogether."

"Everybody thinks you died in Leudonion after running away."

"I did run away but death was not to be my fate, praise the Great Mother. I was twelve years old – *twelve!* – when our father sent me away to be the bride of King Leudon. I was his portal to the great Votadini tribe of which our grandfather Cunedag is still remembered as their last great ruler."

Her eyes were fixed on some invisible point

beyond the far edge of the lake as she thought back to days long gone.

"Leudon was already grey, even then, and I cringed at the thought of his touch. We were wed in the Great Hall at Din Peldur, the chief fort of my husband's new kingdom. I remember the throngs of guests, the leers of the sycophants who hoped to buy my husband's favour with expensive wedding gifts. The feasting was long and grand but I touched not a bit of it. The sight of food turned my stomach and my thoughts were focused on the coming nuptials and what I had to do.

"I had learned from the serving girls at my father's Lys how I could forgo the ordeal of bearing the child of a man I hated. They taught me how to fool a man and his chambermaids. Before I left for the north, I procured a vial of pig's blood.

"I let old Leudon fumble about. He was so drunk that he did not know if he was inside me or betwixt my legs and I made sure it was the latter. Once he was snoring beside me I sprinkled the sheets with the pig's blood.

"It worked that first night but I knew I would be found out sooner or later. Either that or he would consider me barren and a wasted marriage. I decided that it would be better to die alone and starving than to remain another minute in his power. I ran and headed south-west, toward home.

"My journey was long and hard but eventually I found my way back to Ynys Mon, the island of my birth. My mother had been expelled from the Morgens. They hold virginity sacred and our father had stolen that from her. She lived apart as an anchoress and it was to her that I fled, hardened, world-warned and eager to make my own way.

"She taught me all she had learnt during her time in the order and, after a while, I went to them seeking induction. Modron smiled upon me. Normally one of the Morgens must die so that a new member might be inducted and the eldest of the order had been sick for a long time. I did not have to wait long. And so, I became Anna of the Morgens and my training began.

"I learned quickly, thirsty for knowledge and eager to serve the Great Mother. I earned the trust and respect of my peers, many of whom were far older than I, and before my twenty-fifth winter, I took my place as head of the order."

"How is it that a woman of twenty-five years was permitted to rule women old enough to be her grandmother?" Arthur asked.

"I am not permitted to reveal the secrets of our order to an outsider," Anna replied. "Suffice to say that the incumbency of a high-priestess changes like the seasons. It is for Modron alone to decide when a high priestess's time is up and a new one is to be chosen. Some of the older Morgens have been high-priestess twice over before me. They had their time and now it is up to me to lead our order through these days in which we find ourselves."

"Was it you who suggested the alliance with King Meriaun?"

"It was. Under Modron's guidance."

"And the Gaels. Tools, you said?"

"Means to an end. The Gaels possessed a great treasure which I knew would be a boon to us in our efforts. The Cauldron of Rebirth, one of the great treasures of Albion, a gift from Modron herself. It came from Erin with Diugurnach and his followers. Where he got it is not important for it had been among the Gaels for generations. After Efnisien destroyed it in Bran's great war an age ago, it was re-forged in Annun and sent back into our world. Now it is ours, a gift to be used in the war for Albion."

"You're resurrecting the dead," said Arthur, "to help our cousin usurp our brother. I still don't understand why."

Anna laughed. "You are not required to, Brother. It is all far beyond your ken. Not even we Sea-born know all of Modron's intentions. It pleases me that you came to us now, in the quiet before the storm. I am pleased that we might know one another but it is ultimately irrelevant. The wheels are in motion. Modron will be reborn and a new age will dawn. You are but a witness and should count yourself lucky to see such times."

She looked at him and he looked at her, this half-sister whom he had never met. Once she had been no more than a sad story of a lost girl. Now she was a crazed high-priestess of a perverted order and Venedotia's greatest enemy.

They had circled the lake and were re-entering the village on its southern side. Those same, vacant-eyed locals watched them in awe. They were clearly devoted to the Morgens and wholly subservient to them. Anna beckoned the two youths who had delivered Arthur to her. They approached in a grovelling, servile gait that sickened him.

"Take this boy back to the guest quarters," she told them. "Feed him and do not treat him ill. He is very dear to me."

The youths took Arthur by the arms and led him back to the hut he had awoken in that morning. Arthur looked over his shoulder and saw his sister smiling at him from the shores of the lake, her expression unreadable, as were her intentions.

"You should have sent word of your coming," the captain said as they began the long, steep climb up the narrow mountain ledge. "We would have sent an escort to meet you."

There was no 'my lord' or 'your highness' in the gruff captain's address, Cadwallon noted. Wherever King Efiaun of Dunauding's allegiance lay, it was clear he did not consider him to be his Pendraig. Still, they had not been attacked upon approach and had received an armed escort to Efiaun's royal seat. That counted for something perhaps. An undecided mind at best.

"There was no time to send a messenger ahead of us," said Cadwallon. "We come straight from the battlefield and time is short. And we saw no companies bearing the sigil of Dunauding on our way."

"Aye, that is easy enough to believe. King Efiaun has called all his warriors to Din Emrys to guard the mountain, to defend it against … well, *Gaels* some say. What others say I don't like to comment on. Nonsense, to my mind."

So, Cadwallon thought. *Word of the Cauldron-born has reached Dunauding.* "If you fear Gaels," he said, "then I take it your king does not support my uncle Meriaun and his pact with the hounds of Erin."

"I cannot comment on that," the captain replied. "Best you speak with the king yourself."

Cadwallon turned in his saddle to glance at Meddyf who rode beside him. They shared a look. *So there is hope* … it said.

Crowning the summit of a small crag in the shadow of the Giant's Cairn, Din Emrys's dry-stone ramparts followed the natural line of the hilltop, filling in the gaps between its rocky outcrops. It had a rather ramshackle appearance but Cadwallon was not fooled. Din Emrys was one of the most impregnable strongholds in all Albion. There were only two approaches to the mountain retreat. Both passed below the fortress walls for some length making any assault a hard and costly exercise.

Din Emrys had once belonged to an old British family – the Ambrosii – who had made a name for themselves in the Romano-British military and administrative elite. The Lord Vertigernus had stripped the Ambrosii of their fortress and given it to the sons of Cunedag when he had relocated them to Venedotia. The last of the family – the aged Ambrosius Aurelianus – was currently holding back the Saeson advance in the far south, his lineage forgotten and his heritage lost. Nevertheless, Din Emrys still held the name of the Ambrosii in its native British form.

"When we reach the summit," Cadwallon told his escort, "I would appreciate it if you fetched your surgeons quickly. We have many wounded in our train."

"I will pass along your request," said the captain. And then his curiosity got the better of him. "Was it a big battle?"

"Yes. We shattered Meriauned's advance at the Black Falls. No further attack will come from the south." He felt no need to hold back the details of his victory from either friends or foes. News of his success had to be spread one way or another if he hoped to win over the undecided and turn the tide of this war.

He grew aware of the helmed heads of guards peering down at them from the parapets above as they made their ascent. Any army would have to be mad to attempt an attack on this place. He had to keep telling himself that they were still alive because King Efiaun had clearly given orders to keep them so.

The door of the gatehouse creaked open and the tired and wounded column limped in. It was early evening and the low sun gilded the thatch of the roundhouses, stables and smithies. The wind was strong up on the crag and Cadwallon's hair billowed about in his face. Various warriors and nobles had assembled in the main courtyard to examine their visitors. Cadwallon ignored them and gave orders for the wounded to be unloaded from the wagons.

"Where is the lord of Din Emrys while his Pendraig is left to see to the wounded himself?" Cunor demanded.

"Here," came a surly voice from across the yard, as a stocky, fair-haired man approached, the wind whipping his cloak about him.

As the son of Cunedag's last-born child, King Efiaun was only just approaching his middle years. Strong and handsome, his taste in finery was exemplified in his silk tunica, red leather boots and saffron cloak, not to mention the gold rings that made every finger sparkle.

"Cousin Efiaun," said Cadwallon. He refused to acknowledge Efiaun's kingship if Efiaun would not acknowledge his. "We are war-weary and are in need of refuge and aid."

"Of course," said Efiaun. "My roof is yours for as long as you have need of it."

The wounded were escorted to a separate roundhouse while Cadwallon and his followers were taken to the Great Hall and given meat and mead.

"I take it my brother has not come knocking on your door," Cadwallon said.

"Owain? No, we have heard nothing of him. I would have thought he would be marching with you. Before I recalled my riders, they brought me word that you and he had marshalled your father's teulu at Cair Cunor."

"*My* teulu," Cadwallon corrected him. "The Teulu of the Red Dragon. Am I not my father's son and successor; the Pendraig of Venedotia? Please remind me, for signs of your loyalty have been somewhat lacklustre of late?"

Efiaun set his jaw and leaned back in his seat. "With the greatest respect, cousin, you are not your father."

"I praise the gods that I am not, but I am nevertheless the Pendraig – your high-king – and you owe me your support and your warriors. Why did you not heed my call?"

"You speak of an age that died with your father," Efiaun said. "Perhaps it died with Cunedag. This mighty Teulu of the Red Dragon that you claim to have inherited – all I see is a rag-tag band of desperate men seeking shelter."

"This rag-tag band thrashed the teulu of Meriauned not two days ago," said Cunor, his voice testy.

"My penteulu is right," said Cadwallon, "and yet, in a way, so are you. My following is less than half that my father would have commanded and had it not been for King Mor's support, we would have all died at the Black Falls. No, the Teulu of the Red Dragon is as strong as the kings who support it. As strong as the warriors they contribute. As strong as their loyalty to Cunedag's legacy."

Efiaun placed a hand on the shoulder of a young boy who sat by his side. "This is my youngest son. Only twelve winters. I have other children too including a daughter still in her swaddling clothes. They are *my* legacy and I will do all I can to ensure their survival."

"Then join me in ridding Venedotia of its enemies!" Cadwallon exclaimed.

Efiaun shook his head. "You may have won a minor victory over Meriaun's son but Meriaun himself rules Venedotia from the Laigin Peninsula to the eastern fringes of Rhos. And that is not to mention Ynys Mon. That accursed isle vomits forth an even greater threat if the tales are to be believed."

"And do you believe them?"

Efiaun narrowed his eyes. "I don't know what to believe. All I know is that you came down from the north as fast as you could and the people speak of a black horror treading in your wake."

"Old wives' tales," said Cadwallon. "Gaels came from Ynys Mon, nothing more."

"And what of our cousin's alliance with the Morgens? What sort of vengeance for your father's blasphemy are they cooking up?"

"There may be something to that," Cadwallon

admitted. "But it is words and curses only. Let them stir their hate. What need have we to fear a cult of old hags?"

"Hags who have found the Cauldron of Rebirth, so it is told."

Cadwallon sighed. Bad news travelled faster than any teulu could ever dream of doing. "A rumour, nothing more. Even if they did have some sort of cauldron, do you really believe it could be the cauldron of legend?"

Efiaun was silent.

"I have dispatched a company to investigate and, if possible, destroy whatever alliance Meriaun has with the nine sisters. That ought to put to bed all these rumours of the dead walking. In any case, it will at least divert Meriaun's eye to Ynys Mon while we muster our forces in the south and press the advance."

"You seek to advance on Cair Dugannu? You're impossibly outnumbered."

"Meriaun's Gaelic mercenaries are tearing up the Conui Valley as we speak. If we can cross the mountains and make the Pass of Kings in good time, we can come upon Cair Dugannu on its western side without warning. But you're right in saying that our numbers are thin. I need allies. So what do you say? I can't win without you."

"I will give you shelter," Efiaun said, "as you are my kin, but I want no part in this war. Meriaun has sworn that he will not attack those who do not stand against him. Why should I jeopardise my people in supporting a war that you cannot possibly win?"

Cunor slammed his fist down on the table and it

was not just the women who jumped at his sudden explosion. "You trust the word of a traitor?" he demanded. "You honestly believe he won't turn his eyes upon Din Emrys once he has crushed the rest of us? You might think you're safe now up here in your mountain retreat but what about when Meriaun's Gaels are stealing your crops come harvest and you don't dare step down off your hill?"

"Our granaries are full to bursting," said Efiaun coolly.

"Meriaun will wait, believe me. He'll starve you out eventually. Have you ever seen a siege won by starvation? It's not pretty, I can tell you. They start to eat their dead when there are no more rats left …"

"That's enough, Cunor!" said Cadwallon. Efiaun was visibly angered by the outburst and he didn't want his fiery penteulu to cost them the hospitality of their host, although he well understood Cunor's anger. This man sat here comfortable in his cowardice while Cunor had dispatched both his son and his foster-son to almost certain doom in a desperate attempt to turn the tide of the war.

"Won't you reconsider? Cunor speaks truth. There will be no safety for you if we are defeated. But if we win we will have re-forged the lands of our fathers into a Venedotia once more united under the dragon banner."

Efiaun visibly seethed after Cunor's accusation of cowardice. "I am not interested in a Venedotia united under the dragon banner," he said. "I am interested in the safety of my family."

He got up and left the hall. His warriors and kin followed suit leaving the newcomers alone.

"I'm sorry if I spoke out of turn, my lord," said Cunor, his face red.

"Not at all," Cadwallon replied. "I was of half a mind to give him a tongue lashing myself."

"The fool is frightened," said Meddyf. "He has to be made to see sense. We must bolster his courage somehow."

"Hard to do that when all is set against us," said Cadwallon.

The following day brought what felt like a miracle to Cadwallon and his weary but loyal followers. A horn blew from Din Emrys's watchtower, warning of an advancing host. Cadwallon joined King Efiaun at the ramparts looking east. Sure enough, a column of horsemen and their baggage train was approaching along the valley floor, following the river that flowed from Lin Emrys.

Cadwallon squinted at the fluttering banners and, just as Efiaun was giving the order to rouse the fortress and man the ramparts, he held up his hand. "Hold!" he cried, excitement getting the better of him. "That is not the banner of an advancing enemy. That is the Bear of Rhos approaching! My brother lives!"

"It must have been quite a victory in the Conui Valley," said Cunor at his side. "He has more men than he set out with!"

There were also more banners, trailing in Owain's column. Cadwallon could not make them out at this distance but he felt a joy swelling in his heart as he dared to hope for what he had not thought possible.

Meddyf shared the same hope, for upon hearing the news she exclaimed; "My father! My father must be with them!"

Cadwallon all but had to restrain her from leaving the fort and running down the steep pathway to greet the approaching host herself. They waited in the courtyard until the gates finally creaked open to admit the host.

"So many of you have come!" Cadwallon exclaimed, embracing Owain. "So many banners! I dared not hope for such a victory!"

"It was a long, hard slog but we rallied enough support to drive the Gaels back north," said Owain. "They were their own undoing, really. People tend to get irate when you steal their crops and rape their women. You were right; they just needed a standard to follow."

"Doesn't everyone?" Cadwallon said with a grin, clapping his brother on the shoulder.

Meddyf pushed past them when she saw her father dismounting and handing the reins of his mare to a stable boy. She ran into his open arms.

Maeldaf was a tall, broad-shouldered man with greying black curls and a wide mouth bristling with white stubble. He lifted Meddyf up as if she were still a girl and kissed her on the cheek. After he set her down she seemed to remember herself and quickly smoothed down her cloak.

"It's been too long, Father," she said, unable to stop herself from beaming ear to ear.

"Aye, that it has, lass," he agreed.

Young Drustan stood by his side, spear in hand. Cadwallon was surprised how much older he looked since he had seen him last. His hair was long in the Pictish style and his face was thick with a beard that defied his years.

"Drustan, you've grown!" said Meddyf. She kissed him and he shied away with embarrassment.

"I'm sorry I was delayed and didn't meet up with you on the road," said Maeldaf. "But I couldn't abandon our people to face the Gaels alone. Luckily your canny husband sent enough of his cavalry to aid us."

"*All* of my cavalry," Cadwallon corrected him, as he grasped the hand of his father-in-law. "And I can't tell you how much it means to me that you held that valley on my account for so long and against such odds. Thank you Maeldaf."

"Thank them," said the old warrior, extending his arm to the assembled warband. "It was their willingness to stay and defend their homes instead of fleeing into the hills that won us the valley."

And it was then, as he looked into their faces, that Cadwallon understood how desperate things had been in the Conui Valley. "They're all so young," he said, marvelling at the unshaven faces arrayed before him. Most were no more than boys armed with simple weapons and little to no armour. Their faces were frightened, haunted by the fast growing up they had had to do over the past few days. There were a few old men and the occasional woman dressed in her father's or brother's tunica and breeches, spear held in dainty but firm hands. There were almost no men between fifteen and fifty.

"These are all that's left of the valley people who were not killed by the Gaels or fled from their advance," Maeldaf explained. "These are the ones who refused to flee, refused to bow down. They have lost their homes, their families too, most of them. Fathers butchered, mothers and sisters raped and enslaved. Such outrages instil a fierce stubbornness in common hearts. They were prepared to stand their ground until death claimed them but then they saw the bear banner of Rhos coming up from the south and they knew that our Pendraig had not forgotten them. These boys and girls and old men stand with you, Cadwallon. They stand with you if it means their death for what use is life when all that gives it meaning is trampled on and burned by our enemies? They are with you to the end."

"As am I," said a voice to Cadwallon's right.

Cadwallon turned and saw Efiaun standing pale-faced beside him.

"I am ashamed, cousin," he said. "My eyes have been blind and my heart cold. I thought to save my people from the Gaels' fury but I see now that the only way to stop them is to defeat Meriaun. I do not want to live as a client king to the kind of beasts who have done this …"

"Then you will fight?" Cadwallon asked him.

"Aye, my Pendraig," Efiaun said. "For better or worse, Dunauding is with you. We march for the Pass of Kings as soon as you are ready."

Arthur

Arthur had given up straining against his bonds. He had been tied to the wooden frame several hours ago and his hands had gone numb. He didn't know why he had been erected like a scarecrow by the shores of the lake at the edge of dusk. Why hadn't they left him in his hut with his leg manacled? The Morgens seemed intent that he should bear witness to whatever it was that currently had the whole settlement in a state of solemn industry.

It had gone very quiet. The sun was setting. He gazed across the great mirror of the ocean to west. *This is as far as the Romans ever got*, he mused. He truly was at the edge of the world. Beyond that ocean lay Erin, land of the Gaels, which even the Romans had been unable to conquer. And beyond that, who knew? More ocean, like a sheet of glass going on and on into a shimmering infinity? Or more lands? More tribes, more wars and more desolation? Was that all the world was: one vast, endless existence of chaos and conflict?

He thought of his companions and hoped that their fates would be better than his. He thought of wise Menw, bull-headed Cei, strong but kind Beduir, wiley Gualchmei, stoic Cundelig and lustful but good-natured Guihir. He wished them all well and hoped that they would meet their gods in the ways they hoped.

He was convinced that his days on this earth were near their end. He had no doubt that Anna – or one of her sisters – would cut his life short with the edge of a blade before the sun rose once more. What for him then? Would he meet God or would he voyage through the mists of Annun to the Isle of Apples for an audience with Modron the Great Mother? He had always felt torn between the Christian faith and Albion's old gods and now, in the clutches of this ancient order, at the edge of the known world, he was even less sure of his path.

They came just as the sun dipped below the sea and the darkness began to descend; a line of torches dancing like fireflies. They bore bundles of wood which they piled up on the lake shore, before kindling it and standing back to watch the flames grow higher and higher. The glow was reflected in the waters of the lake and it was as the flames began to die down that the Morgens emerged from their roundhouse and made their way down to the shore.

Anna led them and, even in the deepening gloom, Arthur could see that they had added a new layer of greasepaint to their faces which rendered them stark and livid in the torchlight. They carried something large between them and as the light caught it, Arthur could see that it was round and bulbous in shape like a pregnant sow.

The villagers formed a circle around the fire and an iron tripod was erected over the glowing embers. The object the Morgens carried was attached to it by a chain to dangle freely over the low flames.

A cauldron.

But this was no rusted pot. Even at a distance, Arthur could see that this was a treasure of kings. The flames picked out intricate designs beaten into the bronze panels and he could see faces, many shimmering faces, as if the lives of a thousand generations were trapped within its surface.

Water in clay amphorae was brought forward by servants and poured into the cauldron until it was brimming. The villagers parted to allow five naked figures to enter the circle. They were all men, Gaels in the prime of their lives, broad-chested and powerful in the arms. They were not bound and seemed perfectly willing. Anna ordered them to kneel down before the cauldron which they did dutifully.

Arthur blinked. From his vantage point on his wooden frame, he could see all that occurred within the circle of villagers, and he supposed that he was intended to. Were these men to be sacrificed? A group of warriors armed with spears stood nearby, presumably to prevent any disruption to the ceremony.

The water in the cauldron had begun to steam. The Morgens opened leather pouches and scattered what looked like leaves and roots into the liquid. Anna stirred and pounded them with a fat wooden pole. Then the chanting and percussion began. Voices called out arcane incantations while hands pounded skin drums to an intoxicating beat.

The naked Gaels remained kneeling, heads bowed, while the Morgens began to daub their bodies with white greasepaint. Then, on top of that, they painted swirling designs in blue woad, all to the beat of the drums and chanting voices.

The ceremony continued late into the night and Arthur realised that he must have dozed off, for the stars were now bright in the sky and the faint touch of dawn paled the horizon to the east. He felt drugged, lulled to sleep by the incessant drumming and chanting. How had they managed to keep this up all through the night? There was a feeling of exhaustion over the assembly but still they continued as the climax of their efforts undoubtedly drew near. The fire beneath the cauldron had died out and was white ash blowing on the wind.

Anna bade the supplicants rise and they did so, one by one, to wait with arms slack for the next part of the ritual. The other Morgens came forward to affix masks to their painted faces. The light of the torches glinted off white bone and Arthur remembered the boiling bones in the cauldrons by the roundhouse; bones stripped clean of flesh and livid white.

The chanting grew in rapidity until it was a crescendo and Anna beckoned the first of the Gaels to come forward. He stepped up to the cauldron and she dipped a cup into its milky, steaming liquid. She held it to his lips as the chanting became deafening in its intensity. The man drank, gagging at the taste but forcing it down like a child being given his medicine by his mother. When the cup was empty, he staggered away, clearly suppressing the urge to retch.

One by one, the others stepped up for their medicine but by the time the last of them was wiping his mouth, a change had overcome the first to drink. He was hunched over as if in agony and clawed at the earth, fighting something that wasn't there. That he was drugged was obvious, but the effect of that drug was a mystery to Arthur as he looked on, fearful of what might happen next.

The sun was rising. The day was being reborn, and before the first rays glinted off the surface of the sacred lake, the change over the five Gaels was complete.

Arthur understood the sorcery of the Morgens now. He knew the cauldron's secret. He saw who the Cauldron-born were and why Cadwallon had feared them ever since that night they had taken Cair Dugannu. They weren't the dead brought back from the Otherworld. They were as alive as he was but driven insane by the root-magic the Morgens cooked up in their cauldron.

The warriors who had been loitering outside the circle all night blew their horns and barked out orders. The naked men screeched and shambled towards them. The villagers stepped on each other's toes to get out of the way; terrified of Modron's new-born. The warriors kept them at a safe distance with their spears and directed them towards the woods. Then they were off at a jog, vanishing into the darkness of the trees.

Silence descended over the lakeshore. There was no more drumming or chanting. The torches burned low, one or two of them guttering out. The villagers wearily ambled back to their huts while the Morgens remained by the ashes of the fire.

Anna ascended the slope towards Arthur, drawing a knife as she went. Arthur realised that his time to die had finally come.

With several fast slashes, Anna cut through the ropes that secured his hands and feet and he fell forward to land face down in the reeds.

"There are few fortunate enough to witness our sacred rites," she said to him, sheathing her knife.

"Why?" he croaked, his throat dry. "Why me?

Why not just kill me?"

She did not answer. The other Morgens appeared on either side of him and they lifted him up. He was too weak to resist. His hands and feet screamed with pins of fire as the blood in his body began to circulate about them more freely. He knew that he couldn't walk. They carried him back to his hut and reaffixed the manacle to his leg.

"You will remain here for some time," Anna said to him, as they began to file out. "I will see that you are well looked after in my absence."

"Your absence?"

"I am journeying south, across the straits. The final battle draws near. I want to be there to oversee the fruition of Modron's plans. I will return to you, Brother, and we shall discuss your fate at another time."

She left him and it was then that the real feeling of desperation and loneliness consumed him. It would have been better had she plunged her knife into his heart than to keep him alive as a prisoner, chained and unable to help while the fate of everybody he knew was decided.

He thought of the five Cauldron-born he had seen transformed before his very eyes. They had headed off in a north-easterly direction, not a southerly one. That meant they were probably headed for the Lys to finish the job he and his companions had thwarted.

He thought of kind Gogfran and Guenhuifach and the flame-haired Guenhuifar. *Gods, Guenhuifar!* He had witnessed the birth of their doom and had done nothing to prevent it.

He tugged at the chain that bound his leg to the

post. The bowl he had eaten his meal of barley porridge from lay beside his pallet. Nobody had come to collect it in the build up to the ceremony. He seized it and began to dig into the hard-packed earth around the base of the post. He scraped and chiselled, heaping the dirt to one side. It would take him a long time but he was determined to free himself and do his best to escape the clutches of the Morgens. He might not be able to save Guenhuifar and her family but he could at least die fighting his way to her instead of waiting to be murdered by his own sister upon her return.

The day bloomed through the smoke hole above and he could hear much coming and going outside of his hut. Nobody checked on him and he assumed all were busy in preparation for Anna's journey south. His hands were raw with blisters and his tunica was drenched in sweat. The mound of earth beside him towered over his pallet but at last he felt as if he had reached the bottom of the post. He could feel its edge beneath his fingertips.

He tossed the bowl aside and began to scrabble with his fingers, scooping out the earth beneath the post, loosening it in its hole. At last he was able to wobble it about which made the whole roof of the house shake. He tried to keep that to a minimum so that nobody outside would see that anything was amiss.

He got to his feet and seized the post. Straining, he lifted it up a few centimetres, just high enough so he could scoot the ring of the manacle out from under the post with his foot. He set the post back down in its hole and heaved a sigh of relief. He was free at last.

He bunched up the manacle links and held them in one hand so they would not jingle and crept over to the doorway.

Peering out, he could see a few people moving about down by the lake but there seemed to be no one in his immediate vicinity. He slipped out of the hut and moved around to its northern side. The woods were close to the settlement – those same woods he had come through – but now that daylight was strong and skies blue, those shady trees did not seem half so frightening. He was confident that if he was able to make it to the treeline undetected, he could find his way through the woods and onto the trackway back to the Lys.

He dashed across the compound but swerved to the left as two villagers emerged from a nearby hut. A pile of firewood promised some cover so he made for it, keeping his head low.

He slid onto his side as he rounded the woodpile and crashed into the legs of a figure standing directly behind it. The figure toppled over and quickly rolled, drawing a short knife. Arthur struggled into a crouch and gripped his leg manacle ready to swing it at his foe. He knew it was too short to have much range or do any damage but it was the only weapon he had.

Then he realised whom he had crashed into.

"Guenhuifar!" he exclaimed in an excited whisper.

She wore her hunting breeches and tunica and her hair was bound back. Her bow and quiver were over her shoulder. "What are you doing here?"

"Trying to rescue you, you fool!" she said. "But if you go charging about like that you'll get us both killed!"

"But what are you doing on this side of the island and how did you know I was captured?"

"I don't have time to explain now. We have to get out of here. Your friends are ready to charge the village and give me the distraction I needed to free you. I was trying to find out where they were keeping you but then I saw you bounding across the compound like a spooked hare."

"Look, Guenhuifar, we have to get back to the Lys. The Morgens have dispatched the Cauldron-born to look for us. They'll slaughter your family. We may be too late as it is, but I swear I will die to avenge them."

She held up a hand to hush him. "My family are safe. They are with Cei and the others. I can't tell you everything now, we have to get moving."

She poked her head above the woodpile to scout out the situation before ducking back down. "There is an old man headed towards the hut you came from."

"Probably my keeper," said Arthur. "He'll raise hell when he finds me gone."

"Then we make a break for the trees as soon as he goes inside. Are you ready?"

Arthur nodded. He still had so many questions for Guenhuifar. Why had *she* come for him? Why had Cei allowed it? A mission of stealth should have been given to Gualchmei who was the most adept at creeping about. He then noticed for the first time that it was Gualchmei's Persian bow and quiver Guenhuifar carried over her shoulder. "It was you who sent those fire arrows on the village the other night, wasn't it?"

She nodded. "Gualchmei's shoulder is still not

strong enough to bend his bow. He's not too steady on his feet either so I volunteered."

"Volunteered?"

She ignored the inquisitive look he was giving her and looked over the top of the woodpile again. "Come on, the coast is clear."

She took off towards the treeline, crouching low. Arthur hurried in her wake, hoping against hope that nobody in the settlement would look in their direction.

They made the trees without being spotted and then it was a mad dash through undergrowth, leaping over fallen trees and tearing at the branches that snagged their clothes in their effort to reach Cei and the others before they began their diversion. They circled the settlement, keeping close to the fringes of the wood.

They came upon the companions squatting in a dell carpeted with bluebells; they didn't spot them until they'd all but trampled over them.

"Modron's tits!" cried Cei in surprise. "We were just about to unleash merry hell on that settlement and here you two come ahead of schedule! Guenhuifar, how did you manage it?"

"He all but freed himself," said Guenhuifar. "I arrived just in time to help him out of the place without being spotted."

Arthur beamed at seeing his companions again and there were many hugs and much shoulder slapping. Arthur spotted Gogfran and Guenhuifach huddled together in the thick bluebells with the ever loyal Cadfan nearby, spear in hand. "I think it's about time you all told me what's been going on," he said.

"The day you left a friend of mine came from the settlement to the south of the Lys," said Guenhuifar. "She came to warn us of yet more Gaels on their way, probably to reinforce the lot we made short work of. We decided to head east and leave our home for the Gaels to pick over. I scouted ahead and spotted the plume of a campfire in an area far from any settlement I knew of. I decided to take a look and, sure enough, I found what was left of your companions sitting in plain view for any party of Gaels to stumble across. They told me of your foolhardy plan and how it had gone astray. Instead of finding the lake of the Morgens, you, Cei and Guihir had been escorted into one of the largest Gaelic settlements on Ynys Mon."

"Against all sense, we decided to assault the settlement to get you out," said Menw.

"Guenhuifar lent her bow to our efforts," said Beduir. "But then you three fools headed off in the wrong bloody direction and we lost all trace of you. Late the following day we found Cei and Guihir stumbling out of the forest on its eastern side."

"What the hell happened to you, Arthur?" Cei broke in. "One minute you were with us and then nothing."

"I'm not sure myself," said Arthur. "All I remember was something striking my head like a bolt of lightning. The next thing I knew, I was waking up in chains. But listen, the Morgens have dispatched the Cauldron-born east. They're probably looking for us."

"The Cauldron-born?" Cei asked. "You saw them?"

"Yes … in a manner of speaking."

"Then they are real then?" asked Gualchmei, his eyes wide.

All of them were wide-eyed, anticipating his confirmation of all their fears. "After a fashion," was all he could say.

"I think you had best start at the beginning," said Menw. "Tell us everything that happened after you awoke in the Morgens' lair."

Arthur told them, keeping his words concise and his narrative lean. Time was short but he felt that he owed it to his companions to inform them of what they really faced. When he revealed the high-priestess to be Anna, his long-lost sister, Guenhuifar started.

"Your sister?" she exclaimed. "If she was the daughter of Enniaun Yrth then that would make you—"

"His bastard too," Arthur interrupted.

"You are royalty then. A descendant of Cunedag."

"Hardly. My father never acknowledged me and my half-brothers have conveniently forgotten they are related to me. I am fatherless and always have been."

"And you all knew about this?" she asked of his companions.

They nodded solemnly. "It makes no difference," said Beduir. "Arthur is one of us, through and through."

But Arthur could see that Guenhuifar looked at him differently after the revelation. It was the same look he had seen in the eyes of many who did not know him; almost an accusatory look barely checked by polite restraint. He didn't know what people expected of him. He could be neither praised for his heritage nor persecuted for it. It was entirely out of his control. And yet he somehow felt ashamed under Guenhuifar's gaze.

"Tell us what happened next," said Menw.

Arthur finished his story, going into particular detail about the ceremony and the transformation of the Cauldron-born.

"So it is all a trick then?" said Cei once Arthur had finished. "The Cauldron-born are no more than drugged Gaels, mad on bloodlust. The Morgens and their so-called sorcery is a sham!"

"Sham?" asked Menw. "Their sorcery may be no more than root-magic but it seems to have been doing the trick, no? We face truly ferocious foes. They may not be the dead brought back from Annun but the cloud of fear the Morgens have brewed with their cauldron has all but brought Venedotia to its knees."

"But it's lies, all of it!" said Beduir.

"Yes," Menw admitted. "Did you really expect our enemies to be truthful? Fear and lies are their allies. But our work here – Arthur's work – has undone the Morgens' magic. We must fetch this cauldron back to the mainland so that all will know that it is no more than an iron pot and its spawn mere flesh and blood."

"Did you know?" Arthur asked him. "Did you ever suspect that we were not up against the forces of the Otherworld?"

"Suspect? Hoped, more like. I may be wise but even I do not know all there is to know under the sky. But even had I known, my word would not have been enough to sweep away the doubt that has gripped our Pendraig's heart and the fear that has wreaked its havoc throughout Venedotia. Only the cauldron itself, brought back from beyond the veil between worlds, will be proof enough. This voyage of ours will be a long-remembered one."

"The cauldron is travelling south," said Arthur. "Anna too. My sister …"

"Your sister intends to deliver the cauldron to Meriaun at Cair Dugannu. The final battle must be drawing near. We must take comfort in this knowledge for it means that Cadwallon still lives and he is not alone."

"Meriaun intends to unleash the Cauldron-born on the Pendraig and his teulu," said Cei. "We must stop him. We must stop Anna and seize that cauldron."

Menw's eyes twinkled at his words. "At last you begin to understand, Cei mab Cunor. It may only be a symbol, but symbols have Otherworldly power. Yes, it is just a cauldron, but we must stop that cauldron from reaching Cair Dugannu at all costs."

"She has half a day on us already," said Arthur. "And we sit here jawing. Let's move!"

The companions rose and began collecting their gear. "She'll most likely head for Aberffraw," said Guenhuifar. "It's the largest settlement on Ynys Mon and provides the fastest route across the straits. We can buy or steal a boat there that will carry you across."

"We?" said Cei. He glanced at Guenhuifar and then to her father and sister. "There is no reason for you all to accompany us to Aberffraw. We cannot protect you."

"No, you cannot," said Guenhuifar, her tone cool. "But your arrival here has seen us driven from our home and made us enemies of the Gaels. Nowhere is safe for us now." She glanced at Arthur. "Besides, if you are prepared to do all that you must to defeat the Gaels and win back Venedotia, then I will do what I must to help you."

"I thought you didn't care for the Sons of Cunedag," said Arthur.

"I don't," she replied. "But this civil war that is tearing Venedotia apart is no good for Ynys Mon. If Cadwallon is victorious on the mainland then perhaps there is a chance that the Gaels will be driven back to Erin."

"It sounds like you are almost won around to our cause," he said with a smile.

"I just want my family to live in peace and safety, nothing more."

"We need to get going," said Menw. "Anna will try to sail through the straits at slack water before the tide is at its highest. It's the safest time to cross. That gives us four hours, or thereabouts."

"I fear I will slow you down," said Gogfran.

"He's right," said Cei. "We must be fleet if we are to catch up with her. We cannot carry stragglers."

"You'll need my help to procure a boat in Aberffraw," said Guenhuifar. "And I'm not leaving my father behind."

"Anna will be long gone with the cauldron by the time we get your father to Aberffraw!" exclaimed Cei.

"Cadfan and I will accompany my father," said Guenhuifach. "You lot go on ahead. We'll meet my sister at Aberffraw later this evening once you lot are on your way."

"Fine," said Guenhuifar. "Guard him well, Sister. I will see that our companions pass the straits in good time. We must leave now."

They left Gogfran in the dell with his daughter and servant and took off at a jog. They ran through the forest until the trees petered out and the long, low slopes of high grass and marsh rolled out before them. Guenhuifar led the way, fleet as a young deer, bow and quiver bouncing on her shoulder and her tawny plait flailing out behind her like a horse's tail in the wind. They followed the curve of the coast, on and on, until the sky became blood-streaked with the onset of dusk.

When they ran out of breath, Guenhuifar allowed them a short reprieve and they walked for a while, breathing deeply. Arthur walked by her side while the others lagged behind, passing a waterskin around.

"Why didn't you tell me you were the son of a king?" Guenhuifar asked him.

"Because it wasn't important," he said, trying to control his breathing so that he did not gasp and puff as he answered her.

"Some might think it is."

"Well, I don't. Perhaps I'm the only one who doesn't, except my half-brothers."

"They don't accept you? Because you're a bastard?"

"Why should they? Just because some king has a bit of fun with a naïve nobleman's daughter, leads her along, telling her she'll make her his queen and then ditches her, it doesn't mean that sixteen years down the road her base-born son is entitled to anything." He realised that he had snapped at her and regretted it. He felt peevish. She was the first person to actually put what everybody else was thinking into words. She had a strange kind of bluntness, like she didn't care what anybody else thought. She was going to do and say exactly what she wanted.

"It just seems strange ..." she went on.

"What does?"

"That Cei is the one to lead your party while royalty must step aside."

"I told you, I'm not royalty. And Cei is the penteulu's son. He is the natural choice to lead."

Guenhuifar looked back. Cei was struggling along with the others, his face ruddy beneath the afternoon sun. "But is he the best choice? I've seen how you are with your companions. You could lead them just as well as he could, if not better."

"Now you sound like my mother," Arthur muttered, and immediately wished he hadn't.

They picked up the pace and kept it up until the curve of the island swept away to the east.

"There!" said Guenhuifar at last, drawing up and pointing to a ringed and ditched settlement on the banks of a thin river that wound its way down to a sandy cove. "Aberffraw."

They gasped for breath and wiped at the sweat that ran down their faces. The water skin was passed around. There were only dregs left.

"Won't we stick out a bit in a place like that?" Cei asked.

"Not really," Guenhuifar replied. "This is the largest port on the island and plenty of traders come here from Albion and from even farther afield. But it still pays to be cautious. I'll do the talking as I am a local. If anybody speaks to you directly, let Guihir answer in Gaelic. No point in letting it be known that seven British warriors are wandering about."

They entered the village through its northern gate and the guards on the spiked palisade barely paid them a passing glance. The place was busy enough and the air hummed with both Gaelic and British voices.

They found an inn in the form of an oblong timber hall with a warped shingled roof which had once been some sort of Roman administrative building. This appeared to be the hub of business in the settlement, and they wove their way past the spearmen who loitered in the colonnaded entrance, to emerge in a bustling atrium centred around a fire pit set in the cracked tiled floor.

"Find a seat and stay put," Guenhuifar told them. "I'll ask around if anybody has a boat to spare."

"I need ale," said Cei, as he headed over to an empty table. All heartily agreed that certain luxuries could be accommodated after all they had been through.

Several heads turned to examine them as they sat down but no challenge was offered. If their weapons aroused any curiosity then it was probably assumed that they were Gaels in the company of some captain under Diugurnach.

The ale was sour but cheap and they even managed to persuade the surly innkeeper to let them have a couple of roasted birds from the firepit. They devoured them like starving beggars, licking the meat juices from their fingers.

They were on their second clay flagon of ale by the time Guenhuifar returned. "A fisherman I just spoke to has seen a cloaked woman and five Gaels heading down to the bay. They carried something heavy between them, wrapped in cloth and borne on wooden poles."

The companions rose as one, their brief respite forgotten and the scent of their goal in their nostrils. "She must have been alerted to our presence," said Beduir. "Slack water is over an hour off."

"No," said Menw, casting his eyes up at the scudding, grey clouds against the deepening red of the sky. "There is a strong northerly wind. I don't know why I didn't think of it before! That wind will drive more water through the straits and cause an earlier slack water. We may even have missed it!"

They tried to leave the inn as inconspicuously as possible although Arthur knew he was not alone in wanting to bolt out of the place as fast as he could. If they could stop Anna before she set sail, the cauldron would be theirs and the Morgens' plan defeated!

They broke into a run as they left the settlement and approached the river. It was little more than a muddy trickle at that time of day but it would soon swell with the incoming tide. They followed it down to the bay. Several fishing boats were beached on the mud awaiting the tide but all were too small to accommodate them.

Grassy dunes swept away to the right of the estuary and on their left, a long golden beach met the curling waves. In the far distance, across the rushing straits, the mountain ranges of their homeland could be made out.

"Look down there!" cried Beduir. "A boat!"

Down in the churning shallows, a small craft bobbed about. In its hold sat a bulky object wrapped in cloth while five Gaels unfurled the sails and steered the craft out past the breakers. At the stern sat a figure in billowing black robes.

"Damn them!" said Cei, as the wind filled the small square sail and carried the boat out. He looked towards a collection of ramshackle huts surrounded by piles of netting. Several fishermen stood by, watching the evening's events with interest. "Get over to those fishing huts and see if anybody has a boat. I'm not losing that cauldron now!"

They hurried over to the huts and the fishermen fled, not wanting to stand in the way of whatever seven hardened warriors and a girl with a bow wanted. A boat was found with a mast and sail that looked promising enough and they began hauling it down towards the gradually encroaching water.

"Up there, look!" cried Guihir, his eyes fixed on the dune tops behind the fishing huts.

Cei cursed. The outlines of several warriors could be seen etched against the darkening sky. "Our presence in the village did not go unnoticed after all," he said. "Hurry!"

A spear thrown from the dunes whickered through the air and planted itself in the beach a few paces from Arthur, sending up a spray of sand. Guenhuifar unslung her bow and drew an arrow from her quiver.

"Watch it, Guenhuifar!" Arthur called. "Don't make yourself such an easy target!"

She ignored him as a second spear hurtled its way towards her, whistling over her head. She took aim and loosed her arrow at the man who had thrown it. The shaft lodged directly between his eyes and he fell back and out of sight without even a cry.

"By Christ, woman, but you can shoot!" said Beduir.

They were nearly into the shallows now and Guenhuifar loosed another arrow in the direction of the Gaels. They had ducked out of sight and were trying to creep around the dunes and come at them on their left flank.

Arthur felt the chill of the water seep into his breeches as they splashed into the waves and the boat rose beneath his hands, buoyed by the tide. The waves lifted and dropped the little vessel with such force that it threatened to overturn. Guenhuifar slung her bow over her shoulder and splashed towards them to help push them out.

"Those Gaels will be upon us any second if we don't get this boat out past the breakers," said Arthur, glancing up at the beach.

Sure enough, the dark figures of the enemy could be seen running across the sands towards them. "Come with us," he said to Guenhuifar. "We can't leave you here to face them. They'll kill you."

Guenhuifar hesitated. "My family …"

"You're no good to them dead," said Arthur, grabbing her by the arm. "It's us the Gaels want, not them. Your family will be safe in Aberffraw for the time being. Come with us, Guenhuifar, I beg you. Come with us and help us win this war." The waves lapped around their thighs and she stared at him, her eyes filled with indecision. "When it is all over, you will return to your family and live out your days in peace. I promise."

"That is a big promise, Arthur mab Enniaun."

"Come on!" bellowed Cei from the boat. Beduir

and Cundelig were already unfurling the sail and the little craft bobbed about, listing and reeling as its crew found their seats.

Guenhuifar turned her gaze away from the beach and scrambled up into the boat, assisted by Cei and Gualchmei. Arthur followed, rolling into the keel just as the Gaels splashed into the shallows.

Their curses were drowned out as the wind caught the sail and the boat rose and fell as it crested a wave. Up ahead, they could see the other craft, small and black, following the coastline of Ynys Mon as it curved around to the south-east and entered the straits. It was nearly high tide and the current was strong.

"She dares try and pass the straits at high tide?" Beduir marvelled.

"The northern wind caught her unawares and she is trying to outrun the tide," said Menw. "Foolish, but we are no less so for following her."

"On!" cried Cei. "There is no going back now! On and after her!"

The straits narrowed and the current picked up. The waters grew choppy and Beduir struck the sail. They had no need of it now.

"She's heading into the Swellies!" said Cei.

"She has little choice," said Menw. "And neither do we. We can't fight that current."

"This is madness!" said Gualchmei. "Look at those whirlpools! We'll be hurled about like a spinning top!"

"Nothing for it, lad!" cried Menw. "Just hold on and pray to your gods!"

They did just that. The current caught them and sucked them along, jolting them back and forth as conflicting currents fought for dominance over the little vessel.

The water foamed and swirled about them as the boat rocked and bucked. Salty spray lashed their faces and slopped over the bulwarks. Rocks, treacherous and jagged could be seen poking through the water, threatening to rip a hole in their keel while the eddies that formed behind them sucked and twisted.

A large wave rolled up and slammed into the side of the boat, pushing it sideways. Arthur heard Guenhuifar scream as the boat lurched to one side. As water filled it, he lost his purchase on the slippery wood. He slid towards the bulwark and struck it hard. The wind was knocked from his chest and he tumbled over the side into the foaming torrent.

The water was cold and the current strong. He struggled to fight his way to the surface, his lungs choking for air. He reeled, end over end, not knowing which way was up. For a moment he heard the cries of his companions but then water filled his ears and blocked them out. Panic gripped him and all he could think of was Manawydan's large, watery hands clasping him around his middle and dragging him down, down into the blackness.

PART IV

"The heavy blue chain held the faithful youth,
And before the spoils of Annwn woefully he sings,
And till doom shall continue a bard of prayer."
- The Spoils of Annwn, The Book of Taliesin (trans. Mary Jones, 2015)

Arthur

Arthur felt grass, soft and warm under his cheek. There was a pleasant smell too, of apple blossoms in spring. He rolled over and saw blue skies above, clear without a cloud to spoil the perfect azure. He sat up. His clothes were dry. His last memories were of drowning in the straits. Now he was here in the sunshine surrounded by small dark apple trees engulfed in white blossom.

He got up and looked around. The orchard stretched for as far as he could see; rolling green hills dotted with apple trees. White petals drifted on the gentle breeze.

"Pretty, isn't it?" said a voice beside him.

He turned to see a girl of about his age in a white dress standing next to him. She had auburn hair that looked on the verge of flowering into the fiery redness of adulthood. She put him in mind of Guenhuifar, only younger.

"Where am I?" he asked.

"In my country," she replied.

"Am I dead?"

"No. But you will be if you remain here for too long."

"Who are you?"

"I am the grass and the trees and the deep, dark earth. You are Arthur mab Enniaun Yrth, son of the Pendraig and you seek my cauldron."

"*Your* cauldron?"

"Come, it is time for you to return to your companions and complete your quest."

"How?"

She walked over to a tree which bore a single apple, red and ripe. She plucked it. "Take a bite," she said, holding it to his lips.

She held his gaze as he bit down into the crisp fruit. As his teeth split the surface, the apple's juices filled his mouth and he had never tasted anything so sweet. The breeze grew in strength and the branches of the apple trees bent and swayed. Their petals blew free and engulfed him, picking him up and carrying him away from the girl in the white dress.

He could see nothing but white petals and suddenly he felt cold. The petals washed away from him and he realised that they were petals no more. They were foaming, white waves rolling away from him.

He was on a lone stretch of muddy beach. The skies were grim and the hills grey. He knew this coast. It was the northern coast of Venedotia. The tide was going out and it was morning.

He staggered to his feet and looked about. He felt frozen to the bone and standing upright made his stomach heave. He bent over and vomited seawater. When he was done coughing and retching, he tried to make sense of what had happened.

He must have been washed ashore after he fell out of the boat and lain here unconscious all night. He remembered his dream about the orchard and the girl in white. It must have been a fever dream. And yet, surviving the straits was a miracle in itself. He had no answers and knew he wouldn't find them on that grim beach.

His stomach, now emptied of seawater, cried out for food and he climbed up off the mud and into the thick gorse and long grass. He had to find Cei and Guenhuifar and the others, but first he had to find out where exactly on the stretch of coastline he was. If he wasn't careful, he could wander close to the enemy at Cair Dugannu.

He headed east, hoping to find some sign of the boat, wrecked or not. He saw nobody. The beach vanished as cliffs sank down to meet the water and he was forced into the woods that grew thick on the clifftops.

His thoughts were interrupted by the sound of a large animal either in pain or fear. He had been around horses all his life and to him the awful sound was the sound of a brother in pain.

He followed the noise and came to a large hawthorn bush. In among the spiky tendrils was a beautiful white horse. It was a young one – only a foal – its white mane and tail tangled up in the coils of the bush. It was clearly trapped and frightened. It rolled its eyes and tossed its head from side to side in its effort to free itself but succeeded only in tearing its skin. Red blood streaked the downy whiteness of its flanks.

Arthur looked around for signs of its herd but the foal seemed to be alone. He wondered if it had strayed from its fellowship or perhaps they had abandoned him, unable to free him from his thorny prison. It did not look starved so its herd could not be too far away.

He approached slowly, wading through the thickness of the bush, palm outstretched while he made the sounds he had learned from boyhood that would calm a panicked horse. "Easy, boy," he soothed. "I'm going to get you out of this."

The horse tried to back away as Arthur drew the knife at his belt. He placed his palm on the foal's neck to calm it. He could feel its sharp breaths and fast heartbeat and he patted the soft white coat. Beneath that shining down, powerful muscles flexed. This horse might only be a foal, but he was a strong lad.

With a few quick cuts the mane was free and Arthur moved himself over to reach the tail. Soon the foal was able to bolt from the hawthorn bush and cantered around the clearing, tossing his shaggy mane and shaking his head with joy.

Arthur laughed as he sheathed his knife, his spirits lifted at the sight of the freed animal. It truly was a magnificent beast; sturdy, handsome and of the purest white but for a speckling of grey on its hindquarters. It trotted a little way ahead of him and stopped, twitching his ears and flicking his tail.

"Well, so long little one," said Arthur, as he made to leave in the opposite direction. "Go and find your family. I must look for my own."

But the foal whinnied angrily as Arthur left and reared up on its hind legs, kicking outwards with its front hooves.

"What is it, boy?" asked Arthur, surprised at the horse's objection.

The foal blinked his long lashes and nuzzled his nose against Arthur's chest.

"Well, I suppose our way might lie together," he said. "For a while at least."

They left the forest and crossed green hills. The foal led the way, seemingly intent on some direction unknown to Arthur. They followed the coast until a large bulge of land could be seen poking out into the sea. Arthur recognised it as the limestone headland which thrust out from the Creuthin peninsula, shielding Cair Dugannu.

"We should go no further, friend," said Arthur to the foal. "Up ahead lies the mouth of the Afon Conui and the lair of the enemy. Those Gaels will kill me and set you to stud for their mares if they find us."

But the foal would have none of it and wandered on ahead, ignoring Arthur's best efforts to draw him back. He was intent on going a little further and veered towards the sands below them.

Arthur followed reluctantly. He kept his eyes open for Gaelic patrols, ready to flee for the cover of the woods if he spotted any. Then he froze.

Down on the beach was a vessel with a splintered mast and torn sail. It had been dragged up into the shade of the cliffs where it would only be visible to somebody approaching from the west.

A campfire had been built on the sand and two people squatted by it, tending a couple of roasting fish. Arthur recognised them as Cei and Guihir and nearly gave out a whoop of joy despite the need for caution.

"You did it, friend!" he said, patting the foal on the flank. "You found my companions!"

He half ran, half slid down the sandy embankment and, as he hit the wet beach below, Cei and Guihir rose up, drawing their weapons. When they saw that it was him, they sheathed them and ran to greet him.

"God be praised!" said Guihir. "We had all but given you up for dead!"

"We thought Manawydan's watery grave had

received a new tenant," said Cei. "However did you survive?"

"I am not sure myself," admitted Arthur.

"Who's your friend?" Guihir asked, glancing at the white foal which had made its way down to the beach and was nosing the curl of the tide.

"I found him tangled up in a hawthorn bush," said Arthur. "And he led me to you. I think he may have seen your shipwreck earlier today and knew that I was looking for more of my kind. A truly remarkable animal."

Arthur glanced at the vessel they had stolen from Aberffraw. It was hopelessly wrecked and it was hard to believe it had carried his friends to shore at all. "What happened? Where are the others?"

On cue, Menw and Cundelig emerged from the makeshift shelter they had built under the brow of the cliffs, stretching and rubbing their joints.

"We awake seeking our breakfast and find our lost comrade has returned to us," said Menw. "And not alone, either."

"Beduir, Gualchmei and Guenhuifar are out looking for you as we speak," said Cei. "They set out before dawn to scour the coast for you. Wherever did you wash up?"

"On a muddy strand further west," Arthur replied. "I must have been unconscious all night. I had the strangest dreams …"

"Indeed?" asked Menw. "I would very much like to hear them. It is not everybody who is fortunate enough to survive a tumble into the straits at high water. But first I must feed my belly. I see Cei has done us proud and procured a feast from the waves!"

It was sarcasm but not of a cruel sort. Cei was no fisherman but he had managed to catch a couple of mackerel which crackled and spat over the flames.

They devoured the two fish and, when they were licking the juices from their fingers, Beduir, Gualchmei and Guenhuifar appeared on the clifftop above them.

"So, the lad thinks he can have us running around all morning looking for his body while he sneaks into camp and eats our breakfast!" said Beduir, a wide smile on his face.

"You've led us a merry chase, Cousin!" said Gualchmei as they descended to the beach.

"As have you me," said Arthur. "I've been wandering about all morning wondering if I was the only one of us left alive."

Guenhuifar said nothing, but a half-smile on her face told Arthur that she was relieved to see him alive. He wondered why that made him feel happier than even finding his comrades did. She carried Gualchmei's bow and a brace of coneys over her shoulder.

"Guenhuifar couldn't find any Gaels to shoot so these poor creatures had to do," said Beduir. "Just as well, by the looks of things. Somebody needs to give you lot fishing lessons."

Guenhuifar set about gutting and skinning the coneys while the others scavenged for more driftwood to burn. Menw sat down beside Arthur.

"I think it's time we had a chat, lad."

Arthur told him everything; about his dream, about the orchard and the girl in white. Menw listened intently, his dark eyes barely blinking until

Arthur had finished.

"I think the goddess has looked upon you favourably," said the old bard at last. "Few who wind up in the straits come out alive. And fewer still travel further than the boundaries of our world and return."

"What do you mean?"

"I think you've been to Annun, boy."

"Annun? I was delirious, surely! I haven't been quite myself since that slingshot to the head …" he fingered the stitches in his left temple.

"Perhaps," mused Menw. "Or perhaps you drifted beyond death to the Isle of Apples and Modron herself sent you back to this world to finish what you have started."

"Modron?" asked Arthur. "The Great Mother? But she was just a girl!"

"She can take many forms," said Menw. "Just as the earth looks different from summer to winter, so too can the goddess, she mirrors the land."

"She reflects the seasons?"

"It's not quite as simple as that. She reflects the land but what hidden cycles she follows are her secret."

Arthur thought back to the meeting with his sister. "Anna spoke of Modron being reborn. She seems to think we are on the verge of a new age."

"Aye, well, if anybody has any insight into the mind of Modron then it is the Morgens. They are her priestesses after all."

Arthur found it difficult to reconcile the horrors he had seen on Ynys Mon with the pretty girl in the white dress. The idea that the goddess should save his life while her priestesses had nearly taken it was a confusing thought. It all seemed rather more complex than good versus evil.

The others had returned and stoked the campfire for Guenhuifar's coneys. "We can't take that beast with us," said Cei, glancing at the white foal that stood by watching them patiently, twitching his ears. "He'll need feeding before long and we don't even have food for ourselves."

"He's coming with us," said Arthur. He felt a strange attachment to the small horse he had rescued. They had both been lost and, in their search for their respective companions, they had found each other.

"A white foal," said Menw rubbing his beard. "Mabon mab Modron. Very interesting."

"Mabon mab Modron?" Arthur asked. "The youthful god?"

"Aye. Just as Modron is the divine mother, so is Mabon her divine son. The two deities are symbolic of man born of mother. Always must Mabon be freed from his prison in order to reach manhood. In older times Modron and Mabon were often represented by a mare and her foal."

"So, Arthur rescued a foal from a thorn bush," said Cei. "A coincidence."

"A *white* foal," said Menw. "White is the colour of youth, both for man and his mother."

"Pah! Symbolism and superstition."

Menw ignored him. "I believe that Modron sent her son to aid you, Arthur. Just as she sent you to aid her son. You and the white foal are one and the same. *You* are Mabon, Arthur. This quest has been your *mabinogi* – your coming of age tale. You were a boy when you passed through the waters to Annun, to

Ynys Aballach, and you have returned to us from the Isle of Apples a man."

"My *mabinogi* …" Arthur repeated, feeling a little foolish. He liked the old tales as well as any but was a little embarrassed by the way Menw drew parallels between them and his own life.

"We encountered a shepherd who gave us news from Cair Dugannu," said Guenhuifar, as she set the coneys on sticks over the flames. "Three nights ago, the fortress all but emptied itself of troops. Meriaun marched south with all banners flying."

"By Christ there must be a battle brewing somewhere in the mountain passes," said Cundelig, feeding Hebog a scrap of rabbit's liver.

"If they left three nights ago," said Gualchmei, "then Anna will have arrived at Cair Dugannu after they left. She and the cauldron are probably still there."

"*If* she survived the straits," said Cei.

"If we did then you can count on her having done the same," said Menw.

"Whether it is at the bottom of the sea or within Cair Dugannu's walls the cauldron is as good as lost to us," said Cei wearily. "We must head south and skirt Meriaun's teulu to make contact with the Pendraig and tell him that we have failed. Perhaps we can make amends by laying down our lives for him in the final battle."

"We might not have to," said Arthur. They all looked at him. "If Meriaun and his teulu have marched south then Cari Dugannu will be severely undermanned. The cauldron will be vulnerable."

"You're suggesting that we seven storm the royal

seat of Venedotia?" asked Cei incredulously.

"Eight," added Guenhuifar.

"You're not a warrior, lass."

"No, but my aim is deadlier than any of yours. And it sounds as if you need every advantage you can get."

"Why would you risk your life for our mission?" Arthur asked her.

She shrugged. "As I said on Ynys Mon, I have already gone too far down this path with you. The Gaels will never leave my family alone unless they are defeated. I don't care about your precious cauldron. I just want to see them driven back into the sea."

"And you are prepared to die for that?"

"For my family? Yes."

"I do not doubt the courage of anybody here," said Cei. "Including yours, lass. But this is suicide. Meriaun may have marched south but he will hardly have left his back door open. There'll be a detachment of Gaels guarding Cair Dugannu. Possibly Diugurnach himself. We must forget this foolish idea. South to battle is the only road left open to us."

"It's a long march," said Cundelig. "And how are we to know where the Pendraig's teulu is? Even Hebog can't scour every valley and dale in Venedotia. It's more likely that we'll be picked up by Meriaun's scouts than find our own people."

"Our guide speaks the truth," said Menw. "By the time we find the Pendraig, the battle will be over. Lost more than likely and we will be left drifting on the wind."

"It will be a hard fight, there is no doubt as to

that," said Arthur. "But we need not attempt a frontal assault on Cair Dugannu. If we could somehow sneak inside and capture the fortress from within, we could end this war before its final battle begins."

"It's just a bloody cooking pot, Arthur," said Cei. "You said so yourself."

"It is a symbol," said Arthur. He glanced at Menw. "And symbols win the hearts of men more than the truth. We have but to show the enemy – and our friends – that Cair Dugannu is ours and that the power of the cauldron is broken. You'll see how stout the courage of Meriaun's following is then."

Cei sighed. "I suppose dying up here is as good as dying down south. And I'm pig-sick of chasing this old pot about. Very well, Arthur. You have the right of it once again. Let's do this. My only question is how?"

"As to that," replied Arthur. "I have one idea."

Meddyf

A humid drizzle began to mist the trees on the other side of the river as they descended the hill and began to cross the grassy valley floor. The old Roman fort occupied a bend on the Afon Lugu. It was little different to the half dozen or so forts the Romans had built to subdue the rebellious Britons of the mountains. Its square plan, rows of barrack huts and vaulted praetorium put Meddyf in mind of Cair Cunor although Cunor's fort was much better maintained.

Cair Lugu was a tumbledown old place that had not been inhabited since the Romans had left. As they approached its ivy-cloaked walls and crumbling gates, Meddyf wondered why King Etern had bothered to quarter his teulu here instead of camping them on the plain. The ruined fort would offer little protection should her husband decide to march on it.

He must feel vulnerable to hide behind such shabby walls, she thought. *There has to be a weakness here; something that we can exploit …*

"It's not too late to change your mind, my lady," said Cunor beside her. "You can still turn back …"

"No," she said, her face hard against the drizzle. "We go on."

Cunor's words of caution echoed the discussion that had consumed Cadwallon's war council the previous night. She knew that all the men felt honour-bound to try and talk her out of it but all of them – including her husband – knew there was no other way.

Cadwallon had set out the day before in a north-easterly direction with the intention of turning north-west through the lee of the Giant's Cairn and heading through the Pass of Kings which led into the flat coastal lands beyond. Maeldaf and his valley scouts had returned bearing news that Etern's teulu had marched from Cair Cunor and was following the Afon Lugu into the mountains on their right flank.

"The old bastard is planning to cut us off at the pass," said King Efiaun, as they made camp in the Y-shaped valley that night.

"He's too old for this game," said King Mor. "And too slow. We'll reach the pass by noon tomorrow. He'll still be struggling through the mountains by the time we march on Cair Dugannu."

The mood in the tent was light and Meddyf had not seen the men so jovial in as long as she could remember. The end of this war was in sight. By tomorrow evening they would be out of the mountains and the stretch of coastline would be all that stood between them and Cair Dugannu. *All that stands between us and home.*

But, as with every step of this campaign it seemed, God mocked them. King Mor's scouts returned from the north-west arm of the valley with news that Meriaun's teulu had entered the pass from the other side. Their ranks, bolstered by their Gaelic mercenaries, were filling the pass with their tents and the lights of their campfires dotted the black valley like the night stars.

"This was arranged!" said Cadwallon, hurling his wine cup to the ground in frustration. "They mean to pin us between hammer and anvil!"

"And they'll do it too, by all the gods," said Cunor.

"We can't fight them on two flanks."

"And if we fall back to Din Emrys, they'll converge here and storm that mountain retreat together with a force the like of which has not been seen since Cunedag's time," said Owain gloomily.

"Not with all of Venedotia's teulus together could they crack my fortress," replied Efiaun with his characteristic defiance.

"No but they could starve us out in a matter of weeks," Cadwallon reminded him. "We are too many for your granaries to feed. We should have set out earlier!"

Efiaun grew sullen and silent, his shame at his own tardiness to support Cadwallon weighing heavily upon him. If they had made the pass perhaps as little as a day earlier, they would now be facing Meriaun on open ground, instead of penned in the mountains with an enemy host on each flank.

"We outnumber Etern's teulu three-to-one," said Cunor. "If we march by night we could easily be upon them by sunup tomorrow …"

"To what end?" Cadwallon asked. "It is Cair Dugannu I seek to claim not Etern's seat. And I will not waste my men by attacking him and leave myself vulnerable to Meriaun's counterattack. No, we must break through that pass!"

"Etern must somehow be bargained with," said Meddyf. "The old fool has nothing to gain by supporting Meriaun."

"He supports him out of spite for your husband and his line," said Mor. "Etern always hated Enniaun and he resents you, my lord, for being his son."

"But he'll be no better off if Meriaun wins this

war," said Meddyf. "He'll still be king of Eternion and Eternion alone."

"Like I said," said Mor, "he supports Meriaun out of spite, not logic."

"Well that spite must be blunted," said Meddyf. "Or this war is lost. We must have something to offer him, something that will sate his petty jealousy."

"What have I?" Cadwallon asked. "I don't even have my crown …"

"There must be something! We have to at least try to parley with him …"

"You're right," admitted Cadwallon. "There must be a salve for this bitter rivalry my father caused with his brothers." He gave out a sigh as if being forced down a road he did not want to walk. "I will ride east to discuss terms with my uncle."

The other lords voiced their outrage at such a foolhardy notion.

"My lord, you cannot walk into his hands!" said Mor. "You are the key to their victory. If Etern gets ahold of you he will hand you over to Meriaun without a second thought."

"Send someone else to parley with this traitor," said Owain. "You cannot put yourself in such danger."

"Who could carry my authority?" said Cadwallon. "Whom would he see as his equal enough to discuss terms with?"

"I'll go," said Meddyf.

The lords in the tent stared at her.

"I must protest!" exclaimed Mor.

"He'll hold you to ransom as quick as—" Cunor began.

"No," Meddyf insisted. "I would present a valuable hostage it is true, but he would not dare hold me against my will with my husband's teulu less than a day's march from him. Oh, I am sure he feels safe enough now knowing that a victory over him would be a pointless one politically speaking, but he also knows that my husband would throw all to the wind and march on him if any harm should come to me."

The men were silent as they all considered this.

"I don't like it," said Cadwallon.

"Nor I," Meddyf admitted. "But what other choice do we have?"

"My lord, I beg you to send me in our queen's stead," said Efiaun, but all knew his words were mere courtesy. It had to be Meddyf. Only the life of the Pendraig's queen was valuable enough for him to throw away the whole war to save.

Cadwallon was silent for a long while before he spoke. "I want Cunor to go with you," he said. "And I will have every warrior ready to march at the blast of a horn. If my uncle tries any treachery, I'll redden the Lugu with his teulu's corpses."

Cadwallon's oath brought little comfort to Meddyf as the gates of Cair Lugu creaked open, their rusted hinges and wavering timbers threatening to burst asunder at every inch. An armed reception awaited them upon the parade ground and Meddyf and Cunor were escorted to the praetorium.

Despite being summer, a fire crackled in the brazier in the main hall and King Etern sat wrapped in a blanket. His once golden hair was now white streaked with sickly yellow. His face was pinched and veined and he regarded them with beady, hungry eyes as they approached.

"What's this then? Terms of surrender?" he demanded. "Does my brave nephew send his wife to treat in his stead? Oh, I know she comes with protection, Cunor, did you think I'd forget your sullen face? I must say, I'm enjoying your family home immensely, though you didn't leave me much. Even the kitchens had been emptied. Still, when this war is done, I'm thinking of razing Cair Cunor and using its stones to build some stables."

Meddyf felt Cunor tense at her side but the loyal penteulu kept his cool. "We are not here to surrender but to ask you to reconsider your support of Meriaun," she said.

"Reconsider? Does the wolf reconsider his dinner when asked to by the sheep?"

"My husband is not so easily beaten as you might think. Efiaun of Dunauding is with him as is Mor of Rumaniog and many bannermen from the Conui Valley. He could trample this fort within the day and still have enough men to face Meriaun."

"If that were true, then why doesn't he?" Etern asked. There was a hesitation in his voice that suggested uncertainty.

He didn't count on Dunauding joining the war against him, she thought. *This is new to him.*

"My husband wishes to heal the wounds between Cunedag's descendants, not rend them utterly. You swore an oath to his father; your own brother."

"Aye, and he's dead, gods rot him. I swore no oath

to your husband."

"My husband is your brother's son," Meddyf persisted. "The rightful heir to Venedotia. Why turn your back on your father's dynasty now?"

"*I* turn my back?" Etern seemed ripe to explode. "It was my proud and splendid brother who turned his back on me – on all of us! Did he really think we would bend the knee to his son; a whelp who never raised a blade in the conquest of this land?"

"My husband raised his blade to defend Venedotia when the Gaels returned. He fights that battle still."

"And I raised mine to forge it when your precious husband was still sucking on his mother's teat! I am the last of us, the last of Cunedag's sons who watered this land with our blood! If anyone should wear the Pendraig's crown then it is I!" He was overtaken by a sudden bout of coughing which turned his face purple and attendants rushed to offer him water. He waved them away. "Oh, don't look at me like that," he said to Meddyf once he had recovered. "I know what you're thinking. An old wreck like me wouldn't wear the crown for very long even if he did get it on his head. And you're right! My time has passed, I admit that. But what of my line? I have never been blessed with sons but I have daughters who will carry sons of their own. What for them? Why should my brother choose his own descendants for the throne while mine inherit nothing more than a scrap of a kingdom on Venedotia's outskirts that is little more than a buffer state to keep back the dogs of Powys?"

"The Teulu of the Red Dragon has always come to Eternion's defence in the past," said Meddyf.

"After my people have borne the brunt of Powys's

raids," Etern spat.

"What has Meriaun offered you?" she demanded.

She had expected something – more land, the spoils of conquest perhaps – but when Etern sat back in his chair and sighed, his vindictive face sagging a little, she understood the truth. Meriaun had offered him nothing but vengeance; a petty, fleeting thing in exchange for helping him win the throne.

"Is it the lot of your descendants to continue to hold Venedotia's borders in check while Meriaun sits upon your father's throne?" she asked him.

He looked at her with puzzlement. "Can your husband offer me anything better?"

"As a matter of fact …" she began and then checked herself. She had no right to say what she was currently considering. Only her husband had the right to make that kind of offer. And yet, Cadwallon was not here. *She* was. And as well as carrying her husband's authority, she remembered his words to her that morning. *Find a way. Offer him anything we can to turn his loyalty.*

"We have a son," she said. *Forgive me, husband. Forgive me Maelcon.* "A fine lad who will be upon the cusp of manhood in a few years. I understand you have a pair of daughters, young and fair."

"What of them?" Etern asked, his beady eyes lighting up with greedy curiosity.

"You said so yourself, you are too old to wear the crown of the Pendraig for long. But your grandson might wear it for many years. There are other ways to secure it for him than war."

"A union, eh?" Etern smirked. "Just to be clear, we are talking about your eldest son, am I right? I know that you have two and trickery is rife these days …"

"My word is as good as my husband's and he holds the honour of the Red Dragon higher than anything," Meddyf said firmly. "I speak of Maelcon, our eldest and heir to the throne."

"I'll want your husband's final word on this. No offence, Lady Meddyf, but this is men's talk. I don't know why he didn't come here himself …"

Meddyf smiled. "As you said, trickery is rife these days."

Arthur

On the eastern banks of the Afon Conui Arthur and his companions waited, screened by the reeds that grew close to the water's edge. The moon was bright and the sky clear. Despite the warm summer night, Arthur felt a chill penetrating deep into his bones. It may have been the recent swim across the Conui that had soaked them all, followed by several hours lying on its muddy banks amidst the wavering reeds but Arthur knew better. Up there, within the spiked walls of Cair Dugannu, many things waited for them. The end of this war. The cauldron. *My sister.*

"What if Guihir has been captured?" asked Gualchmei. "Or killed? Will we still press the attack?"

Arthur shook his head. "We'd be slaughtered before we made a dent in those gates." He sighed. "No, our entire plan rests on our master of tongues gaining us entry."

"He'll think of something," said Beduir. "He hasn't let us down yet."

"There's always a first for everything," Guenhuifar muttered, as she rubbed Gualchmei's bow with an oiled cloth. Gualchmei's shoulder had healed enough to hold a blade and so he had loaned the Persian weapon to her. Her deadly aim would be needed in the fight ahead.

The white foal Arthur had rescued grazed nearby. It had followed them without being asked and had even crossed the Conui, proving itself to be a fine swimmer at low tide. Arthur knew it could not come with them up to the gates of Cair Dugannu but he had not the heart to hobble it. It was so wild and pure and untainted by the hand of man that he would hate to be the one to bridle or saddle it.

"Look!" hissed Cei. "There is the signal!"

Up ahead they could see one of the torches on the west gatehouse winking as something obscured it once … twice … three times; the signal that Guihir had succeeded and the gate was open to them.

"Stay, boy," Arthur whispered to the white foal. "I will be back for you, I promise."

The foal blinked and turned his head away from Arthur, almost as if in understanding. As they made to leave the horse remained and gazed at the river.

They hurried up the grassy slope like phantoms, keeping to the shadows of the trees. When they reached the palisade they slipped in through the open gate. Guihir climbed down from the rampart to greet them.

"Well done," Arthur said, clapping him on his shoulder. "What did you tell them?"

"That I had come from the great army further south with news that the engagement had gone well but some of Cadwallon's riders had been spotted heading up the Conui Valley and that they should be prepared for a minor counterattack on the fortress."

"True, funnily enough," said Beduir with a grin. "But not in the manner you described!"

"I spun them some war stories and they gave me meat and mead and a place to sleep in the Great Hall," Guihir continued. "I left as soon as I was sure everybody was snoring. There are a few more guards on the palisades so we don't have much time before the western watch's absence is noticed."

"Any news of Anna and the cauldron?" Cei asked.

"Aye, it's here," Guihir replied. "This lot are terrified of it. They don't like having it in the fortress and are happy that it's to be carried south tomorrow."

"Where are they taking it?"

"The Pass of Kings is what I heard. Apparently Meriaun is massing his forces there to hold off Cadwallon and his allies. It is set to be a bloodbath."

"Where is the cauldron kept?" Arthur asked.

"Somewhere in the royal chambers behind the Great Hall."

"We'll need to master the fortress before we start poking about for it," said Menw. "Who is in charge?"

"It's Diugurnach. He's sleeping up at the hall with a few of his captains. There are only a couple of guards at its doors."

"This should be easy," said Cei.

"Not so fast," said Arthur. "This whole plan rests on us killing Diugurnach before anybody else in the fortress is alerted to our presence. If we don't make it into the Great Hall without being spotted then all is lost."

"It's your plan," said Cei with a shrug. "Just let me at the bastard."

They snaked their way through the settlement that lay between the twin hills. Some attempt had been made to rebuild the roundhouses that had been torched during the initial attack. They were unfinished and eerily silent; monuments to the people who had been slain by Meriaun's foul treachery. Arthur swore that the shades of those who had inhabited those charred ruins would be avenged that night.

The shattered gate to the north hill was unguarded. The eight companions hurried up the trackway and around to the side of the Great Hall. A pair of torchlights illuminated the entrance, bouncing light off the iron helms and mail coats of the two guards.

Arthur glanced up at the palisades. There was a guard making his leisurely way along the ramparts, easily visible by the moonlight. That same moonlight would make them just as visible to him if they tried to rush the entrance to the hall. He turned to Guenhuifar.

"An arrow please. Right in the gullet of that bastard up there."

Guenhuifar nodded and drew a shaft from her quiver and nocked it to her string.

"The rest of you," Arthur said. "Follow me. We make our move as soon as that guard falls."

Their heads nodded in the gloom. Guenhuifar's bowstring creaked as she drew the fletching of her arrow back to her ear. She waited a couple of heartbeats and then let it fly. They all watched the deadly barb sail through the night and strike the guard in the neck, as fine a shot as ever. If he cried out at all they did not hear it and were confident that nobody else in the fortress did either. The man sank to his knees and fell face first onto the walkway, rolling off it to land heavily on the ground below.

"Now!" Arthur hissed.

They drew their blades and charged the guards at the doors to the hall. They were spotted immediately but, by the pale, shocked faces of the guards, Arthur assumed they looked like spectres emerging suddenly from the gloom. Spears were lowered but Arthur and his company hacked through the shafts and drove in upon the Gaels, sinking their blades into throats and groins, slaying the unfortunate men almost immediately.

They paused at the entrance to the hall to clean their blades.

"There are perhaps a dozen warriors sleeping by the hearth," Guihir said. "Diugurnach has made his quarters in the chamber behind the dais. What do we do – kill the warriors first or try to sneak past them to get at Diugurnach?"

"We'll have to dispose of the warriors first," said Arthur. "But quietly! We must make damn sure Diugurnach doesn't escape."

"Nice and slowly then," said Beduir, placing his hand on the iron handles of the great carven doors.

They eased the doors open as silently as they could but Arthur pined for a measure of oil to silence their complaining hinges. Within the hall the glowing embers of the hearth and the moonlight from the smoke hole illuminated the slumbering forms of several warriors on their furs, chests rising and falling with slow snores.

They crept into the hall, weaving a path around the sleeping warriors. Arthur motioned to his companions to pick a target each. It was a dirty way to win a fight but this war had not been of their choosing. All they had to do was finish it.

Arthur stood over his prey, his sword held point down over the man's throat. He saw Cei and the others doing the same. There were not enough of them to slay all the sleeping warriors at once. They would have to move on to fresh targets quickly once the killing began.

At a nod from Arthur, blades were raised and

thrust downwards.

There was some struggling, a little choking, but for the most part, the targets died instantly. Arthur put his boot on his man's face and tugged his sword free with an ugly sucking sound. He glanced around the hall. A man on the far side stirred in his sleep and rolled over but did not awake.

Something else did awake however; something Guihir had not noticed else he would never had let his companions go through with their plan.

The first Arthur heard of it was a long, low snarl. He glanced across the glowing ashes of the hearth and saw a large, shaggy head with two yellow eyes set within dark circles of fur. It rose up onto its haunches – Arthur had never seen a hound so big. This was one of the great wolfhounds Erin was known for.

"Bugger, why didn't you say anything about a dog?" Cei hissed to Guihir.

"I didn't see the blasted thing!" Guihir replied. "It must have been in Diugurnach's chamber and then came out here to sleep by the fire."

"What do we do?" Gualchmei asked, panic in his voice.

Some of the warriors were stirring, roused by the ongoing growl in the great beast's throat.

"Nothing for it," said Arthur. "We kill the dog as well as the men. Band together! It's going to attack!"

The wolfhound stood up, its vast shape casting a shadow on the dais behind it. It snarled once again and then bound forward, clearing the hearth in one massive leap.

Beduir lunged to meet it, dodging those slavering jaws and slashing at its side with his blade. It tumbled into the others, sending them sprawling under its weight. It scrabbled to its feet, bleeding through its thick, matted fur and turned on Beduir. Beduir backed off, holing his sword point out in front of him as the hound advanced.

It yelped in pain as one of Guenhuifar's arrows found its mark between its shoulder blades. As it turned to try and bite at the shaft, Beduir swung at its exposed neck. The beast went down, its big shaggy head nearly severed from its body.

The Gaels were awake now, scrambling to their feet and reaching for their weapons, cursing the intruders. Arthur and his companions huddled together, facing enemies on all sides. They were evenly matched but the Britons were on enemy turf and the anger at being awoken and seeing the death of their prized wolfhound was evident in the enraged faces of the Gaels.

Swords clanged and slithered together as Briton met Gael amidst the orange glow of the hearth while shadows leapt frantically around the walls. Arthur gutted an opponent and then cried out a warning as the shape of a massive Gael emerged from the chamber at the rear of the dais, naked and brandishing a sword.

This, he assumed, was Diugurnach; a mighty man with tangled hair that fell to his broad chest. The many scars that lined his body were livid in the light. "Watch it, Cei!" Arthur cried and his foster-brother ducked just in time as Diugurnach's blade swooshed through the air above his head.

Cei and Beduir sidled around to the giant's right while Cundelig and Gualchmei engaged him on his left. It was four against one, but the Gaelic chieftain was more than a match for any of them, swiping at them with his broad blade and kicking with his bare feet at any who got too close.

Beduir, always courageous no matter the odds, lunged at him with his sword. The blade penetrated Diugurnach between the ribs and he let out a bellow of rage. Seizing Beduir's sword arm by the wrist, he brought his own blade whistling down and severed the limb at the forearm.

"Beduir!" Arthur cried, unable to run to his companion's aid for the remaining two Gaels who barred his way.

Beduir screamed and clutched at his stump which bled profusely. Menw hurried around to the side and hauled the fallen warrior to safety while Cei, Gualchmei and Cundelig pressed the attack.

Diugurnach was sorely wounded though he fought on with astonishing perseverance. His lungs wheezed for air and his side ran slick with blood. Beduir had scored a mighty victory over their enemy but had paid a dear price for it.

It was Gualchmei who finally brought down the giant, hacking low at his hamstrings while Cei occupied the Gael's attention. Diugurnach roared as he sank to his knees, his ruined legs no longer able to support him.

Cundelig ran his blade in through his back and the great ugly head went back as it gasped for air, eyes rolling and bulging. Cei seized the shaggy mane and struck once, twice at the straining neck. The head came free with a gush of blood and the lifeless body slumped forward.

It was over. As Arthur and Guihir finished off one Gael, Guenhuifar sank another of her arrows into the last one. Diugurnach was dead. The Great Hall of Cair Dugannu was theirs. All that remained was to secure the rest of the fortress.

"Bar all the doors," said Arthur, "except the main one. Don't let anybody in on us. We must challenge them on one front only."

Sure enough, Gaels were converging at the steps to the Great Hall, alerted by the sounds of fighting coming from within. The garrison, such as it was, was preparing to storm the hall. There were not a great number of them but enough to still pose a threat.

While Menw staunched Beduir's bleeding stump with a tablecloth, Arthur seized Diugurnach's head and lifted it up by its hair. He was surprised by the weight of it. "Follow me close," he said to the others.

As one, they moved towards the doors where the torchlight glinted off the mail and weapons of the host outside. As Arthur exited the hall to stand on its steps, he held the head aloft. Faces, pale and uncomprehending gazed up at him, spears and blades gripped in ready fists.

"Do you recognise the head of your chieftain?" Arthur bellowed. "Look upon his dead eyes and know that you are beaten! Cair Dugannu is ours and we hold it for Cadwallon mab Enniaun, the true Pendraig! Throw down your weapons and you will be permitted to live! Stand against us and your souls shall join Diugurnach's in the Otherworld!"

It took only a few moments of deliberation before spears, axes and swords clattered to the ground. They knew it was over. Somehow the Britons had taken the

Great Hall from under their noses and slain their mighty chieftain who had led them from Erin with promises of a kingdom.

As Cei organised the escorting of the prisoners to a secure holding and the posting of guards, Arthur went back into the hall to check on Beduir. He found Guenhuifar and Guihir tending to him. Beduir's face was pale and beaded with sweat. He was barely conscious.

"Where is Menw?" he asked.

"He hurried off muttering something about the cauldron," said Guihir.

Arthur cursed. "He means to confront Anna alone!" He bolted from the hall and crossed the enclosure to the northern palisade. The sun was beginning to rise over the sea to the east, turning the great flatness of the water to speckled gold.

He climbed the stairs to the upper chambers. He had never been to Cair Dugannu before, at least not since he had been a baby and knew little of its layout, but he assumed the royal apartments would overlook the sea.

He found Menw standing with his back to the door in a wide chamber furnished with much finery. Tapestries hung on the walls and the bed covers looked to be of silk. The window opposite the door framed the form of his sister, dark hair aflame with the light of the rising sun behind her. Between her and Menw stood the cauldron.

He stepped into the room and was aware that he was intruding on a meeting of two great powers. High-priestess and king's bard faced each other with the object of their conflict between them.

"I never understood why," Menw said to her. "Why support Meriaun? Why try to overthrow the line of Cunedag and replace one descendant with another? Then, when I found you here in the royal apartments, I understood at last. These were to be *your* apartments, weren't they? You were to rule from Cair Cunor as Meriaun's queen."

Anna's face was rigid and her eyes spat a hate that chilled Arthur to the bone. They had ruined her plans. They had all been complicit in her destruction and she hated them all for it. Whatever dreams or plans she had entertained were as good as dust on the wind now.

Menw rubbed his temples as if greatly tired. "But I still don't understand how you convinced your sisters to go along with your plan. The Morgens have always prided themselves on their status as oracles, interpreters of Modron's whim, impartial in politics. Why abuse that status for the lust of their high-priestess?"

"Lust?" Anna snapped. "You think I lusted after that oaf? Meriaun was a means to an end, nothing more."

"A means to an end," repeated Arthur. "Like the Gaels. Plans within plans within plans. I wonder, sister, are you even sure of your own intentions anymore?"

She turned her head to glare at him. The white greasepaint was flaky and a little of her true countenance was visible behind the mask. "Don't be naïve, *little brother*. I am Modron's representative in this world. I am her voice and her intentions are as clear to me as spring water. The wheel is turning. A new dawn is on the horizon and Meriaun's son, *my* son will herald a new age. He will be Mabon son of Modron, reborn. I am the vessel of his rebirth just as this cauldron is the vessel of all rebirth. From my loins will come the power that will set all to rights."

Gods help us, she's pregnant! Arthur thought.

"You have forgotten your vows, Anna," said Menw. "The Morgens may speak for the Great Mother but they are not her living embodiments. They are certainly not mothers themselves. You overreach your duties …"

"What do you know of the vows and duties of the sisterhood, *bard*?" she said. "Your order is a bastardised echo of the druids who came before you. Your knowledge of the ancient mysteries is as the knowledge of a child compared to its mother's. You are as children floundering in the great wide world. It would have been better for all of you had you not intervened."

"I think we've heard enough," said Menw. He turned to Arthur. "Have Cei find a secure place to detain her. She will face the Pendraig's justice when he returns."

Arthur called down for Cei and Gualchmei and they came up to escort his sister away. As she passed Arthur, she gave him a glare that he would remember until his dying day. "You, of all people should understand," she said. "You, a bastard of the line of Cunedag. Why do you serve them? They'll never accept you as one of their own."

"I do not require them to," said Arthur. "But I serve them nonetheless for they are my family."

As she was led away, Menw approached the

cauldron and placed his hands on its beaded rim. "Such a simple thing," he said. "And yet so very powerful."

"Is it truly the cauldron of legend?" Arthur asked.

The bard shrugged as he examined its decorative panels, running his fingers over the faces of gods. "It is old, very old, I'll grant it that. Who knows what its true purpose was? Perhaps it was just something our ancestors used to dilute wine in. It doesn't really matter, does it? The minds of men have given it a purpose."

"And now that purpose must end. Should we destroy it?"

"No. Not yet. The Pendraig must receive it into his keeping. Only then will the people learn not to fear it. Only then will its spell be broken."

Once the prisoners had been secured and the victors had gorged themselves on salted meats, hard tack and ale from Cair Dugannu's stores, Cei held a council in the upper chambers. They stood around the cauldron and discussed what their next move was to be.

"Somebody must ride south to bring word of our victory to the Pendraig," said Arthur. "If we can make it known that we now hold the fortress and the cauldron, perhaps we can end this war before it claims too many more lives."

"You should go, Arthur," said Cei. "It was your plan. This victory is your doing. My father will believe you." He glanced at the others. "We should remain here to hold this fortress against reprisal from the Gaels."

"I will accompany Arthur," Menw said. "It is

unfortunate that we cannot bring the cauldron with us but we shall have to somehow convince enemy and ally alike that this pointless war must end."

They ended their council and Arthur and Menw went down to the stables. The white foal that had followed them east had been admitted to the fortress and Arthur had seen him fed and stabled. He longed to ride him but knew the animal was still too young to be broken. *One day*, he told himself as he patted the foal's neck. *When all this is over we shall ride together, you and I.*

"Have you thought of giving him a name?" asked Menw, as he saddled a dun filly; almost as if he had read Arthur's thoughts.

"I had originally thought to call him Mabon," Arthur replied. "But after what Anna said to us, it just doesn't feel appropriate. I'm thinking of Hengroen instead."

Menw smiled. "A fine old name."

Hengroen it was and Arthur said farewell to him and saddled a chestnut gelding. Before the noon sun reached its zenith, they rode out of Cair Dugannu and galloped across open fields in the direction of the Pass of Kings.

Cadwallon

The spears flew overhead as the two lines met in the tightness of the pass. They whickered through the air and fell like a rain of vipers into the midst of Cadwallon's front ranks. Men fell screaming, transfixed by the dark shafts. And then, the lines met in an unholy rumble of thunder that echoed up the rocky crags on either side of the valley.

Cadwallon sat with the mounted reserves behind the centre of the teulu. Before him the spears of his assembled auxiliaries prickled the air and beyond their tips crackled the carnage of the front ranks. Owain sat with him along with the mounted riders of Rhos. King Mor commanded the right flank while King Efiaun led the left.

They had all followed his orders without question but he sorely missed Cunor's experience in commanding the teulu. He had learned battle strategy as any royal youth had done and had even led his own cavalry wing in the wars with the Gaels ten years previously but commanding an entire teulu was the job of a penteulu, not a king.

This battle had been thrust upon him before they were truly ready. They had reached the pass around noon of the day Meddyf had set out. They had made camp well within view of Meriaun's campfires and tents. Early the following morning, Cadwallon had been in his tent discussing battle lines with his commanders when the horns began to blow indicating movement in the enemy camp.

He had emerged to see Meriaun's lines advancing through the valley pass, thick with Gaels and bolstered on their left by Elnaw of Docmaeling's teulu, and on their right by the lords of the Laigin Peninsula.

Orders were given quickly to rouse the camp, send out the cavalry wings and cluster the auxiliaries in the centre of the valley to bear the brunt of the enemy's advance.

The pass was a narrow bottleneck and its steep and rocky sides forced the ranks together so they were short and deep. With no room to manoeuvre, it was all but impossible for the cavalry wings to curl around and outflank the enemy. It was equally impossible for Meriaun's host to outflank them and it promised to be a long and bloody battle of attrition.

As the chaos and calamity of war sounded all around him, Cadwallon desperately scanned the enemy ranks for signs of what he feared the most; the Cauldron-born. There appeared to be no woad-smeared skull-faces within the enemy host and Cadwallon allowed himself to breathe a sigh of relief. The battle could go either way but at least they would be facing men that could be killed.

He wondered if that meant Cei and his companions had succeeded in their quest. He supposed that if they had, they had in all probability given their lives in doing so. If they ever made it out of this valley alive, Cadwallon promised the gods that those brave seven would be given the highest of posthumous honours. He would do that much for Cunor, who had sent both his son and foster-son – *my own half-brother*, he remembered suddenly with a pang of guilt – on such a perilous quest.

Where are you, Cunor? We need you now!

After an hour of fighting, the brook that flowed through the valley became clogged with corpses, damming its red waters. It burst its banks and turned the green valley floor to a muddy, hellish mess.

"The right of our front line is thinning," Owain cautioned.

Cadwallon cursed and gave the order for King Mor to lead his cavalry forward. The auxiliaries parted to let them through. Mor led them in a charge that broke deep into the left flank of the enemy and Cadwallon smiled to see the raven banner wavering above the carnage well behind Meriaun's front lines.

A bellow of horns that sounded to their left told them that Meriaun was responding to the sudden attack and the many coloured banners of the Laigin commotes rushed forward, cutting a swathe through the front lines and slamming into King Efiaun's troops.

"Damn!" said Owain. "Our left wing is crumbling! Efiaun is being overwhelmed!"

"Draw them back!" said Cadwallon. "We cannot lose Efiaun!"

"If we pull them back we lose our left flank! And that might lose us the battle. Meriaun has all his spearmen ready to fill the gap and close in on us."

"Then we must support Efiaun," said Cadwallon, finding that his mouth had turned suddenly dry.

He gave the orders and the long aurochs horns bellowed out the signal for the mounted reserves to move out. Owain ordered his own troops to accompany the Pendraig and the dragon banner rippled as it was carried aloft by the standard bearer amidst the streaming manes and tails of horses and the plumed helms of their riders.

They swung left and crossed the stony brook which was treacherously deep now with its pinkish depths. Up ahead they could see Efiaun's force dwindling as the wavering banners of the Laigin commotes cut their bloody vengeance through his ranks.

"Venedotia!" bellowed Owain, sword raised as they thundered towards the havoc.

It was a cry taken up by many voices. Cadwallon screamed it too but his voice was lost in the tumultuous crash of two lines of cavalry meeting.

The hot, mad press of horses and warriors was intensely claustrophobic. The desperate hack and slash was superseded only by the burning desire to press forward, to claim ground at all cost.

But it was too hard. The enemy were too many. Even with the full brunt of the reserves, the teulu had only gained a few feet of bloody, trampled grass and now the enemy, recovered from the initial shock, were pushing forwards once more. Gaelic spearmen flanked the knot of horsemen and began to encircle them, stabbing at hamstrings and haunches.

"We'll all be slaughtered if we don't get out of this!" Owain cried to Cadwallon over the awful din.

"But if we retreat these dogs will harry us every step of the way!" Cadwallon replied. "We stand out ground! We hold this pass at all costs!"

What else was there to do? They had traipsed all over Venedotia and everything, every alliance, every skirmish had led them to this point, to this pass. If they lost it he would lose his crown and if they won it … he would win *everything*. There could be no retreat, no second chances. *No surrender.*

There was some great disturbance further along the line. Mounted warriors were charging the enemy, pushing through Cadwallon's auxiliaries from the rear to get at the Gaels. Cadwallon craned his head to see, and whooped with joy when he saw the banners of Eternion wavering above the newly arrived host.

"Eternion is with us!" he cried to Owain. "Our uncle has sent his teulu!"

The men voiced their elation despite the desperation of their situation. The enemy pressed hard against them, hemming them in on three sides, but help had arrived!

Meriaun's front lines fell back, driven apart by the wedge of Eternion's cavalry. The pressure on Cadwallon's left wing loosened considerably as the Laigin bannermen found themselves exposed to newly arrived and fresh horsemen. Their nerve began to crumble and, banner by banner, they retreated from the battle.

"Do we push on?" Owain called to Cadwallon.

"No!" Cadwallon replied. "They have given us a window through which we can escape! Fall back! Retreat to the brook so that we may regroup!"

They turned their mounts and, stepping over the bodies of the fallen, headed back to the flooded brook. The auxiliaries, weary, wounded and severely reduced, fell in behind the retreating cavalry. Cadwallon turned in his saddle to make sure the enemy had not wheeled about and was following on their heels. They were not. The sun was sinking. The valley was clogged with the dead and everybody had had enough.

Cadwallon spurred his horse into a gallop and found Cunor in the mass of Eternion's horsemen. "Once again you come in the nick of time!" he cried. "And more welcome than you can ever know!"

Cunor scanned the carnage of the valley. "Are you taking over my job, my lord?"

"You can have it! If this battle has taught me anything it is that kings appoint penteulus for a reason. Still, I did not do too badly I hope? In the face of such odds? They came upon us by surprise and I was forced to act."

"I'm glad to hear it was not a battle of your choosing, lord. I was worried you had tried charge the enemy camp without me!"

"There is still plenty more to be done, old friend! Meriaun waits beneath his standard while his forces regroup and plan their next assault. And that is what we must do. But tell me, Cunor, where is my wife?"

Cunor led Cadwallon back to camp where Meddyf awaited astride her mare. She had never looked so beautiful to Cadwallon's eyes. They both dismounted and embraced. Even when they kissed, she did not shrink from his bloodied armour.

"You did it, my love," he told her. "You brought us the help we so desperately needed and not a moment too soon!"

"Etern took some convincing but we have reached an agreement," Meddyf said.

"I'm blessed to have such a wiley negotiator for a wife!"

"His loyalty was not bought cheaply."

She was holding something back, he could tell. "What is it?"

"Maelcon must marry one of Etern's daughters. It was the only way."

Cadwallon was silent for a while. This was unexpected, and a bitter draught to swallow. That he should have to buy his uncle's support like this! "Fine," he said. "If that is what it took. You did well."

"The battle?"

"Inconclusive. The arrival of Cunor broke their impending victory and they have retreated for now, as have we. We are at least now, evenly matched. It could become a nasty stalemate."

"The Cauldron-born?"

"No sign of them."

"Then Cei …"

"Must have succeeded. That is one victory, at least. We must pray for another."

Arthur

As they crested the small rise on the grassy cape of the Heaps, Arthur and Menw were afforded a view of the carnage in the valley pass below them. If there had been any battle lines drawn then they had long since disintegrated into chaos. Knots of horsemen rode back and forth, cutting down fleeing footmen. Sheildmen clustered together and drove off riders with their spears. The valley was littered with the corpses of the slain. If there had been any victory won that day then it had been a costly one.

Arthur could pick out many standards he recognised but all seemed to be fleeing, regrouping and retreating. He could see two camps; one directly below them which he assumed to be Meriaun's as it held the northern section of the pass. In the distance he could pick out the white tents of another camp, smaller and vulnerable in the shadows of the rocky peaks. That had to be Cadwallon's camp. He could see many banners fleeing towards it.

"We're too late," he said. "The battle is over."

"If that is true then who are the victors?" Menw asked him.

Arthur had no clue. The whole thing looked to be a shambles. "How do we get to Cadwallon without passing through that hell?"

"We don't," Menw said. "We must go through it."

"Merion's warriors will peg us for exactly who we are. The Gaels too."

"Not if we use out wits," the bard replied.

The sun's dying flare caught the mountain peaks and stretched their shadows against the cliffs behind them as they descended into the valley and turned south. The stink of blood, iron and opened bowels hit them like a wall as they reached the valley floor. The flies and ravens had not yet begun to feast but it was only a matter of time. Up ahead, Arthur could see that the valley bottom was flooded, turned almost marshy by the swollen brook. Bodies floated in the distance.

They plodded on, keeping their eyes ahead as a group of riders splashed past. Arthur forced himself not to make eye-contact. He focused on their goal; the cluster of tents in the hazy distance. Close, yet deceptively so, for hundreds of obstacles lay in their way.

"Hold!" bellowed a voice behind them and Arthur squeezed his eyes shut in frustration. The riders had wheeled around to inspect the youth and the old man closer. "You two," said their leader; a swarthy man of middling years in a round, dented helm. "What company are you from?"

"King Elnaw's company, friend," said Menw. "And yourselves?"

"King Meriaun's companions," the warrior replied. He peered at Menw. "You're a little long in the tooth for this game, aren't you?"

"I am a healer," Menw replied. He nodded at Arthur. "This lad is my apprentice and bodyguard. We marched with the rest of Elnaw's teulu but were delayed en route. One of the king's bannermen had a nasty fall and I was ordered to remain and tend to him. Now, here we arrive at the battle with our work cut out for us."

"What's in the bag?" the warrior asked, gesturing to the leather sack Menw carried on his saddle behind him. He had stripped himself of all identifying marks of his bardic order before they had set out from Cair Dugannu, including his crane-skin bag, replacing it with a crude leather sack. "My healing herbs, my knives and my tools," he replied.

"You're in luck," said the warrior, "or some poor buggers are, I should say. "We've a score wounded we dragged from the front lines across the valley here. They sorely need your skills after Etern's cavalry trampled and hacked their way through them, damn the traitorous bastard to hell!"

"Etern?" Menw asked. "He has switched sides?"

"Aye, he was supposed to close the trap behind Cadwallon's teulu once it had entered the valley but some devilish bargaining has been going on. His cavalry charged in at the last moment and shattered our lines. It all fell apart after that. Come, we'll escort you."

Arthur glanced at Menw, knowing that they had no choice but to follow the warriors in the opposite direction to Cadwallon's camp. It had been some quick thinking on Menw's part that had saved their necks but he ground his teeth in frustration all the same.

They were led to a makeshift camp on a high bit of ground. Several footmen had been stripping the dead of arms and armour and were piling them up. Nearby, several wounded were lying on the mud, cloaks bundled up under their heads. The warriors dismounted and the chief of them led Menw and Arthur over to the injured men.

"Do what you can for them, Healer," he said. "If there is no hope then just give the word and I'll make a merciful end of it." He tapped the knife at his belt.

"As you say," said Menw, approaching the row of moaning wretches.

"Don't you need your bag of tricks?" the warrior asked.

"Ah, yes," said Menw. He turned to Arthur. "Run and fetch it for me lad, eh?"

Arthur tried to read the expression in the eyes of the old bard but could not fathom it. He turned and walked over to their horses. He heard Menw talking to one of the wounded, trying to soothe him and take his mind off the pain.

"The gods must look favourably upon me," said the stricken man, between gasps of pain. "That they send King Enniaun's old bard to tend to me!"

"What was that?" the warrior demanded. "Enniaun's bard?"

"The poor wretch is raving," said Menw.

"I saw you once before," the wounded man went on. "At Cair Dugannu when I was a lad. It was Samhain and you played your harp in honour of the dead."

"Still your tongue," said Menw, "lest someone has need to honour you before the day is out. You need rest."

"I've a mind he speaks the truth," said the warrior. "And I'm not sure I trust an old man and his 'bodyguard' wandering the battlefield on horses so fine they could only have come from a king's stables. Just where were you two going when we crossed your path?"

Arthur had laid his hands on the leather sack that was tied to the saddle of Menw's horse and was watching the exchange, his heart hammering in his chest. The seasoned warrior turned slowly to look in his direction.

"What's in the bag, lad?"

Menw suddenly cried out; "Flee, Arthur! Ride now and don't look back!"

"Stop him!" the warrior barked, but Arthur had already heaved himself up into the saddle.

Another of Meriaun's men lunged forward to seize the animal's reins and was rewarded by the heel of Arthur's boot connecting with his face that sent him reeling backwards.

Arthur kicked his mount into a gallop. He hated to leave Menw behind in the hands of the enemy but this was his only chance to reach Cadwallon. He could hear enraged shouting behind him and a spear whickered overhead to land in the mud a few feet wide of his frightened horse's hooves.

On he galloped, splashing through mud and water, leaping bodies and skirting the deepest parts of the flooded valley. He was vaguely aware of footmen running and shouting although if they were running and shouting at him he had no idea. The battle still seemed to be going on in parts of the valley and he wished to avoid engaging at all costs.

The cluster of white tents grew closer and the simple defences of the camp became apparent; spiked barricades and flooded ditches for the most part. He reined his horse in within a few yards of a cluster of mounted warriors. They turned in surprise at his approach and urged their horses to surround him. He suddenly found spearpoints directed at him from all sides.

"I am Arthur mab Eigyr of Cair Cunor!" he cried. "I am loyal to King Cadwallon the true Pendraig!"

"Easily said," said one of the riders. "Not so easily proved!"

"Where is Lord Cunor?" Arthur demanded. "He is my foster-father!"

"Aye, he's right," said another of the riders. "I know him from the training yard at Cair Cunor. "It's the penteulu's foster-son, no mistake."

They lowered their spears and began to ply him with questions. Arthur refused to answer any of them until he was taken to Cunor. They eventually gave up and he was escorted into camp.

Upon spotting him, Cunor strode forward to greet his foster-son in a mighty bear hug. Arthur was startled at this for Cunor had rarely shown him or Cei much affection. "You have survived, lad!" the big man said. "But Cei—?"

"Alive," Arthur said. "He is at Cair Dugannu."

Cunor's brow creased. "Captured?"

"No and that is what has led me here in the most urgent haste. Cair Dugannu is ours. Cei holds it for the Pendraig."

Cunor was lost for words. "But how …" he managed at last.

"I had better explain to the king," said Arthur. "We have little time."

Cadwallon was found in his tent receiving reports from his captains of their losses. His face was grave and he held his head in his hands. He looked so very tired. His queen, Meddyf, was by his side and Arthur was surprised to see her in camp with the enemy so close. King Mor was there too, as well as Owain, and another man in fine armour whom Arthur could only assume was one of the other kings Cadwallon had drawn to his cause.

Cunor dragged Arthur before them all and Cadwallon looked up in surprise as if suddenly remembering something that had slipped his mind.

"My foster-son, Arthur is here, my lords," said Cunor. "And he has news from the north."

Wine was brought and Arthur drank gratefully as he related his tale to the assembled lords. Not one of them interrupted him as he told all from their arrival on the shores of Ynys Mon and the wounding of Gualchmei to their desperate flight to the ruined Lys and their plan to steal the cauldron from the Morgens. At last he got to their daring attack on Cair Dugannu and the slaying of Diugurnach.

When he was finished, a silence hung heavy within the tent. He drained his cup of wine and sat back in his chair, more exhausted than he had felt since they had set out. It was done. The message was delivered and the fate of the war was out of his hands. He felt somehow unburdened now.

"Arthur," said Cadwallon slowly. "You and your companions have surpassed all our expectations. In truth, we thought you had all been slaughtered by the Gaels and my conscience has ravaged me for sending you on that desperate mission instead of keeping you with the teulu. But my mind is now set at peace by your sudden appearance here, on the edge of all ruin."

"All is not lost, my lord," said Arthur. "The battle may yet be won …"

"We are, at best, evenly matched," said Cadwallon. "It could go either way—"

"Not if we fight with our wits as well as our numbers," Arthur interrupted, trying to echo the sage words Menw had given no more than a couple of hours previously. How he wished the old bard was here now! He could explain things to Cadwallon so much better than he could. Yet, he had to try. "The cauldron is yours. Use it to your advantage, lord."

"How, when it sits at Cair Dugannu?"

"Meriaun expected to make use of it in this battle. Its absence today will have been sorely missed. Let him know that it is no longer in his possession and neither is Cair Dugannu. Let all your enemies know."

"Deal a blow to their spirits before we deal a blow of arms, eh?" said Cunor. "The lad speaks sense, lord. You could call Meriaun to discuss terms. Even if none are reached, he will walk away knowing that a sore defeat has been inflicted on him already."

"He may claim we are bluffing," said Cadwallon uncertainly.

"No doubt he will, lord," said Arthur. "And that is why we have brought proof."

"Proof? Of what sort?"

Arthur reached down for the leather bag he had brought from Menw's horse. It had been resting against his calf until now. He lifted it up and placed it upon the table before the king.

"What is this?" All heads leaned in to inspect the object.

Arthur opened the bag and drew it down to reveal the object inside.

When the meeting adjourned Arthur was told to go and get some food and some rest. He relished both eagerly for it had been a long day in the saddle. As the assembly began to drift away, Queen Meddyf caught his arm in passing.

"My lady?"

"Tomorrow morning, I ride for Din Emrys where our people have taken refuge," she said. "I shall give your mother news of you."

"Thank you, my lady," he replied.

"She has missed you dearly but never gave up hope of your return. I am ashamed to say that she was the only one. But you proved us all wrong. Thank you, Arthur. Thank you for bringing us hope."

Darkness had fallen but still the camp hummed with activity. Defences were being reinforced, food prepared for the hungry and weary warriors and the screams from the wounded reminded everybody that sleep was a privilege afforded to only the very few.

Arthur was given a pallet to rest on and, after eating his fill of mutton stew, coarse bread and weak ale, he slept the sleep of the dead until dawn.

He awoke to find the camp already roused. Messengers had been sent to Meriaun to call him and his allies to parley. A request had also been sent to return Menw to Cadwallon. Arthur was pleased to hear this for he was greatly concerned for the bard's safety.

A tent was pitched beyond Cadwallon's defences but out of bowshot from Meriaun's. The brook had been cleared of bodies during the night and the valley had drained itself once more. The assembled lords and kings prepared to ride out to discuss Venedotia's fate. Arthur was surprised to learn that he was to join them, and rode his newly brushed and fed mare alongside his half-brothers.

King Meriaun was a strong-looking man in his fifties with black hair cropped close at the sides where it had begun to turn to grey. A scar marred his right cheek and people said it had been given to him by Beli mac Benlli; the Gaelic chieftain he had slain at the young age of eighteen.

Meriaun's face was unreadable as he watched his cousins take their seats opposite him. On either side of him sat his allies. King Elnaw of Docmaeling and some Gaelic captain sat on his left side, the assembled lords of the Laigin Peninsula on his right. Arthur glanced sidelong at his half-brothers. Owain's face was beet-red and simmering while Cadwallon's remained impassive, matching Meriaun's in aloofness as each eyed their own rival for the throne.

"Before we start," Meriaun began. "I have something of yours."

Two of Meriaun's warriors entered the tent, accompanying a man in his middle years. Arthur nearly leapt up from his seat when he saw that it was Menw. The old bard did not appear to have been mistreated and Arthur supressed a sigh of relief.

"Your father's precious bard will remain by my side until we are done talking," said Meriaun. "Think of him as an extra insurance against any of your trickery."

"*My* trickery?" Cadwallon demanded. "That is fine talk for one whose boundless treachery has all but torn Venedotia limb from limb."

"I am not the rebel here, Cadwallon," said

Meriaun. "You were given your chance to surrender peacefully. As for your allies, well, I can hardly blame them for backing what they must have believed was the winning horse, and I should state now that they will face no repercussions for their poor judgement should they chose to distance themselves from you now. But *you* Cadwallon. It was your pride and stubbornness that caused this war."

"You dare to lay the blame at my door?" Cadwallon seethed. "I am Enniaun Yrth's son! I am the rightful Pendraig, the next in line of succession of Cunedag's dynasty …"

"Did you know our illustrious grandfather?" Meriaun interrupted. "I did and I can tell you that Cunedag was a cut and grab man, a brutal, thieving, reaver who respected only raw strength and the will to take what is desired. Why else do you think Lord Vertigernus sent him to re-conquer Venedotia from the Gaels all those years ago? He was a barbarian chieftain and little more. This dynasty, the *line of succession* people so wistfully proclaim is nothing more than an accident of circumstance. Old Cunedag would have laughed to hear you wail about your birth right as if that is all it takes to be a king. He recognised no such thing as blood succession! If he ever felt that one of his offspring was ever worthy enough to inherit his kingdom, then it would have been because he took it for himself and damned his rivals!"

"Albion has moved on from the days of bloody chieftains stealing from each other and slaying their rivals," said Menw. "Your talk is of the ways of our enemies; the Saeson, the Gaels and the Picts. These are no longer the ways of the Britons."

"Who do you think you are fooling, old man?" Meriaun snapped. "That feeble cowardice is the reason Albion is in the state it is. There are no strong chieftains left. There are none willing to do what it takes to rule."

"Except you, presumably," said Cadwallon.

"Aye, except me," said Meriaun.

"You've had your say," said Cadwallon as he leant forward in his chair. "Now I shall have mine. You've already been defeated by something you underestimated. You sought to rule through fear and so you concocted your little arrangement with the Morgens. But you didn't count on the stout hearts of my followers. They have exposed your lies and the charlatanism of the Nine Sisters. You were expecting your secret lover to arrive with a gift that would whip your followers up into a frenzy, didn't you? It must have been disappointing when it never arrived."

"My high-priestess has been waylaid by some obstacle, it is true," said Meriaun. "Perhaps it was the doing of whatever little band you sent to Ynys Mon to disrupt things. But it hardly matters. I have already won. The odds may have been evened somewhat due to Etern's treachery but it won't do you any good. Even if you were to break through my lines, you would still have to face my mercenaries at Cair Dugannu. I have won, Cadwallon. You should do your followers a mercy by admitting it."

Cadwallon grinned. He motioned to Owain and the leather sack was produced. Owain reached in and drew out the head of Diugurnach by the hair.

The blood drained from Meriaun's face although he held his composure well. His Gaelic captain was not so restrained. He cursed aloud and looked like he wanted to punch something. Arthur wondered if Diugurnach had been a well-liked chieftain.

"Cair Dugannu is mine," said Cadwallon. "As is the cauldron and your would-be-queen. Diugurnach is dead as will many more of your followers be if you continue to resist me."

"How?" stumbled Meriaun, his voice choked with rage and disbelief. "No army could have passed my lines and taken Cair Dugannu. What allies have you that I have not checked?"

"As I said, Meriaun. You have already been defeated by that which you did not credit. You can't win. You are trapped here in this valley. I will force you against the walls of Cair Dugannu or into the straits if I must, but I urge you to accept my offer of surrender now."

Meriaun flew up in a rage. "This puffed up bravado is irrelevant! You may have slain Diugurnach, but if you think you have won this war then you are wrong by a great measure! I withdraw my offer of mercy. You and your followers will die today in this valley!"

He turned and stormed out of the tent. His Gaelic captain, still enraged by the grisly trophy, followed him out and then, Elnaw and the lords of the Laigin Peninsula rose, slowly and stiffly, their faces grave and uncertain. They left and Menw stood by, forgotten by his captors.

Cadwallon smiled. "Well, my lords," he said. "I think that did the trick."

"He will be preparing to throw everything he's got at us," Cunor warned.

"I know. And we must be ready. Come, let us ride back to our lines with all haste."

They rose and Cadwallon embraced Menw. "Welcome back, old friend. You did it!"

"Arthur did it," said Menw. "It was he who rode through enemy lines and carried his message to you."

"I'm sorry for leaving you, Menw," said Arthur.

The bard waved his apology aside. "It was necessary. Besides, Meriaun's fools would not dare mistreat a bard. And my time in their company gave me plenty of opportunity to spread a few rumours!" He gave a conspiratorial wink.

"What sort of rumours?" Arthur enquired.

"Oh, just that the Morgens have turned their back on Meriaun, the gods are displeased, that sort of thing. Especially effective as the promised cauldron never arrived. Even the Christians among them ate it up. Did you see Meriaun's face when Owain held up Diugurnach's head?"

"I thought he was going to shit himself," said Arthur with a laugh.

"Instead of a cauldron, he receives the head of his ally and news that his plans are scuppered. By now that tale will be making the rounds of his camp. I tell you, Arthur, symbols are more powerful than spears!"

Cadwallon and his lords lost no time in whipping the camp into battle lines. Spear and bowmen hurried past Arthur to fill the centre of the valley while horses and their riders trotted to the left and right wings to converge under various standards. Cunor had left Arthur and Menw to discuss tactics with Cadwallon but he was soon back, strapping on his war helm.

"You are to ride under Owain's standard, Arthur,"

he told him. "He is leading the left flank along with King Mor. You will be in good company."

"Thank you, sir," Arthur replied, feeling a chill of excitement mingled with fear in his breast. He realised Cadwallon would need every man to win but it had only just struck him that he would be riding into battle for the very first time. He had been training for this moment for as long as he could remember but now that it was here, he found that he both dreaded and eagerly anticipated it in equal measure.

"May Modron continue to smile on you, lad," said Menw, as Arthur climbed up into his saddle.

"Thank you, Menw. Stay safe."

He rode off to join the gathering cavalry on the teulu's left wing. When he got there, Owain bellowed his name and all the riders repeated it with gusto; a rousing salute for the man who had dealt such a stinging blow to the enemy's morale. Arthur felt his face flush with embarrassment.

Somebody handed him a helm and he strapped it on before a spear and shield were thrust into his hands.

"Stick close to me and my house guard, Arthur," said Owain with a friendly smile. "I know it's your first battle but your foster-father would have my hide if you tried to be a hero and got yourself killed under my standard."

The enemy lines could be seen marshalling at the other end of the valley. Before they had completed their manoeuvres, the horns by the fluttering dragon standard blew for the infantry to march forward. It was a slow, steady march and was seen by the enemy who doubled their efforts to get into their formations.

"It looks like Elnaw is commanding the left flank," Owain said. "We await my brother's signal to charge them."

Arthur swallowed. Things were moving too fast. Over the past few days he had got used to surviving danger by hiding, fleeing and evading. Now he was part of an unstoppable force heading towards an immovable object, and for the first time he felt the terror of the lowly soldier of the ranks, his fate tied to the fate of the teulu.

"That's it!" cried Owain at the blast of a horn. "Move out! Hit them hard and hit them true!"

The cavalry started to move around Arthur, and without thinking, he kicked his mount on to keep pace with them. It was one jostling mass of trembling flanks, nervous coughs, chomping bits, sweat and saliva. Man and horse were one, united in their desperate hope to survive the next few hours.

The two lines of infantry thundered together and, as the spears began to fly overhead, Owain bellowed; "Charge! Don't let the bastards outflank our infantry!"

The hoofbeat drummed on the earth like a deafening pulse. Through the helmed heads and horse-hair plumes ahead of him, Arthur could see King Elnaw's cavalry charging at them, head on, spears lowered. He couldn't move as he and his horse felt all but carried between the flanks of his neighbours. He began to panic. *We're too tight! We have to loosen up!*

But such were the tactics of the Bear of Rhos; hit them hard and compact like the blow of a hammer.

And they did hit them hard. The shock of it was

like a punch in the face to Arthur though he was several riders behind the front line. The wave of impact rippled through the entire wing, shoving horses back, causing them to whinny and rear up. Enemy spears thrust outwards, scraping helms and shields, piercing the necks and faces of the unfortunate.

Arthur batted aside a spear with his own and stabbed over the shoulder of the rider in front of him. He was rewarded by a cry and a spurt of hot blood that ran down his spear shaft and cooled on his whitened knuckles.

Owain, mad fighter that he was, pushed deeper and deeper into the enemy ranks; his spear broken or lost, swinging his great sword at any enemy head within reach. Arthur did his best to stay with him but the hot, sweltering press of horse and man was too hard for him to break through. Owain had many loyal riders intent on keeping their lord alive.

A rider on a small, fast horse slipped in beside Arthur and called out Owain's name but to no avail. Arthur recognised his light armour as that of a scout. "What news?" he cried.

"Meriaun's reserves are unguarded!" the scout shouted. "We can come upon their right flank if we can only disengage from this madness!"

Arthur took up the scout's job and forced his mount through the press of horses. "Owain!" he yelled. "Owain!"

He saw his half-brother's helmed head turn around.

"News from your scouts! Meriaun is vulnerable!"

Owain wheeled his mount around and two of his

riders filled the gap he left in the front line as he pushed his way towards Arthur. "What is this?" he demanded.

"Meriaun sits with the Laigin lords," the scout shouted over the din. "There is room for us to outflank them!"

"Lead the way!" Owain bellowed. Then he shouted orders to those in the rear of his cavalry to follow him.

The left wing split in two, half remaining to hold Elnaw's warriors and half following Owain and his scout in a mad dash up the sides of the valley. Several of Elnaw's riders spotted them and followed in hot pursuit. They took a wide curve up the valley wall and down again, bypassing the battle and slipping through the narrow gap Meriaun had left unguarded.

"Venedotia!" bellowed Owain, his bloody sword thrust outwards.

His cry was heard by those on the valley plain and the banners of the Laigin lords wavered as if trembling at the sudden and unexpected attack.

"Venedotia!" cried Arthur, joining the chorus issued forth from the throats of the charging cavalry.

This time there was no buffer of front lines to insulate the blow and Arthur found himself thrust deep into the enemy ranks. He stabbed at somebody's neck but only nicked it as the man reeled in his saddle, blood gushing down his mail.

Arthur was entirely trapped, hemmed in by mounted riders on all sides and, strangely, the realisation that there was nothing he could do about it banished his fear. He might die in the mud that day but powers greater than him – either Modron or the

Christian god – had already decided that. There was no running, only fighting, and all he had to do was fight on as hard and for as long as he could. That knowledge was a blissful and unexpected release.

He could see Meriaun's standard only yards away from him and the smell of victory urged him to fight harder, move faster and dig deeper into the enemy. The war was at its end. Vengeance and victory were in sight.

His arms grew weary with killing, his helm was dented by the blow of a sword and the blood of his enemies had washed his shield red with gore. The first he knew of their victory was the shouts of his comrades who were further back and on slightly higher ground.

"They flee!" Owain's riders cried. "Meriaun stands alone!"

Arthur rose in his saddle and, beyond the heads of Meriaun's reserves, he could see the banners of the Laigin commotes being borne away from the battle, carried north up the valley. They had given up and abandoned their false king.

Behind them the main battle had drawn to a close. The Gaels, their confidence surely broken by the news of the death of their great chieftain, had been all but slaughtered by the right flank led by Efiaun and Cunor, while the enemy infantry had been routed by Cadwallon's advancing lines. It was over.

Arthur didn't see who it was who hauled Meriaun from his horse and struck down his standard but Owain later claimed the feat for himself. The men were elated and their cries of victory resounded in the valley all the louder as if trying to dispel the awful sounds of slaughter that had reigned only moments before.

"You fought well, lad," Owain said to Arthur, as they rode back towards the rear of the ranks. "I don't doubt my brother will find a position of great responsibility in the teulu for you."

Meriaun was dragged before Cadwallon who dismissed him out of hand. No words were necessary between the two cousins. They had both already spoken their piece. The traitor was bound and secured along with all the other lords who had surrendered.

They rode immediately for Cair Dugannu, leaving the corpse-strewn valley and the wagon train of equipment and prisoners to trail in their wake. As they reached the coast, Arthur breathed the sea air deeply, letting it cleanse his lungs after the foulness of the battle in the pass. Gulls cawed overhead and his heart soared with them, knowing that soon he would be reunited with his comrades – *and Guenhuifar* – and that the war would finally, truly be over.

As the twin hills of Cair Dugannu came into sight, Arthur could see a crude pennant fluttering from the palisades. It was red and had the image of a dragon stitched on it. Cadwallon beamed when he saw it.

The gates were opened and there was much cheering from the teulu as it clattered into the courtyard. Cei and the others descended from the walls to greet the returning king. Even Beduir was there, his maimed arm in a blood-spotted sling. He looked much better and Arthur was ecstatic to see him on his feet.

Guenhuifar stood by him and she smiled at

Arthur. He found that he ached to take her in his arms.

"Can a king ask for better followers?" Cadwallon said.

"Or a father for better sons?" Cunor added, as he embraced Cei and Arthur together in a rare but powerful bear hug.

"Let the whole land know that the Pendraig has returned to Cair Dugannu!" said King Mor.

There was a cheer and Cadwallon then approached Cei, his face suddenly serious. "Now then," he said. "It is time you introduced me to my sister. Where is the damned hell-cat?"

Cei's face grew suddenly red as if from embarrassment. "Well, as to that," he stammered. "There have been developments …"

"What happened?" Arthur demanded.

"She escaped, put simply," said Cei.

"Escaped?" Arthur cried. "But how?"

"Look at us, Arthur!" Cei replied. "We are six. Six to hold a fortress! She somehow slipped out of the pantry we had secured her in. None of the other prisoners escaped. Gualchmei was patrolling the walls and he saw her fleeing down the slopes towards the straits."

"Towards the straits?" Menw enquired. "What time of day was this?"

"Just before the tide came in," said Beduir. "If she tried to cross, I don't see how she could have outrun the high water."

"Nor I," replied Menw. "You are sure she attempted to cross?"

"After Gualchmei roused us we rode out and all

but caught up with her at the Lafan Sands," said Cei. "We saw her cross but … well, the tide and …"

"And you did not dare follow in her footsteps," finished Cadwallon. "For that you are not to be blamed. She must have been desperate to escape my justice and preferred to take her chances with Manawydan rather than remain on the mainland. Well, she is probably dead."

"It seems so," said Menw. "Even her sorcery is no match for Manawydan's indominatable whim."

"A shame," said Cadwallon, "that I never got the chance to ask her why; why she hated me with such a passion. But I suppose we will never know."

Arthur felt that he had an inkling as to the cause of their sister's rage but he kept his thoughts to himself.

The following morning the wagon train of supplies, prisoners and the wounded arrived, shortly followed by the women and children from Din Emrys. The effect of their presence suddenly made the fortress shine as if all the death and killing done in the earning of it was just a memory. Things almost felt as if they were back to normal.

Arthur's mother wept to see him and must have kissed him a dozen times over, which embarrassed him no end in front of all the warriors who now held him in such high esteem. "You have placed your foot on the pathway to your true place in the world, my son," she told him. "I am so very proud of you. And your brothers …?"

"They honour me," he said, allowing her to kiss him once more in her sudden increase of pride. "They call me Arthur mab Enniaun now."

She smiled at this.

"And I am to be given a command in the teulu. Cei too."

"What have I always said? You are the true son of a Pendraig. And now you have shown them all!"

Preparations began in earnest for Cadwallon's coronation feast. Regular hunting parties set out to procure fresh meat for Cair Dugannu's stores and Arthur occasionally joined them. Afterwards he would see to Hengroen in his stall and comb his fine mane, wishing the day would come when he could begin the process of breaking him.

It was on one of these occasions that he bade farewell to Guenhuifar who was setting out with a couple of escorts who would ferry her to Ynys Mon.

"You will be back for the coronation feast?" he asked her.

"I should think so," she replied. "My family too. Cadwallon has invited us all."

"You don't seem very enthusiastic."

She sighed. "It's hard. I have spent all my life hating the kings of Venedotia. We have always been alone, my family and I, isolated and forgotten. Now we are to be honoured at the coronation of the next Pendraig. It takes some getting used to."

"Things will improve for Ynys Mon under Cadwallon's reign," he promised her. "He has already spoken of ridding the island of the Gaels. It won't be too long before we will be back and asking your father to open up the king's mead again to celebrate another victory."

She gave him a half smile. "I hear what you say and my father will be only too happy with the news. Personally I just hope this isn't all some dream I might awake from. It doesn't feel real."

"I know. Everything has changed so fast. A few days ago we were on the run, hunted and starving. Now we are the toast of the seven kingdoms. And now you must go."

"And now I must go," she echoed.

"Guenhuifar …" he said, struggling for the words. "Tell me … tell me it wasn't just me?"

"What wasn't just you?"

"Well, I know it sounds silly, as we were in such danger and all, but … I felt *happy*. I don't know why but even though the Gaels were after us and we were cold and always on the move, I honestly felt *happy*. I think it was because I was in the company of my friends. And I was in your company …"

She smiled.

"You saved my life, Guenhuifar. You came to rescue me from the lair of the Morgens, so I suppose that has something to do with it, but I can't help but feel that … well … perhaps you felt somehow the same as me …"

"Arthur," she said, placing her hand on his chest to still his voice. "It wasn't just you." She leant in to kiss him on the mouth.

It was a small kiss, a kiss of companionship but it set Arthur's heart aflame. After their lips had parted she gazed at him and he wished he could read what was behind those green eyes. Then she was gone, leading her horse out to join her escorts in the yard. She smiled at him over her shoulder as they rode out of the western gate and he hoped the days until their next meeting would pass quickly.

Cadwallon would not allow himself to be crowned

until the unpleasant business of justice had been carried out. Meriaun was given a summary trial in which he was found guilty of treason. No allies came to his defence. On the morning before the coronation, he was taken out of the fortress to a stone on the coast and made to kneel with his head upon it. Then, one of Cadwallon's burliest warriors hacked off his head.

The lords of the Laigin Peninsula were allowed to keep their lands but the borders of Dunauding were extended to cover the worst of the offenders. Efiaun was given direct charge of keeping them under control. Meriaun's son, Cadwaldr, succeeded his father as king but, with a decimated teulu, few doubted that Meriauned would pose much of a threat in the years to come. That just left Elnaw of Docmaeling. Cadwallon insisted on his abdication in favour of his son, Condruin; an ineffectual youth who would only ever be a puppet of Cadwallon's to ensure that Docmaeling never rose up against the Pendraig again.

Both Cadwaldr and Condruin were summoned to Cair Dugannu for the coronation. They grudgingly attended and the Great Hall was filled nearly to bursting. True to tradition, it was a bard who officiated and, once Menw had placed the gold diadem upon the new king's head, Cadwallon was carried around the hall on a shield by four of his warriors. All six sub-kings of Venedotia, new and old, kissed his sword as a token of their loyalty.

As his first oath to his subjects, King Cadwallon promised to mount an invasion of Ynys Mon and rid it of the Gaels once and for all. Cunedag's Lys was to be rebuilt and Gogfran would resume his duties as the Pendraig's steward. The island was to become a part of Venedotia once more.

Arthur glanced at Guenhuifar who stood on the other side of the hall next to her tearful father. She looked resplendent in a dress of white with her fiery hair combed and plaited. He smiled at her and she returned it, a flush of colour showing on her neck.

After the final shout of 'Long live the Pendraig', the hall set to with the feasting.

It was after dark that Cunor approached the king and told him of the visitors at their gate. Cadwallon rose and gave the order for the western gate to be opened to them. The look on his face told the hall that he had received some grave news and, when he left, all followed him out into the courtyard to see what was amiss.

Eight figures in white robes entered Cair Dugannu. They looked like spectres but Arthur recognised them instantly although their appearance was much changed. Aside from the white garments, their faces glistened in the torchlight with the pale cosmetic they had slathered over their visages. There were no black skull-like circles around their eyes this time, Their faces were of the purest white as if they had been bathed in milk.

"Damned cheek turning up here like this," said Owain. "Have them cast in irons, Brother!"

"No," said Cadwallon, as he approached them. "That there are only eight of you and that you have come of your own free will tells me that you seek peace rather than mischief," he told the Morgens.

"The wheel has turned," said one of them.

"Modron has been reborn."

"And my half-sister? What of her ill deeds?"

"The Morgen called Anna is no more. We followed her until Modron's plan had walked its path. Now we must choose a new high-priestess. Just as Venedotia has a new Pendraig and Venedotia begins a new era. Long live the Pendraig!"

"What assurances do I have that you will not seek to undermine me as you did before I wore this crown?" Cadwallon said, tapping his gold diadem with his finger.

"You are where Modron has placed you," came the reply. "As is everybody. Accept our blessings and the blessings of the Great Mother."

And with that, the eight priestesses left through the gate and headed down to the river.

"I don't trust them," said Owain. "Not one bit."

"You would be mad to," said Menw. "It would be as wise to trust the tides, the wind and fate itself. They have said what they came to say."

"Are they my enemies, Menw?" Cadwallon asked.

"They walk a path known only to them," the bard replied. "Punish them if you will but as they said, the wheel has turned, the goddess is reborn and we find ourselves at the beginning of a new era. Perhaps it would be wise to seek no more answers than that."

As they filed back into the hall to continue the feasting, Arthur spotted his mother waiting for him by the stairs to the royal apartments. She was holding a long object bound in an oiled cloth.

"Mother?" he asked. "Do you tire from the feasting?"

"Feasts no longer bring me much joy," she replied.

"Once upon a time they did, when I was loved by a king. But these days I would rather take to my bed. I leave on the morrow. Back to Cair Cunor. I have no relish for life at court and I pine for my own chambers and my tapestries. This is your world now, Arthur. But always remember that I will be waiting for you at Cair Cunor."

"What's that you've got there?"

"This? A gift. From a mother to her son."

She handed it to him so he unwrapped it. It was a spear; an old one, but a good one with plenty of strength still in its shaft.

"Now you are a man," Eigyr said, her eyes moist with tears. "Accept this as a token of my love for you as you take your place beside your brothers."

Arthur choked down the lump in his throat and embraced her. "Thank you, Mother. This means more to me than you know."

"Be safe, my son," she said. She nodded in the direction of the open doors to the Great Hall. Music and laughter spilled out from the warmth within. "Go and be with your companions. But come home to me one day. Promise?"

"Promise," he said, a tear suddenly spilling down his cheek.

He watched her climb the stairs to the upper chambers and then he turned and walked towards the Great Hall. He could hear Cei's voice roaring out a song of battle and the voices of the others – Beduir, Gualchmei and many more – joining in. He checked his spear at the gate and crossed the threshold to join his companions.

Venedotia would know several years of peace

under King Cadwallon's reign, and in its rocky hills and grassy valleys a white foal chased the wind, shaking its shining mane. In no time at all, it seemed, it grew into a fine young stallion.

HISTORICAL NOTE

Most of the historical basis for the figure behind the legendary King Arthur comes from a text called the *Historia Brittonum* (The History of the Britons); a compilation of manuscripts believed to have been put together by a Welsh monk called Nennius sometime in the mid ninth century. In relation to the wars with the Anglo-Saxons it states that 'Then in those days Arthur fought against them with the kings of the Britons, but he was a commander in the battles.' It then goes on to list twelve battles, the locations of most have never been fully identified.

Further evidence comes from two ambiguous references in the *Annales Cambriae* (The Annals of Wales) set down sometime in the mid tenth century. These detail Arthur's victory at 'the Battle of Badon' in 516 A.D. and his eventual demise in 537 A.D. at 'the Strife of Camlann' along with somebody called Medraut.

This all seems a far cry from the King Arthur and his Knights of the Round Table of later legend. In fact, these early references don't even make him out to be a king at all. Some sort of 5th century war leader who led a native resistance to the Anglo-Saxon expansions seems likely but how did this shadowy figure emerge from the chaos of post-Roman Britain to become the legendary king of a fictional Camelot in the later middle ages?

Between the early references to the historical Arthur and the romances of the 13th and 14th centuries there was a large body of Welsh poetry and tales pertaining to Arthur. In this tradition he *is* a king but there are many differences to the well-known legend of later centuries. There is no mention of Lancelot, Merlin, the Round Table or the sword in the stone. Instead, the hot-headed Cei and one-handed Bedwyr appear consistently as his closest companions along with Gwalchmei (who became Gawain in later stories). His queen is Gwenhwyfar but he rules from Caerleon, not Camelot.

That such a body of literature and folklore was inspired by a single individual suggests that Arthur, whoever he was, was a figure of great importance to the Britons. There is a supernatural element in these early tales and several other Welsh tales of the period depict bands of warriors chasing after magical cauldrons. The mabinogi of *Bran and Branwen* (as told by Menw in this book) is one such example. The tale of *Culhwch and Olwen* (a story from which I have borrowed many elements including the characters who accompany Arthur on his quest) also deals with a similar vessel and the legendary account of the great bard, Taliesin, is centred around the cauldron of Ceridwen. Perhaps most important of all is the cryptic poem *The Spoils of Annwn*; a surreal account of a band of warriors (including Arthur) who voyage to the otherworld and steal a magical cauldron. As with Bran's expedition to Ireland, only seven of them return.

In Celtic myth the cauldron appears to be a symbol of rebirth and there may be archaeological evidence in the form of the Gundestrup Cauldron which depicts a goddess-like figure dipping warriors into a cauldron headfirst. Parallels have been drawn between the magical cauldron and the quest for the Holy Grail which occupied much of later Arthurian literature.

It was Geoffrey of Monmouth who first penned a comprehensive life of King Arthur. His twelfth century *Historia Regum Britanniae* (History of the Kings of Britain) is an incredible blending of fact, folklore and pure fantasy. It is in this work that Arthur is first given a sister – Anna – who is married off to King Loth of Lothian. Little else is said of her but in later romances Arthur gains a more famous sister; the wicked sorceress Morgan le Fay. Morgan was also first mentioned by Geoffrey of Monmouth who called her 'Morgen' (meaning 'sea-born') in his *Vita Merlini* (The Life of Merlin) but makes no mention of her being Arthur's sister. Instead, she is a wise healer, a shapeshifter and chief among nine sisters who rule Avalon, the 'Island of Apples'.

The idea of nine priestesses ruling an island appears with interesting frequency in Celtic history and literature. The 1st century Roman Geographer Pomponius Mela in his *Description of the World* says that the isle of Sena (Île de Sein) belonged to a 'Gallic divinity and is famous for its oracle, whose priestesses, sanctified by their perpetual virginity, are reportedly nine in number.' The cauldron in *The Spoils of Annwn* is kindled by 'the breath of nine maidens' and the Arthurian hero Peredur encounters the nine witches of Caer Lloyw (Gloucester) in *Peredur son of Efrawg*. In Welsh and Breton folklore there are creatures known as 'morgens' who are reportedly water spirits responsible for drowning men. Paralleling the name of Monmouth's sorceress, we could be looking at a folk memory of a Celtic priestess-hood connected with water and islands that were relegated over time to the status of witches and evil spirits in medieval literature.

The dynasty of Cunedda (I have opted for the older form 'Cunedag' as it appears in the *Historia Brittonum*) was a real (or at least semi-legendary) dynasty that ruled Gwynedd in the late fifth century. His name and the names of his sons appear in the royal genealogies of Wales as the ancestors of the notorious Maelgwn of Gwynedd (definitely a real king).

There is nothing that specifically connects King Arthur with Cunedda's dynasty, but I felt that it was an interesting (and possibly dysfunctional) royal family with plenty of room for a bastard son (and daughter) within its ranks.

Sneak Peek – Banner of the Red Dragon

Caledonia, 482 A.D.

Arthur

The mist hung over the forests like a shroud. Arthur gripped the reigns of his grey mare Lamrei in his gloved fist, patting her pale neck to sooth her nerves while he fought down his own. Behind him his company stood ready, horses whinnying softly, champing at the bit and scraping at the damp earth with their hooves. Every sound seemed amplified in the muted silence of the forests. The jingle of every harness was like the toll of a bell and every nervous warrior's cough a clap of thunder.

He looked out across the wooded valley that lay deep in the Caledonian Forest. Its other side was barely visible in the fog and shade of the tall pines. Somewhere over there Cei was waiting at the head of his own company. Further down the valley waited the combined cavalry of their foster father Cunor and King Leudon, blocking the exit, sealing the trap.

It had been a hard season's fighting. The thick forests of the north concealed an enemy that had dwelt there since the dawn of time, deeply knowledgeable of its paths and valleys, working as swiftly as ghosts in the mist. Blood had been spilt for every inch of ground as the Britons were constantly assailed by small raiding bands sent by King Caw of the Pictish tribes.

The Picts had been united under a high-king before but the fragmented state of the tribes and their incessant blood feuds made it a rare occurrence. The first time had been during the Barbarian Conspiracy of 367 when the Roman garrison at the Great Wall had rebelled. A Pictish confederation under King

Gartnait had swarmed south in an attack coordinated with the Gaels of Erin and the Sacson pirates who plagued the south-east coast. The second time had been during a civil war between Prince Talorc and his aunt Galana who, in accordance with the tradition of matrilineal descent held by some of the tribes, wanted the throne for her infant son. It had been a British army sent by Lord Vertigernus that had crushed Galana's rebellion and placed Talorc on the throne to rule Pictland from his royal seat at Din Eidyn.

But Din Eidyn had once been the home of the Votadini tribe; a client kingdom of the Romans. Their greatest warlord was Cunedag who had been sent by Lord Vertigernus to reconquer the mountainous region of Venedotia from the Gaels several years earlier.

Cunedag had been Arthur's grandfather and although Arthur was but a bastard offshoot of Cunedag's dynasty, he served Venedotia as loyally as any trueborn son.

In the years that followed Talorc's victory over his aunt, the British warlord Leudon set his sights on a northern kingdom of his own and took Din Eidyn from the Picts. In an attempt to legitimise his rule over what had once been the territory of Cunedag's kin, he married into the ruling family of Venedotia. His bride Anna – Arthur's half-sister – had run away from the marriage bed and was now dead yet the kingdom of Leudonion had been secured.

The Picts, never ones to forget an injury, plotted swift revenge on Leudon. Their opportunity came in the form of Caw who banded the tribes together in a confederation with the intent of smashing Leudon's hold over Din Eidyn and driving the Britons back south. Leudon, cowering in the face of Caw's painted hordes, had sent to his lost bride's family for help. King Cadwallon, newly ascended to the title of 'Pendraig' – high-king of Venedotia – heeded his estranged brother-in-law's call and had sent the Teulu of the Red Dragon north that summer.

Now autumn had come and the treetops had turned golden brown, their leaves stripped away to reveal the skeleton of the forest. The Picts had finally been forced into open battle and Arthur hoped that this would be an end to the war. He was sick of the rain and the mud, sick of the cold, whipping winds and sleeping in rough tents, eating bowls of watery stew and stale bread, day after day. He wanted to go home. For many reasons.

A sound reached his ears; a distant tramping of hooves down on the valley floor. He leaned forward in his saddle and listened hard. He could just make out the sound of the oncoming force as it moved slowly through the trees. It was five-hundred strong according to the scouts. He could see movement; spear tips and blue woad on bare skin. The helmed heads of warriors mounted on their sturdy highland ponies. He turned to Gualchmei.

"Get ready for my signal," he said, and Gualchmei passed the message along the ranks. Spears were gripped tightly and shields were lifted up and down as the warriors prepared their shoulder muscles, revolving their arms in their sockets, loosening up for maximum mobility. The sound of the oncoming Picts was louder now, a low rumbling growl of movement. The trees down in the valley began to sway as the mighty force shouldered its way past. A horn bellowed on the other side of the valley, Cei's horn; the signal to attack.

"“Company!" roared Arthur, holding his spear aloft. "Forward!"

As one, Arthur's company followed their captain down the slope of the hill and into the valley. Earth and pine needles were kicked up by hooves as they gradually picked up speed.

"Keep the line steady!" Arthur bellowed. "As one!"

Trees whipped past them, a fuzzy blur of greens and browns. The enemy was in sight now; a massive force of mounted Picts flanking a column of spearmen. Savage war-hounds strained at their leashes, their ears pricking at the sound of on-commers.

Hundreds of heads turned to look in startled surprise at the charging Britons. The hounds bayed and gnashed their jaws and the spearmen tugged on them as they hurried to form a defensive line. But they were too slow and undisciplined. Arthur struck out with his spear as he led his men into their right flank, blinking as a gush of blood spattered the right side of his face. The spearmen went down under the hooves of the Britons and the Pictish cavalry flanks turned in an attempt to hem them in.

Horses whinnied in fear and pain and the war-hounds barked and tore savagely at their flanks. Spears punctured armour and flesh while shields shivered and split under the impact of heavy swords and axes. The Picts, never ones to stay surprised for long, fought back with a furious energy.

Arthur parried a spear stroke and thrust his own iron-tipped shaft into the chest of his attacker, knocking the stricken man from his saddle. He could hear the distant sound of Cei's horn and grinned as the Pictish host turned in shock to face another company of Britons descending the valley on the other side. Caught between two pincers, the Picts fought bravely, refusing to give up any ground to their attackers.

Then came the sound of another horn, deeper, more resonant. It was as if a death-toll had descended from the fog and all in the valley turned to see its source. Emerging from the southern end of the valley was the third cavalry led by Cunor and King Leudon. Above them the banner of the red dragon wavered, nostrils flaring, tail billowing out behind it like a ghastly apparition from the mist accompanied by a roaring of horns. This was the final stroke for the Picts and their captains turned in their saddles and bellowed out the order to retreat.

The Britons roared with triumph and urged their steeds onwards, cutting at the heels of their enemy. They chased the Picts up the valley, slaying any who were too slow to escape their stabbing spears and swinging blades. Arthur heard Cei bellowing to him above the slaughter.

"By Modron's tits, we have them on the hop! Did you see that prince of theirs? We wiped that blue smirk off his face!"

"Hueil? No, I couldn't make him out." said Arthur. Hueil was Caw's eldest son and had led most of the attacks against them throughout the season. "Were you near him?"

"Aye, but I couldn't get a good swing at him. His bastard captains formed a ring about him. But I'll get him next time! They have nowhere to run now. It's only a matter of time."

"Time is something we are running short of," said a voice behind them. It was Cunor, Cei's father, his steed foaming with sweat and his standard-bearer struggling to keep up with him. "We have waited all season for this battle and now that we have these bastards pinned down, winter threatens to take them away from us. I want the heads of Caw and Hueil on poles by the end of the day."

"They'll be heading for the river," said King Leudon beside him. "Caw will most likely be somewhere beyond it with the rest of the confederation. What we faced today was merely Hueil's vanguard. There is a fording point further east."

"Then we must push onwards and cut them off before they cross the river, father," said Cei. "If we stop Hueil reuniting with the rest of the Picts, Caw will be more vulnerable."

"Agreed," replied Cunor. "But beyond that river is unknown territory. I don't want to risk blundering into any of their ambushes."

"The river is wide and deep further west," said Leudon. "If we could push them in that direction, then they won't be able to cross and will be forced to fight."

"Very well," said Cunor. "But we must secure that crossing in case they slip by us. Cei, Arthur, your companies are light and fast. I want you to ride for the crossing as fast as you can. Reach it before the enemy does and hold it until we arrive. With any luck we will be able to crush Hueil between our two forces."

"Yes, sir!" replied Arthur and Cei in unison and they trotted off, hailing their standard-bearers to regroup their companies.

"Follow my lead," said Cei to Arthur as they set off up the valley. "If my company comes across any pockets of resistance, ride yours around on my left flank and engage."

They proceeded northwards and the valley levelled out into flat ground. The forest grew thicker and the two companies had trouble keeping their men in an orderly formation.

"Get those stragglers on our right flank closer in!" called Arthur to Gualchmei. "I don't want anyone vulnerable to ambush!"

The sound of Cunor's horns dwindled into the distance as Arthur and Cei rode on. Soon they could hear the rushing of the river and Cei sent scouts ahead. They reported back with news that Hueil and his company were already in the process of fording it.

"Damn them!" shouted Cei.

"We're too late!" said Arthur.

"We have to cross and cut them down before they regroup with Caw."

"Your father's orders were to wait for him at the ford."

"If we let Hueil reach his father this war could drag on and on! And I don't know about you, but I want that blue bastard's head on a spear before sundown!"

"Cei, we could ride straight into a trap!"

"Arthur is right," said Beduir, Cei's cousin. "We don't know how large Caw's following is. There could be thousands waiting for us across the river."

"Then that is why we must cut down Hueil before he reaches them! And Beduir, you are in my company, not Arthur's. You do as I say!"

Beduir shrugged apologetically at Arthur and followed Cei as he led his company across the river. Arthur watched in silent disapproval. He knew there was no point in trying to make his pig-headed foster-brother listen to reason when the scent of blood and victory was in his nostrils.

When he was halfway across the river, Cei turned in his saddle to call to Arthur. "Remain on the southern bank and wait for my father if you wish, Arthur. But I'm going to bring back Hueil's head!"

"This is a bad idea," said Gualchmei at Arthur's side. "Both companies are vulnerable divided."

Arthur nodded. "He is a fool, but he is not under my command. Where is Cundelig?"

"Here, sir!" the lead scout replied, trotting over to him. Hebog, his peregrine falcon, sat on his gauntlet, leather hood pulled down over its eyes.

"Take a group of your scouts to the other side of the river and keep pace with my block-headed brother. We can at least watch his back that way."

Cundelig saluted and crossed the river with three of his scouts on their light, fast horses. Arthur waited with the rest of his company on the riverbank, watching the swirls and eddies of the dark water.

Cundelig had barely been gone a few moments before he and his scouts returned, splashing across the ford in great haste.

"Sir!" he blurted. "Cei and his riders have plunged on into the woods in a northerly direction. We spotted a large company of Picts coming from the west and I mean massive. It's a good bet Caw is with them. We only just managed to get back across the river without being seen."

"It was a ruse," said Arthur, panic rising in his gut. "They will be coming up behind Cei. He'll be trapped!"

"Lord Cunor and the rest of the teulu are still on their way," said Gualchmei. "There is nothing we can do."

"The hell there isn't!" replied Arthur. "That's my foster-brother out there. I'm going to get him out somehow. If we can trick Caw's force into coming after us instead of Cei, then we may have a chance to ambush them here at the ford. I'm going to split the company into two units. You shall lead the first, Gualchmei. Ride west as hard as possible and draw Caw's attention. I shall take the second unit and conceal ourselves on that ridge across the river. When the enemy pursues you across the ford, we shall charge their rear."

"Sir," said Gualchmei. "We are a small enough force as it is. Dividing us is extremely risky. Even if we spring a successful ambush, we'll be hopelessly outnumbered."

"We only need to draw them away from Cei. The first party does not need to engage the enemy at all, merely bait them. But we need to move now if we are to prevent them from getting at Cei. Off you go and good luck. And remember, only draw their attention. Do not risk yourselves in combat."

"Yes, sir," replied Gualchmei and he rode off, leading his small group of men across the river.

Arthur waited until the river was clear before leading his own men across. The rise on the other side was thickly wooded and provided excellent cover for his men and their horses. Atop it, he could see the rear of Gualchmei's unit weaving through the trees below, following the river west. As they vanished into the gloom, Arthur felt the haunted wilderness closing in on him. He had less than twenty-five warriors, they were alone and on the wrong side of the river in uncharted territory.

All because of Cei.

It hadn't been the first time his foster-brother had charged into danger without a thought for the consequences. He was a hot-headed, gung-ho oaf. But Arthur loved him and would risk all to save him. It was selfish to risk the lives of his men perhaps, but there it was.

It wasn't long before the sound of horns calling for chase to be given drifted through the trees towards them. Arthur heard the hammering of hooves and Gualchmei's unit thundered into view, curling around to cross the ford. The Pictish vanguard followed closely, hooves churning the earth and war dogs threading their way in and out, jaws slavering for the kill. They had taken the bait!

The press of infantry hurried along in their wake; hundreds of them dressed in an array of colourful wool, mail, leather and skins. Every inch of bare flesh was either tattooed or painted with the blue dye of the woad plant depicting the sigils and totem animals of a dozen clans.

As the stragglers were wading into the foaming waters, Arthur yelled the order to charge at the top of his voice. They crashed down the slope and the Picts turned, startled at an attack on their rear. But the danger posed by Arthur's paltry twenty-five riders was slim in the face of their superior numbers.

Arthur roared an oath of defiance as they slammed into the rear of the enemy. They cut through the infantry like butter, swinging their great cavalry swords and axes down on unprotected heads, cracking them open like turnips. They drove deep into the enemy ranks so that the shallows of the river wetted the fetlocks of their horses.

Across the river, Gualchmei had wheeled his unit around and was charging the enemy head on, trapping the Picts in the bottleneck of the ford.

Brave lad, thought Arthur. *He is prepared to lay down his life for his comrades.* A retreat south was open to him but he had chosen to die with his teulu. That kind of loyalty could not be bought.

The river turned red and grew bloated with the corpses of the fallen. The Picts were momentarily trapped and many braved the deeper parts of the river. Some made it to the banks while others lost their footing and were swept away by the strong current.

Up ahead, Arthur could see King Caw; a plume of raven feathers cresting an iron helm that wobbled as he hacked and slashed his way through Gualchmei's ranks. Near to him Arthur saw Hueil, roaring defiance and urging the Picts onwards. He must have cut westwards after crossing the ford to bring news to his father while Cei was led on a wild goose chase deep into the forests.

They had no chance of holding them at the ford. Gualchmei's unit was being overrun. The Picts would win through but Arthur did not regret his decision. Drawing the enemy away from Cei and spoiling their trap had been the only choice open to him.

A bellowing roar sounded from the south-west and the Britons cried with joy at seeing Cunor and Leudon at the head of the teulu, riding hard towards the ford. The red dragon standard was as a splash of blood amidst the muted greens and browns of the forest. The Picts saw that the tables had turned suddenly and began pushing against Gualchmei's unit all the harder, not to destroy them now but to break through, to flee.

"We have them!" Arthur cried. "Push on! Cut down their king! Don't let him escape!"

They crossed the ford, threading a path around the sodden corpses that leaked red tendrils into the pinkish water, and climbed the bank to re-join Gualchmei's unit. Cunor and Leudon had slammed into the right flank of the fleeing Picts and battle rang out among the trees for as far as the eye could see.

Arthur led his company into the rear of the fleeing enemy but the battle was over almost by the time they got there. Cunor was wheeling his mighty mount around, waving a bloodied sword in the air.

"You did it, my lad!" he cried upon seeing Arthur. "I don't know how you held that ford against such odds but you did it!"

Before Arthur could explain, Cunor interrupted him. "Caw is dead! I saw him hacked down by Leudon's household troops. The head of the tattooed snake has been lopped off! Where is Cei?" he asked at last, noticing his son's absence.

Arthur saw the look of concern cross his foster-father's face and hurried to allay his fears that his son was slain. "Cei was not with us at the ford. When we arrived, Hueil and his warriors had already crossed. Cei led his company across the river in pursuit of him while my company remained to wait for you. My scouts brought me word of a large Pictish force coming from the west. It was a ruse to ambush us once we had crossed the river."

"What happened?"

"I split my company and we lured the Picts across the ford and then ambushed them."

"Saving my son," said Cunor, his face grim. "Well were the hell is he?"

"Sir!" said Caradog, captain of the first company, galloping over to them. "Prince Hueil has escaped. He is has rallied the remaining Pictish cavalry and they are fleeing south."

"To what end?" asked Gualchmei. "Without their king they can't pose much of a threat to the southern kingdoms. They'll disperse and attempt to sneak back to their tribal lands. It's over!"

"No," said Arthur. Hueil is as canny a leader as his father was. He'll remain a standard for them to flock to."

"You're right, Arthur," said Cunor. "This war isn't over until I have Hueil's head along with his father's. You must go after them, son."

"Me?" Arthur said.

"Aye. You have the fastest horses. We will finish mopping up here."

"Cei returns!" Gualchmei exclaimed.

Cunor turncd an angry facc to thc ford whcrc his son was leading his company through the water.

"I told you to remain at the ford!" Cunor exploded as Cei drew near.

"Father," Cei protested. "Hueil was within our grasp! I couldn't let him get away! Not when we were so close to winning…"

"Hueil headed west and re-joined his father," said Cunor. They would have bitten you in the arse had it not been for Arthur's quick thinking! You deliberately disobeyed my orders!"

Cei's face reddened. "Father, I…"

Cunor turned to Arthur. "Get going. Don't let Hueil escape."

"Yes, sir," Arthur replied and began rounding up his company.

"Hueil has fled south?" Cei enquired. "Father, let me go with Arthur…"

"No! I want you here with me where I can keep an eye on you!"

Arthur did not wait to hear any more. Water skins were passed around and those who were still fit to ride mounted their horses and set out.

They rode south all afternoon until the sky above the treetops grew blood streaked. The men and the horses were tired yet still they forced themselves on with the knowledge that their enemy would be just as fatigued.

They can't run forever, Arthur told himself as he urged Lamrei on, sympathising with the creature's flagging strength.

They passed through the neck of Albion where the

great island narrowed into the tribal territories of the southern Picts, squeezed between two powerful British kingdoms. To the east lay Leudonion with its chief forts of Din Eidyn and Din Peldur. To the west lay the kingdom of Ystrat Clut, ruled by King Caradog; an old Briton who was a little too friendly with the Gaels and the Picts than his countrymen thought decent. This was compounded by his refusal to aid King Leudon in his war against the northern Picts. Eventually, as darkness descended, they were forced to stop and rest.

"Hueil will be doing the same," said Gualchmei. "His horses will be no fresher than ours."

"I want to be ready to move out at first light," said Arthur.

After they had fed and watered the horses and brushed down their sweat-streaked coats, they collapsed around their campfires and boiled their meat. Arthur posted sentries and sent Cundelig and a scouting unit further south to see if they could find out how far away Hueil was camped. With the stars like dust in the black sky, the men began to snore as they sank into a well-earned rest.

Arthur remained awake, staring into the glowing embers of the campfire. His thoughts were of home, of Venedotia and the hair of one woman which burned in his mind as red as the heat of the flames before him.

He and Guenhuifar had grown close over the past two years. Much of Arthur's time had been spent on Ynys Mon with the teulu in their effort to drive away the Gaels. It had been a long campaign but they had succeeded, despite several fresh invasions from Erin along Albion's north-west coast. King Cadwallon, the Pendraig of Venedotia and Arthur's half-brother had rebuilt Cunedag's old lys in the north-eastern corner of Ynys Mon and had made Guenhuifar's father steward of it as he had been of old. Many celebrations had taken place in Cadwallon's new royal seat and Arthur and Guenhuifar had found their eyes meeting more and more often over the heads of the revellers in the smoky hall.

Without ever revealing their feelings for one another to anyone else, they had enjoyed stolen moments of secrecy and forbidden kisses beneath the moonlight when the autumn wind was peeling the dead leaves from the trees. Whether he was in his bed at Cair Cunor, or in a muddy field facing a horde of howling Gaels or Picts, Arthur's mind yearned for those soft lips and that thick, auburn hair. They had not openly expressed their love to each other but it was there all the same; a glowing ember that smouldered away, biding its time, threatening to burst into flame at any moment.

"Arthur!" called one of the sentries, hurrying over to him. "Cundelig and his scouts have returned!"

Arthur got up and went to the perimeter of the camp where Cundelig was dismounting, his exhausted horse shaking with fatigue.

"Arthur took Cundelig by the shoulder. "You have returned so soon! Are they close?"

"Any closer and we could hurl insults at each other," said Cundelig. "The ground slopes down through the trees over there to the shores of a great lake. Hueil has made camp beneath the shelter of the trees at the water's edge. He commands but a fraction of the warriors we saw him ride away with."

"Where are the rest of them?"

"Deserted? Fled back to their homes? Who knows?"

"Ha!" said Gualchmei, joining them at the camp's edge. "He's a sitting duck!"

Arthur was not convinced. "He must have come this far south for a reason. My guess is that he has sent his warriors out to rally local support. We are in Damnonii territory and we have the Britons of Ystrat Clut to the west of us."

"Ystrat Clut has long been friendly to the southern Picts," said Gualchmei. "King Caradog refused to send his warriors to aid Leudonion."

"And we don't know how loyal the Damnonii are to Caw's confederation but if they rally to Hueil's standard with the support of King Caradog, we could be facing a resurgence here in the south."

"By Christ, we've got to take him and take him now!" said Cundelig. "Else all will be undone!"

"Aye," Arthur agreed. "The lads and the horses need a couple of hours more sleep but I want to fall upon Hueil's camp before dawn. They don't know we have followed them this far and won't be expecting us. Once we have Hueil, we ride east for Din Eidyn. We can hand him over to Leudon's people there and he can be used as a bargaining chip to end this war."

The dawn attack on Hueil's camp went according to plan. Arthur marshalled his cavalry on the top of the slope just as the sky was beginning to pale in the east. They were all still tired, stiff and sore from the previous day's fighting but the sight of the small cluster of campfires down by the shores of the lake was more refreshing to them than either sleep or a good meal. That pathetic encampment was all that stood between them and the end of the whole blasted war.

Arthur gave no orders for horns to be blown. He wanted the surprise to be saved until the very last second. He led them himself, spurring Lamrei down the slope, dodging the trees, spear gripped in his right fist.

As they emerged from the trees in a thunder of hooves, the alarm of the sentries could be heard, but only briefly. They tore through the outer perimeter, skewering and hacking down any Pict who stood in their way. Campfires were scattered by hooves in a flurry of embers and ash. Arthur sent the wings of his company to envelop the camp on all sides, leaving only the lake at the enemy's rear.

The panicked Picts splashed into the shallows and tried to swim for it but Arthur's men dismounted and waded in after them, reddening the water with down-thrust spears. Those who remained on land were captured and herded together.

"Where is Hueil mab Caw?" Arthur bellowed, wheeling Lamrei about as he scanned the faces of the prisoners.

They remained silent but it was a futile gesture. Hueil was known to Arthur and his men. They had seen his blue-painted face roaring at them over the din of the battlefield several times that summer and would recognise it now.

"Here!" said Gualchmei triumphantly.

Hueil was plucked from the gathered prisoners and hauled before Arthur. The woad on his face was cracked and peeling now and the effects of tiredness and defeat showed in his wild, dark eyes.

"Arthur mab Enniaun," said Hueil, drawing himself up defiantly. "You have the upper hand today, it seems. The gods take pity on you at last!" He grinned through his blackened teeth.

"Fortunes of war change like the tides," said Arthur. "And today is not your day. Fetch him along!"

"What of the others?" Gualchmei asked.

Arthur glanced at the unarmed Picts who were clustered together like sheep. "They are of no use to us," he said. "Kill them."

The enemy did not scream or beg for mercy as Arthur's men set about their butchery. Such things were the very depths of dishonour for a Pict and they died as Arthur knew they would, fighting with their bare hands until their last breaths. Hueil watched the awful scene without emotion. These were his warriors, his companions. They had done him proud in life and now they did him proud in their deaths.

They ate what they could of the Picts' meagre supplies before setting out east. Hueil was led on a horse, his hands bound behind him, saying not a word.

It was before noon that the scouts came hurrying back with news of a Pictish host approaching from the east.

"Damnonii?" Arthur asked.

"By the looks of their markings, I would say so," said Cundelig. "A thousand strong on foot. They must have marshalled their entire tribe."

"Is there any way around them?"

"If we could make it to the banks of the Bodotria Estuary, we could follow it to Din Eidyn but it would be risky trying to cross that distance so close to their scouts. They have dogs and our horses are tired. We would not avoid an engagement if we were spotted."

"Back north, then?"

Cundelig rubbed his chin. "Possible. But we might run into whatever is left of Caw's warband fleeing south with Cunor on their heels. Even refugees would outnumber us."

"Then there is only one way open to us then," said Arthur. "We go south. To the Wall."

"The Wall?" Gualchmei exclaimed.

"It is quite a distance but we can find safety at Din Banna."

Din Banna was one of the sixteen forts the Romans had built at regular intervals along the length of the Emperor Hadrian's great wall.

"They won't be looking for us yet so we have a head start on them," said Arthur.

They turned their mounts in a southerly direction and tried to cover as much distance as possible before night fell. To the south the lands opened up into a vista of rolling moors bearded with purple heather and cut through by flowing watercourses. There was little cover and when they camped that night, Arthur forbade the lighting of fires for they would be spotted miles off. They had no food left and slept in discomfort for only as long as they had to before setting out once more.

At first light Cundelig sent Hebog up and shielded his eyes with his hand as he watched the bird's movements to the north of them.

"Damn!" the scout cried.

"What is it?" said Arthur as he mounted his horse.

"A large host approaching from the north. They've seen us!"

"Ride!" shouted Arthur. "We ride straight for Din Banna and stop for nothing!"

The Wall had stopped functioning as a wall long ago. Unmanned and unmaintained, sections of it had crumbled in leaving gaping holes through which the Picts regularly slipped through to raid the kingdoms of the Northern Britons.

Straddling the road that led from west to east, Din Banna was as a rock against the tide, walled on all sides with its old Roman watch towers manned and its granaries full.

After the Wall's garrison deserted Din Banna, the settlement on its eastern side had remained occupied and had grown after King Gurust of Rheged refortified it, making it the northernmost defence of his kingdom.

Gualchmei called out a greeting as they approached the small wooden bridge that spanned the overgrown ditch at the foot of fort's walls. The great double arched gates creaked open to admit them and once every rider was within the ruined northern section of the fort, they were slammed shut and bolted once more.

Arthur swung himself down from his saddle and heard the relieved laughs and jests of his men at finding refuge. He wished he could share in their relief, but they were not out of the woods yet.

"Where is the camp prefect?" he demanded of a nearby soldier.

"Here!" said a short man in scale armour as he strode towards them.

"See that our horses are fed and stabled, they have had a long journey."

"You're Venedotians, aren't you?" the camp prefect said. "What news from the war?"

"All but over and its last engagement is to happen here."

The prefect's face paled. "*Here*?"

Arthur directed the man's gaze to the prisoner who was being lifted down from his horse. "That is Hueil mab Caw. We captured him in battle but were forced to flee south. There is a large band of Damnonii on our trail."

The prefect gawked at him. "You brought Picts to the Wall?"

Arthur looked at him curiously. "I was under the impression the Wall was built to withstand Picts."

"But, but the rest of your teulu? Where is the mighty dragon standard of Cunedag?"

"Mopping things up in our wake," said Arthur. Caw is dead. His son is the last figurehead of the Pictish confederation. That is why we brought him here, where they cannot get at him."

"But Din Banna is severely undermanned! Most of the garrison went with you lot to fight in the north!"

"Nevertheless, a Pictish warband a thousand strong is marching upon us. Bring everybody from the settlement within the walls. Find every bow and spear in the fort and place them in the hands of every person able to use them."

The camp prefect cursed and hurried off to see that it was done. As the frightened villagers began to trickle in through the east gate, supporting the elderly and herding livestock, Arthur walked along the walls and surveyed the defences. Some of the towers had crumbled away but the parapet itself was in good repair. There was even a couple of catapults that seemed to be in working order.

He had barely completed his survey before the horns began to blow from the northern watchtowers. He ran the length of the parapet to its northern face.

The Picts were emerging from the trees in clusters beneath their banners. They took up a howling war cry intended to intimidate.

"Fewer than a thousand," said Gualchmei as he and Cundelig joined him on the parapet. "Perhaps your eyes are getting tired, Cundelig."

"There are fewer of them because they have divided themselves," said Arthur. "They want to surround us."

His prediction was confirmed as the warning horn was taken up on the west wall and then, after an interval, on the east.

"They have slipped through the gaps in the Wall further along," said Arthur. "They don't want us escaping with their precious prince."

"Shit!" said Gualchmei as he gazed at the horde of woad-painted warriors that chanted and hammered on their shields. "They're surrounding the fort! Can we withstand them?"

"Perhaps," said Arthur. "But we will only last as long as the fort's stores do."

The Picts attacked as one, blowing their aurochs horns to signal an assault on all sides. Arthur bellowed for bowmen to be placed evenly along the walls and he and his men began distributing spears.

"Don't let any of the buggers get their ladders close!" Arthur instructed the terrified soldiers and villagers who lined the parapets. "And hack through any grappling hooks that gain a grip. If even one of those bastards gets up here, our defences will be penetrated and the whole fort may fall."

Arrows sailed out from the fort's walls to disappear seemingly without significance into the mass of warriors below. The catapults hurled stones into the mob but still they came in attempt after attempt to climb the walls with their ladders and hooks. They seemed to be frantic. They knew their prince was within the fort and gleefully hurled themselves at its defences in their effort to free him and save what was left of Caw's confederation.

The assault went on until dark. The catapults ran out of ammunition and hung slack. With the onset of night, the Picts retreated out of arrow range to rest and recover. Arthur ordered the distribution of food. He and his warriors having barely eaten since the previous night, gobbled down hard tack biscuits, bacon and beer. They were dog tired and Arthur ordered them to sleep in shifts until dawn.

The following morning the assault began afresh and the situation looked desperate. They were low on arrows, had few spears between them and the Picts had brought forth battering rams cut from trees during the night, sharpened and fire-hardened to slam again and again at the north and west doors.

"Much more of that and those doors will give way," Gualchmei called to Arthur over the din. "We can't spare extra men to put over the gates else we thin our defences on the walls!"

Arthur nodded grimly. It was only a matter of time. Their fates were tied to that of the fort and before a second night fell the Picts would gain entry and overrun them. He made a decision that he had been grappling with all night.

"Bring me Hueil," he said.

Gualchmei blinked at him and then hurried off to carry out his orders.

The Pict was brought up to the walls and he surveyed his attacking countrymen with an arrogant smile. "You can't win, Arthur," he said. "The Damnonii believe in my father's dream. Every true-born Pict does and will gladly water the ground with his blood in order to see you Britons pushed out of the north for good."

Ignoring him, Arthur grabbed him by his hair and forced him to his knees, his head hanging over a stone in the parapet. "We may all die here," he said, "but so will you. Your countrymen will never hail you as their leader. I'll see to that"

He drew his sword and, as he gripped it with both hands, Hueil turned his head to look at him with wide eyes as comprehension dawned.

Arthur swung down with all his might, once, twice, his blade connecting with the stone on the second blow. Hueil's head tumbled over the parapet as blood gushed from the stump of his neck to wet the stone with gore.

The act had been witnessed by hundreds of Picts and they gave up an ear-splitting cry of rage. Curses burned the air and they drove the attack harder, this time for vengeance for now that Hueil was dead, all was lost to them now. All that remained was a deep desire to bathe in the blood of the defiant Britons.

"Well, that's that then," said Gualchmei in a resigned tone.

"I couldn't let them have him," Arthur replied. "We face the last of their fury now but at least this war is done."

They held out for the rest of the day, using their arrows sparingly. The end was coming but the desire to postpone the inevitable was strong.

A little after midday the Picts on the northern side of the fort dispersed with great urgency. A bellowing of horns drowned out the war chants that had dulled the ears of Arthur and his comrades for over a day.

Mounted warriors burst from the trees, driving the Picts before them. The Britons on the walls went wild as the banner of the red dragon erupted from the green like a burning brand to drive away their attackers. Arthur roared with joy to see Cunor leading the charge with Cei and Caradog close behind amidst hundreds of their countrymen on Venedotian steeds.

The Picts fled to the western side of the fort but a group of them turned and clustered to the left of the fort's gates, trying to form some sort of defence against the horsemen. As Cunor led the advance against them, the Picts that had fled swarmed around to outflank him.

"They're going to try and blindside him!" Arthur cried. He gripped the stone parapet with whitened knuckles. He bellowed as loudly as he could; "Cei! Beduir! On your right flank!"

Beduir had seen them and was desperately trying to drive a wedge between the charging Picts and

Cunor. It was too late. They were within spear-throwing distance and a javelin whickered through the air.

Arthur roared impotently as he saw the spear tip erupt from his foster-father's chest in a spurt of gore, its wicked point glinting. Cunor gasped and swayed in his saddle as Beduir led his followers into the Picts and hacked them down. Cei was at his father's side in an instant, seizing the reigns of his horse and supporting him, preventing him from falling.

"Open the gates!" Arthur called. "Let them bring the penteulu in!" He found the camp prefect and ordered him to fetch the surgeon.

Cei organised two columns of riders to protect the gate as it swung open. Leading Cunor's horse, he galloped down the avenue and into Din Banna.

Arthur clattered down the ladder to ground level and rushed to help Cei lift Cunor down from his horse.

"The injury is serious," said the surgeon after a moment's inspection. "He has lost a lot of blood but from what I can see, the barb missed his vitals. I need to get him indoors so that I may treat him properly."

"Help him," Arthur said to two nearby soldiers. He turned to the surgeon. By the gods, you'd better keep him alive!"

The Picts had dealt the only serious blow there were able to and now most were either dead or were fleeing towards the woods. Arthur ordered the teulu to enter the fortress and the gates were barred once more.

"No point chasing Picts into the woods," he said. "They won't be attacking again in a hurry and we will be long gone by then. Cei, what happened in the north?"

"We won," said Cei. "Caw's warband are raven meat now or else limping back to their tribal lands. Leudon has returned to Din Eidyn with many prisoners. We have a few ourselves travelling with the wagons. We were meant to go to Din Eidyn but when you did not return, father ordered us to ride south with all haste. By the gods, Arthur, you've led us a merry dance! We found the remains of a Pictish camp on the shores of a lake and the waters red with the blood of their slain. We figured you had carried on south but all the way to the Wall, Arthur?"

"We had no choice," Arthur said. "Hueil sent out his riders to muster the Damnonii who gave chase as soon as they spotted us. We nearly didn't make it to Din Banna."

"And where is Hueil?"

Arthur nodded up at the headless corpse that still leaned over the parapet, its arms bound behind it.

"Just as well," Cei said. "He was too dangerous to be allowed to live."

The ravens descended in droves to feast on the awful scene without the fort's walls. Arthur organised food and water to be distributed to all and Din Banna's occupants relaxed into their bittersweet victory.

The surgeon patched up Cunor as best he could but the penteulu was weak and barely conscious.

"We can't stay here," said Cei. "For one thing, the granaries won't feed the teulu for very long and I don't know about you, but I want to smell the mountain air of Venedotia again."

"Can we move him?" Arthur asked, nodding in the direction of the infirmary.

"It will be a slow march, but we must."

"Very well. We spend the night here and tomorrow, homeward." He fumbled at the laces of his cuirass. "Gods, what I wouldn't give for a hot bath, a warm meal and a soft bed!"

Manufactured by Amazon.ca
Bolton, ON